MW00911543

Mars 185

by

David M Czaplicki

Miranda,

Enjoy the Journey to Mars!

David M Czaplicki

Copyright 2006 by David Czaplicki

All rights reserved. No part of this book may be reproduced or transmitted in any form or by any electronic or mechanical means, including photocopying, recording, or by any information storage and retrieval system, without written permission of the publisher & author, except where permitted by law.

ISBN: 978-0-6152-1364-4

Publishing History
January 2007: NF Publishing
June 2008 : White Solar Press

Cover Photo:
Picture of Mars, *Courtesy of U.S. Geological Survey*

Dedication

Dedicated to my father, Roman, for all his support and inspiration, both in writing and in life.

1

Carlos Mendez climbed the large red dunes overlooking Roman, the first independent city on Mars. It was his city, his dream, and it was just a bit over a half a year away from completion. Carlos could feel the wind race over him, a mild 50 kilometers, he figured. Not bad, considering the storms could get to be over 500 kilometers.

The sun was setting, and the sky took on a light blue haze. The bright lights of Roman sparkled against the dark red rocks and sand. A ridge of mountains, dwarfing most mountains on Earth, lay due north. It was an incredible sight that only a few men had seen. Out in the middle of this harsh new frontier was a dream coming to reality, the dream called Roman.

It would take Carlos over an hour to get to the top of the ridge. Even on his busiest days he seemed to end up here, just to look out over the city. His transport would carry him out across the roads leading to the dunes. He would cross the dunes, which seemed to change daily from the high winds. The color of the sand appeared to change along with their contour. The different shades of reds and brown were alone a site that seemed to be painted by the Gods. Once he crossed the dunes, he was forced to climb the rocks to the top of the ridge.

Carlos snapped on his helmet, opened the door of the transport and began his trek up the cliffs. His frequent walks here had begun to form a path. Carlos checked his oxygen supply, it was a good hour before he needed to be back in the transport. It had been a tough day and Carlos found the view overlooking Roman a spiritual experience. About halfway up the cliff he turned around and looked at Roman. He could see the lights of the machinery that were heading for the garages. On the west ridge he could see the bright lights from the laser blasters, that could turn the hard Martian stone into sand. The five domes of Roman glowed against the dark brown. He looked back up to the top of the cliff. He would get an even more spectacular view from the top. He found it a place to reflect on the days work and plans for the next day.

As he approached the top he spotted someone else looking down at Roman. Carlos walked over to him. "Hello," Carlos said as he pressed the COM link on. There was no response? Possibly the person had their COM link off. Carlos walked over and tapped him on the shoulder. As the person began to turn, Carlos tried his COM link again "Hello," Still no answer. The figure turned, but Carlos was unable to make out a face through the visor. He glanced at the name badge on the suit.

"You!" Carlos exclaimed. "You would be the last person I would expect here!" The figure just stood still. "Well, maybe your not such a ..." Carlos was unable to finish his sentence. The figure had pulled a sharp object from his side and cut through both layers of Carlos suit, Carlos hearing the ripping of his suit. He prayed that only the outside suit was torn, then he still may have a chance. But as a burning sensation took over, Carlos knew he was a dead man.

* * *

Nick Gambino couldn't believe it. He reached for his cup and swallowed the remainder of his cold coffee. Carlos Mendez dead. But how? He looked out of the jet window as questions raced through his head. Things seemed to be falling apart. Delays and spending over budget were increasing daily. The project was almost over half of a year behind schedule. Nick slid his fingers through his dark hair as the pilot's voice came over the intercom. "We will be landing at Phoenix Airport in approximately 12 minutes. Temperature is a scorching 96 degrees."

The stockholders were not happy about the delay on Mars, and now with the news of Mendez death they may want changes, internal changes. Nick's boss, Ed Brocton, had the pleasure of dealing with them. Ed Brocton had taken over Calprex when it was a small company designing modules for space stations. He became very aggressive and surrounded himself with hungry, hardworking employees. Calprex got its first big break almost twenty years ago when it was chosen one of the nine companies used in building the moon's space stations. Calprex became a big time player and a hot commodity. Stocks went up, jobs increased and Calprex was on its way. Ed Brocton had always maintained a family atmosphere and had given much to the company in return for their loyalty.

But hard times had hit over the last five years as Calprex lost parts of the contracts to smaller specialized companies. Calprex was caught up in picking up a section of sub-contracts. The stockholders weren't happy, and they wanted some changes. They insisted that he bring in an outsider into the company. They wanted the man who had changed the industry over the last half a dozen years, the man who was actually one of the reasons Calprex had lost business, Tom Afidan.

Brocton respected Afidan's knowledge but was not a fan of the way he did business. But with sales down, Ed Brocton didn't have much of a choice, and Afidan did make an impact immediately. Sales went up, productivity increased, payroll went down, and because of this, he was able to get more contracts in full. Brocton couldn't argue with the results. The problem was he just didn't like him, didn't trust the guy.

Ed Brocton still had many friends in the industry and over the course of years was negotiating for Calprex the awarding of a contract for one of the first independent bases on Mars. Small stations on Mars were built, and Calprex was passed by for other companies. Over the last few years Calprex had designed some new innovative ideas and was finally awarded to build the first city on Mars, the city of Roman. At first, Afidan thought the idea was too big and risky, but the stockholders saw green in this venture, and so Calprex broke ground.

Nick remembered how he and Ed had personally picked Carlos to oversee the building of Roman, a dream Carlos had shared with them. His puzzling death continually filled Nick's thoughts. How did it happen? The specifics were sketchy. Ed had called a meeting at their facility in Arizona to decide who should replace Carlos and to find out exactly what had happened.

Nick worried over it possibly being the opportunity Afidan was waiting for, the opportunity to take control of Calprex. Within the hour Nick had landed, and his vehicle arrived at the gate of Calprex. He rolled down his window to show the guards his credentials. The hot dry desert air quickly filled his car. A large older gentleman walked up to Nick.

"Sir, some ID please," he said in a rough voice.

Nick handed him his card.

"I'm sorry Mr. Gambino," he apologized. "I didn't know it was you!"

"That's okay, you're just doing your job." Nick assured him. "Busy day at the gate?"

"Yes, it is as a matter of fact, especially for a Sunday. What's going on?" he answered a little bewildered. "Nothing to worry about, just a meeting," Nick replied.

"Well, have a good day Mr. Gambino."

Nick pulled through the gate, and down the narrow road, that led to a large hanger. As Nick's car approached the hanger, the doors of the building opened. He proceeded to drive his car in. The road led into the hanger, continuing down into a dimly lit tunnel where the road descended underneath he desert. He finally arrived at a parking area where he again was stopped for identification.

"Go ahead, Mr. Gambino. They're all here. You're the last to arrive."

"Thanks, John," Nick parked his car and went to the elevators, using his magnetic card, that enabled him to go down. Twenty levels down and the elevator doors opened.

"Good morning, Mr. Gambino."

"Good morning, Nick" came another voice.

"Good morning, everyone. Does anyone know where Ed is?" Nick asked as he walked through the room, glancing around for a response.

"He hasn't left here in over a week," came a voice.

"He's in the blue conference room," said someone else as Nick continued on his way through the room.

At the end of the room was an older woman sitting at a desk.

"Betty, how are you? They got you here on a Sunday, too?" Nick asked.

"Nick, how have you been? I've been here straight through. Someone has to keep an eye on Ed," she replied with a smile.

"He's very fortunate to have someone like you, Betty."

"Thanks, Nick. You can go right in."

Nick continued down the hall and opened the doors. All eyes turned toward the door as it opened. The blue conference room had a traditional conference table.   The room was, of course, done in a blue decor with a rich cherry wood accent. Every chair at the table was filled with the exception of Nick's, the one to the left of Ed.

"Nick, thanks for getting here so soon. I know it was a long flight," Ed said.

Ed had dark circles under his eyes. His age was showing as the pressure increased through the years. Nick had known Ed for almost thirty years. They had all aged, but Ed maybe a little more. His hair was thinning and he had gained excessive weight. There were also numerous creases in his face.

"No problem at all. I just wish we could all meet on better terms," replied Nick.

The room was somber. Carlos Mendez was with Calprex for years and loved by all. Nick sat down next to Ed. Tom Afidan flanked the other side of Ed, and another twelve members sat around the table. Nick didn't even like the sight of Afidan. Nick figured he was close to sixty. He was of average size, probably in better shape than most men his age. He had a receding hairline and slicked back what hair he did have. His two large piercing eyes could intimidate most people. Afidan had a large chin and crooked nose that had been broken at least once. It was not a face one

4

could trust. Ed stood up and swallowed hard. He tried to hold back the tears.

"We know why we're here. We don't have the specifics on Carlos's death. Tom does have a few details and will fill us in later. The major question is who replaces Carlos. We have to send the replacement in 72 hours. The positioning of Mars and Earth are optimal, and if we send Carlos's replacement within that time frame they should be there within two months."

Tom looked at Ed, then glanced back to the group as he spoke to them. "We don't need to send anyone right away. We have competent people there. Gary Ivory, who is in charge of our Security, can oversee everything until a qualified person can be selected. This is a monumental decision. Let's not rush this."

Nick looked around the room to see who was buying Tom's song and dance, then spoke up. "Tom, Gary Ivory has only been with Calprex for a few years. We need someone with a little more experience, Calprex experience. He works for security. I'm not sure that makes him qualified."

"Nick, Gary Ivory is extremely qualified. I hand picked him myself a few years back."

"We want one of our people, not yours, Tom." Nick snapped back as Tom stood piercing at Nick.

Ed looked to the room. "Any suggestions, anyone?"

"Greg Johnson," came from a voice in the back.

Quickly Tom rebutted "Greg has a medical situation that could give him some problems down the road. He can't go racing in space now."

"How about Tina Holt?"

Tom quickly spoke up again. "Tina has two children. I don't believe she'll leave them for two years, and Mars isn't the environment to raise a family."

The names continued as Tom rejected them all. Ed looked desperately around the room. He did not want Ivory running the show. Ivory was a puppet for Afidan. The room was quiet when Nick stood up.

"I believe I have the answer. We can send Brett Roberts."

Nick's eyes met Ed's, was it hope or worry they shared about Brett?

"Brett Roberts! He doesn't even work for us!" Tom exclaimed

"He did, for almost twenty years. He is still a company man." Nick said.

"Listen, Nick, he doesn't know anything about Roman. You just don't want Ivory!"

Ed looked around the room. "Brett Roberts left Calprex about five years ago for personal reasons, but he's qualified for this position. He did similar work on the Moon for us, and he is a person we can all trust."

"His personal problems, are they taken care of?" said someone in back of the room.

"Will he come back?"

Nick stood up. "If you agree, I can get him on the shuttle within three days."

Except for Afidan all were in agreement.

"Then it's done. Can you get a hold of Brett? Do you know where he is?" Ed asked

"Yes," Nick said, wanting to believe his own words.

*　*　*

It was a cold February morning as the Calprex jet landed on the icy runway in Central New York. As the jet taxied toward the terminal Nick wondered why anyone would want to live in such a cold place. Nick knew why Ithaca, New York had become the home of Brett Roberts.

The plane came to a stop and Nick gathered his belonging as he took one more peek out the window. As Nick made his way down the stairs he felt the cold breeze cut through his jacket. He walked to the doors leading to the gates.

As Nick made his way to the checkpoint he could see Brett Roberts waiting for him. This was going to be a hard sell. Nick walked through the gate towards Brett.

"Nick, how are you? You look good," Brett said in the deep voice that Nick was so familiar with.

"Ask me that when I leave," Nick chuckled. "So how are you doing?" Nick said, studying Brett Roberts.

Still a good-looking man, but the years were beginning to show. Brett's face seemed to have aged quite a bit from what Nick had remembered, but then he hadn't seen him in years.

Brett stretched out a hand and wrapped the other around Nick. "It's been a long time, too long," Brett said emotionally. "What brings a southern boy like you up here to New York? It must be important for you to fly out on short notice."

"Brett," Nick looked into his eyes. "It's important, very important."

"Let me get your bags, Nick."

"I didn't bring any. I can't stay."

"You came all this way and you're not spending time up here with me? I don't get it?"

6

"Brett, I need you to come with me. Come back to Calprex."

The two walked through the airport as they spoke.

"Calprex? God Nick what do you need with an old timer like me? All those young hot shots. And what about Afidan?"

"That's why we need you. Ed needs you." Nick stopped. "Carlos Mendez is dead."

Brett's eyes met Nick's "What happened? Was it on Mars? I heard he was heading your project up there."

"Yes. Mars was his dream, Brett, but you knew that. We don't have the details on his death yet. Ed needs to find a replacement, now."

"I can understand that, but why me?"

Nick stopped "It goes back to Afidan. He's trying to take over Calprex. Ed is finding it difficult to find people he can trust. I'm finding it hard to find people I can trust. Everyone is so intimidated by Afidan it's incredible. Half the people who joined the company in the last few years are puppets for him."

Brett stopped, looked down at his feet and then turned to Nick.

"Nick, I'm finally getting my head on straight, I can't go back out there. I don't even know the details of what you're doing."

"It's similar to the position you held on Moon Base One, Brett. A little more overseeing in Roman. You'd be our eyes and ears."

"Jesus, Nick, Ed could send anyone to do that."

"Not really. Your experience and reputation will give you much more leverage. Hell, Brett, most people in the Space program look at you as a hero, I know I do. We really need you."

"When would you need an answer?"

"I needed it five minutes ago. We need to leave in a few hours. You'll need to be at the space station within the next 36 hours."

"What about the class I'm teaching at the University and the house and my belongings and packing? There's a lot to do." Brett explained, "Even if I do go."

The two continued to walk through the terminal. "We can take care of it all. Don't worry. You know we'll pay you what ever you want."

"Cut the crap, Nick. The money isn't even an issue." The two walked out into the cold, crisp air and headed for Brett's car. Brett looked at the white fluffy clouds and then turned back to Nick.

"Look, we'll have to take a ride to my house. I need to pick up some things. Then I guess I'm flying back with you."

The two drove out of the airport and headed south towards Seneca Lake. As they descended on the highway, Nick could see Seneca Lake with the snow-covered hills in the background.

"Some view, Brett. It's definitely breathtaking. A bit too cold for me though. I'm a bit too much of a southern boy to live up here. I'll take the humid 80's anytime."

They passed the south point of the lake and turned up the hillside towards the campus. The two drove through Cornell University on the way to Brett's home. The sidewalks were swept clear of the freshly fallen snow. The students were briskly walking from one building to another as they drove through college town. Brett pointed out a small diner, Joe's Kitchen. "That's where I had my first date with Kathleen. God, it seems like yesterday. I can still remember what we ate, even the waitress's name."

"You told me about it a few times, so this is the famous place. Still around after all these years."

"Yes," Brett replied, as he seemed to get choked up. "I love this place. Guess that's why I came back here. A lot of great memories."

They continued through the university, entering then a maze of properties overlooking the Lake. The car turned after a row of evergreens, and down a small dead end street. They turned up the winding driveway to Brett's small log cabin nestled in the trees. A covered sailboat was perched against a large shed toward the back of the yard. They got out of the car and walked up the porch. Nick looked out over the mountains and Seneca Lake that lay below them. Nick took a few steps onto the wooden deck.

"Brett, this is a magnificent sight!"

Brett was already in the cabin when Nick turned back to him. He proceeded to follow him inside. The fireplace was burning and a large throw rug lay in front. The mantle was covered with pictures of his family. He followed Brett into the study, which was filled with nautical memorabilia. A large picture of Moonbase hung above his desk. The far wall was filled with numerous bookshelves, Nick glancing at them as Brett began to pack.

"Nick, can I get you anything to eat or drink? This may take some time." Brett continued to collect some CD's from the other room.

"No, I'm good." Nick said as he watched Brett go through his things, "We can have our people out here to close everything up for you. You can even make a list of any items you don't have time to pack now and we'll make sure you have them by the time you leave."

"I know, just want to grab a few things."

Brett put his palm pilot in his coat pocket and placed a few more pictures in his bag.

"So who's running the show up there, running Roman?"

"Well, Gary Ivory, one of Afidan's people. He's in charge of security of Roman, and when Mendez was murdered, he took charge."

Brett was packing a duffel bag and looked up "Murdered! I thought it was an accident?"

"Well, Ivory's report says an accident, but there have been way too many accidents and I think Carlos was onto something and they knew it."

"Who knew it? Ivory? Afidan?"

"Brett, I don't know. Wish it were that simple. There are a lot of factions on Mars. You have people looking for religious freedom, political freedom. You name it. It's a chance to start fresh. Unfortunately that is not always good."

"Yeah, I've heard about some religious confrontations up there. But why would any of these factions want to get rid of Carlos?"

"I don't know. That's why we came to you. We want you to find out."

Within a hour they were on their way to Arizona in the corporate jet.

* * *

Brett sat on a stool in one of the Calprex medical suites. He heard the door open and raised his head as Ed Brockton walked in.

"Brett, God I'm so grateful to you. I'm sorry I couldn't meet you at the airport. How are you?"

Brett walked up to Ed and the two shook hands, then embraced. "Well good, but if I get one more needle in my arm, one more test!"

"Hell, even if you didn't pass the physical, I'd still send you." Ed's large smile faded into a somber expression.

"I know Nick filled you in on a lot of material on the flight down here. We don't know how Carlos died. Gary Ivory, who is in charge of security, is very close with Tom Afidan, so the answers may come slow. I'm afraid Ivory is in charge till you get there so I don't know what will be left to find when you get up there. Of course you have unlimited authorization and will take charge when you arrive at Roman."

"Is there something you're not telling me? Do you think there was foul play involved with Carlos death? Nick thinks it's a possibility," Brett asked with some concern in his face.

"I'd like to think there wasn't, but there are just too many things going on up there. I don't trust anyone or anything, and when you arrive there I'd recommend the same for you. This project is one of the greatest achievements in mankind, and there's been a number of accidents in the last six months. Too many to be just accidents."

"What kind of accidents?"

"Look, I've sent files that you'll have access to on the voyage. Every report that came from Roman, every profile on every person there. One thing with the reports, keep in mind who filled them out. I have also downloaded everything from the original concept of Roman, the blueprints to responsibilities of all the contractors."

"Well, I would say it appears that you left no stone uncovered. But you seem worried."

"Worried is an understatement. I feel something is going on up there. Something doesn't add up. I'm sorry I have to run but I have to make a few calls and check on a few things. I'll see you before you leave. Thanks again."

Ed left the room quickly. The nurse came in with another series of vials.

"Let's try the left arm this time, Mr. Roberts!"

2

As the shuttle climbed up into the black sky Brett Roberts's heart pounded with excitement. Space with all its hardships was the only constant Roberts had encountered in his adult life, a constant of the unknown, constant danger. The shuttle had taken Brett Roberts up to Space Station Alpha, which was one of the hubs Calprex used in their Mars project. It was one of the older space stations built in the late twenties. The station was a combination of modular units built on Earth and sent up on booster rockets. As more stations were built over the years, it was found to be more economical to build the station completely on site.

Space Station Alpha was a multi-national project, which at the time of completion showed great unification in the quest for space. As the years passed and the station grew in need of numerous repairs and updates, disagreements on who would pay for the improvements divided the countries that had worked together years ago on its conception. In the end a private corporation purchased Space Station Alpha along with numerous other stations in the same situation.

Now Space Station Alpha was transformed into a hub for freighters loaded with supplies for Mars. As the hatch of the shuttle opened, Brett could smell the musty recirculated air of the station. He knew in time one wouldn't even notice the smell, but it was hard to take for a few minutes. Since the station was used for transporting materials, no artificial gravity was built into the station. Brett pushed his way through the opening and down a small corridor. He was met by a few of Calprex's people, and they guided him through a maze to get to the appropriate docking bay.

Even though Brett had spent many years in the space industry, he felt clumsy as he bumped into walls and grabbed on to items to help push his way from one location to the other. His escorts seemed to move effortlessly as they glided from one corridor to the other.

He was headed to the Freighter Novelette. It was a smaller freighter, but was much quicker than some of the other older models. The

Novelette was, as all deep space crafts were, powered by cold fusion. Although cold fusion had been discovered in the late 1980's, most of the scientific community scoffed at its possibility.

The early experiments with cold fusion were unsuccessful. Man had always used thermonuclear fusion, the type of fusion found in a hydrogen bomb, as well as the Sun and other stars. Cold fusion however could take place at normal room temperatures using an electric current. The first obstacle was to find the correct ratio of deuterium into a body of metallic palladium. Deuterium is a form of hydrogen, which contains only one neutron and one proton. When neutrons are released from a deuterium-tritium fusion reaction, there is an increase in the energy of the nuclei. Once this was found, nuclear fusion could produce usable amounts of energy at room temperature and the possibilities were endless. The energy problem of the Earth was solved, and deep space exploration was possible. Ships could travel to planets in half the previous time. While back on Earth energy companies slowly integrated cold fusion, the space industry went full speed ahead.

The freighter carried a varied payload, from food and water to materials needed to construct the City of Roman. The engines of the Novelette were in the rear of the ship. A large cargo area preceded the engines. This area was almost one kilometer in length, quite small compared to the new freighters. The bridge was the nose of the ship. It was the smallest part of the ship, but from there everything was controlled. The bridge was oval in shape with multiple portholes and sensors. It held a crew of twelve but could run efficiently on eight.

Circling the ship was the "donut," so nicknamed by the crew. It was in this circular part of the ship that the passengers were carried and were the quarters for the crew when they were off duty. Once the Novelette reached cruising speed, the donut rotated around the cargo area, and at a speed that would produce gravity for its passengers. Four corridors led from the "donut" to the cargo area, and also led to the bridge.

An older type freighter, but this ship would get Brett Roberts to his new home. Brett had spent a couple of years on the moon years ago. Back then he was a novice, not knowing the hardships that were to follow. This time he was ready for anything. He was about to embark on a voyage lasting 62 days. He knew little of what his responsibilities were and that he would face numerous internal problems along with the harsh conditions of Mars.

A small transport from Alpha Space Station took him to one of the hubs on the donut. With no centrifuge yet, Brett floated onto the freighter and was given his seat number as well as his sleep area. The ship had the metallic smell, but was much more tolerable than the station.

"Mr. Roberts, we will be leaving within the hour" came a voice from his earpiece. "If you could buckle in at 1430 as we check all systems. We hope to take off at 1500. You still have time to drop some of your belonging off in your quarters, but you must be in your seat for take off."

Roberts checked the cubicle that he would spend two months in. Everything seemed to be there. He made his way through a long circular hallway and up to observation area 5. He took a seat and buckled himself in and closed his eyes, closed his eyes and dreamed.

* * *

The sun was shining, and summer was approaching. The flowers were blooming and the air smelled of life. Spring was in full bloom in upstate New York. Three young men raced across Cornell University campus.

"How did you do on the exam?" asked one as they scurried across the old brick path.

The young man a bit smaller than the other two exclaimed, "Aced it! All that studying paid off."

The large, dark-haired one replied with a smile, "Off to the pub. Celebration time. I'm buying. That was my last exam this semester."

But the smaller one did not hear him. He was focused on something else, someone else. "Hey, who is she? You guys know?" A young blonde walked by. She was the most beautiful girl he had ever seen. She had on a short lavender skirt, and a sleeveless blouse. She wore a necklace and glittering earrings. She turned toward the boy as if she knew she was being watched.

The young man looked into her big, warm blue eyes. She had full red lips and rosy cheeks.

The larger boy replied, "Who, where? Hey, where you going?"

But it was too late. He was off, racing over to the young lady.

"Hello," he said breathlessly, "I know this is going to sound like a line, but…" She had a glowing smile and her eyes pierced his soul. "But, you may be the most beautiful girl I have ever seen."

"Well, it certainly sounds like a line," she said with a smile. "A good one though."

"Are you going to class? Do you have more exams? Today? Would you have time for a cup of coffee or a soda, anything?" the young man rambled on.

"I do have one more exam, but that isn't till Thursday, so I guess I have time for one cup." Her smile grew as she watched him fumble over his words.

"My name is Brett, Brett Roberts," he said

The girl put out her hand, "Hello Brett Roberts. I'm Kathleen Stalivic."

* * *

Brett woke to the rumble of the engines as the Novelette pushed away from Space Station Alpha. He knew his journey to Mars had begun. Brett opened his eyes and found the observation area full of passengers. Sitting across the aisle were two young Asian men. Couldn't be much older than twenty-five, just kids, although nowadays everyone seemed like a kid to him. They talked quickly and seemed to be discussing Mars geology as they showed each other graphs and charts. To his far right were a half of a dozen of men of Arabic descent who all sat there quietly.

"Good day, Mr. Roberts. Hope I didn't wake you" came a rough voice to his left.

"No, not at all." Brett turned to the gentleman seated next to him.

"No I must have zoned out. Didn't hear a thing"

The gentleman was a huge man with a head of deep red hair, and a full red beard to match. He held out his hand. "I'm sorry. I have the upper hand. I know who you are. My name is Terry McGregor, with Relins Incorporated. We're handling construction of the living modules within Roman. We have over three thousand units finished, many of them being used," he declared excitedly.

"I saw a picture of you, wanted to find out who I would report to on Mars. We really are proud of what we've accomplished. We are right on schedule and have many different plans to accommodate the needs of its user."

"So, Mr. McGregor, what…"

"Please call me Terry" he interrupted.

"Okay, Terry, what's your reason for the visit? Sounds like everything is going well."

"Very well. We are actually looking at helping out with building more living units as well as designing a new plan for some of the administrative offices. I have some plans with me."

"Sounds costly to send someone up with the plans, could have downloaded them."

The man roared with laughter, and with his large beard he almost look like the mane of a lion.

"Oh, I'm also a replacement. My counterpart, Kelly Reherd, is due to go back. We try to keep a fresh person up there."

"Sounds like a good plan." Brett was anxious to get to work himself. He could feel the ship accelerate as the G-force pushed him back into his seat. Terry McGregor sat back himself as they accelerated.

"Mr. McGregor, first deep space flight?" Brett noticed him turning green.

"Hmm, yes. Does it show? I understand the first hour is the toughest. After that it's no problem"

"Yeah, that's about right. After that you just have to keep yourself busy. Two months is a long time."

"Well I do have a lot of work I can get done from here. Transmitting reports, work schedules, all the things that keep everything going smooth. What about you, Mr. Roberts? Have enough to keep you occupied?"

"Hmm, yes. Two months may not be enough time to complete it," he said as he sat back and thought about where to start.

* * *

Gary Ivory quickly walked through the corridors, he heels of his boots springing against the new metallic floors. He entered the Security office and went into his private office, securing the door behind him. His monitor was blinking ... "Incoming Message."

He hit accept. The computer voice clearly said "This is a private message... would you like a scrambled line?"

"Yes," he replied

"Password please?"

"History Alpha 1," he spoke back into the computer.

"Voice verification complete."

The face of Tom Afidan came onto the screen. "Gary, I have sent files for you to download. Most of them are pertaining to our operation, as well as one on Brett Roberts. I'm not sure if there is anything in there that you can use. We have come so very far and you cannot let Roberts or anyone stop us. He is arriving on the Novelette, which should arrive in a few months. Make sure that you are ready for him. He has been reviewing layouts, project operations and Mendez death. Keep him busy. Keep him away from the North area. If all goes as planned by the time anyone finds out anything, it will be too late. Do whatever it takes and keep me posted. Make sure you use a secure channel." Gary loaded a CD in and downloaded the files.

"Would you like to save this message?" asked the computer

"No, I would like it deleted and removed from the memory banks."

With a click it was complete. Brett Roberts was not about to stop Gary Ivory. No one was about to stop him.

* * *

The morning sun was falling on the forest as Brett Roberts walked down the path to the creek. He could smell the pine as his feet disturbed the blanket of needles. He could hear the birds overhead chirping, and the squirrels playing in the branches above.

"Dad, come over here! Take a look at this" called a young boy.

The boy stood over 5 feet, tall for a ten-year-old, making up for his height he lost in his low weight. His blond hair glistened in the sun.

"Alexander, where are you?"

"Here, Dad! Look at these tadpoles, hundreds of them."

Alexander had loved nature since he was old enough to crawl. It wasn't hard to get caught up in his excitement.

"Dad, there are more here this year than last. I think they're Pickerel frogs."

"You think so, Alex? Why is that?"

"That's all I caught here last summer, remember?'

"All I remember, Alex, is that they were green."

Alexander quickly scooped his bucket in the water and then gathered some tadpoles in his net and put them in the bucket.

"Too bad Mom wasn't here, Dad."

Brett felt the same way. He always missed Kathleen more when he was with Alexander. He was feeling guilty for being family, a family divided.

"Well, maybe we can talk her into coming with us next year."

"That would be great, like old times!"

Alexander continued to fill the bucket with tadpoles.

"Dad, can you carry them to the cabin?" Alexander asked.

"Yeah, I think you have enough, don't you?"

Brett lifted the bucket of tadpoles and the two went down the trail towards the cabin.

"We didn't have much of a breakfast. What do you want for lunch?"

"I'm not really hungry, Dad. I want to get the tadpoles in containers and label them. Maybe we can eat later."

Brett had given up trying to get Alexander to eat, or anything else for that matter. When Alexander had found something to do with science, nothing else mattered.

"This is great here, Dad! I could live here forever. It's got everything here." Brett agreed it had everything, everything but Kathleen.

The ring of the intercom woke Brett. The gravity on Novelette was less than that of Earth as he cautiously got out of his bunk.

"You have a message coming in. Would you like to take it?" Came a voice from the computer.

"Of course." He said as he rubbed his hands across his face and pushed back his hair.

The face of Kathleen appeared on the screen. He raced his hands across his hair again.

"Kathleen, how are you? I was afraid you didn't get my messages."

"I got your messages. Guess I was procrastinating talking with you. You know things don't go well back home when you're up in space. Here you are off again." Her eyes still made his heart pump with excitement as he listened to her voice. "Brett, I hope I didn't wake you? You look well." There was a slight pause between the two as the signals were delayed a few seconds as the Novelette raced father away from Earth.

"No, I was getting up anyway. You look great as always. I'm sorry I couldn't talk with you in person before I left. It was kind of a quick thing."

She smiled, "That's all right, I wouldn't have talked you out of it anyway. You seem to be happy the most when you're out there, out there in space."

"It was a sudden thing. Should be back in a couple of years if all goes well. But we can keep contact of course," he said as the guilt started to come over him.

"I know, but nothing exciting going on back here, Brett. You and your son were the dreamers of the family." She forced another smile, yet he could feel her pain.

"Kathleen." He paused as he gained his composure. "I was happiest with you. You and Alex."

She looked at him as a tear fell from her eyes, "I know. You take care of yourself and don't take any foolish chances up there." The two looked at each other as tears filled their eyes.

"I promised my sister I would take her to the city for her birthday, Brett. I have to go."

"Well, give her my best and please take care of yourself. I... I still love you."

"I know." The monitor picture went blank. Brett wiped the tears from his eyes. As the computer terminated the connection another one came on. Brett clicked it, no audio, and just a message.

"BEWARE OF ALL. DO NOT TRUST ANYONE OR ANYTHING.

A FRIEND"

"Computer, who is the sender?"
"Unknown," came the voice of the computer
"Where did it originate? From Earth?"
"Unknown."
"Can I reply"?
"No."

The next month Brett had reviewed blueprints, reports, safety studies, personal files as well as anything pertaining to Roman. The city of Roman was composed of five domes, Capricorn, Virgo, Libra, Aquarius and Scorpio forming a circle. Each dome was over two kilometers across and had a series of walkways and tunnels connecting each other. Two smaller domes, Gemini, were in the center which contained water pumps, recycling stations, waste despoil and maintenance garages.

The entire city was surrounded by a large monorail system. The monorail traveled at high speeds, which actually produced a gravitational force equal to that of Earth's. Everyone was to spend approximately 20 hours a week on the monorail to help reduce deterioration of muscles and bone mass.

One could enter the monorail at any dome station where a transport would connect to the moving monorail. The monorail was over 50 meters wide and contained work out facility, dinning establishments, offices, a library, and numerous activities that one could do in their free time.

In all its grandeur most of Roman lay underground. The underground consisted of multiple levels of living quarters, workstations, laboratories and public areas. The bottom levels contained elaborate farms, which grew potatoes, wheat, rice and soybeans. Rabbits and chickens were also raised for consumption. It was a self-sufficient city with new hope for starting a new way of life.

As he went through the lists of people, he was surprised to find some old friends were stationed at Roman. Ali Patel, who was one of the foremen with construction equipment on the moon station, was now in charge of all heavy machinery. Tony Garsia was one of the physicians based in Roman. Also, Rebecca Marceau and Dale Oshioki, who were both geologists, were stationed in Roman. A few other names sounded familiar, and some others were based on the moon at the same time as Brett, but he couldn't place them.

The long voyage would soon come to an end. For Brett it was going by much faster. He had so much to go over, and he still felt unprepared.

He remained uncertain as to what his exact responsibilities were. He still had little information on Mendez's death.

Over the course of the journey, their destination was only a small bright light in the sky. As they got closer to Mars, it began to fill the sky. Although it was only two-thirds the size of Earth, without oceans and seas it had more geography to cover. The Tharis volcanoes included Olympus Mons, which is the largest mountain in the solar system. Everything on Mars was large. The Valles Marineris was a canyon as long as North America.

As they approached Mars its physical features became more visible. Brett was able to observe large dust storms that were hundreds of kilometers in circumference. One could make out what once could have been riverbeds, gorges and shorelines. But Mars now was a dry dead planet. The ultraviolet radiation, the oxidizing nature of the soil, made for a sterile world. A dead world yet Brett felt something he had not felt in awhile. He felt alive. Maybe Kathleen was right.

Brett spent a few hours every day in the observation area working out on the exercise equipment. The observation areas became the focal point on where people meet. Terry McGregor would always strike up a conversation. He was very excited about his work as well as going to Mars.

"Well, it won't be too long now, few more weeks. It's gone by much quicker than I thought. There are some great people on this ship. Well, except for the six over there." McGregor pointed over his shoulder to the six Arabs sitting at a table in the back.

"Oh, had a problem with them?" Brett replied as he studied the six. He had to agree with McGregor that there seemed to be some unity on this ship with the exception of them.

"Not a problem. Just something isn't right with them. You know what I mean? Don't get me wrong. I'm not prejudice. They won't even say good morning."

"Terry, there are all types of people out there. Don't let it get to you." He still glared at the six. McGregor was right. Something wasn't right.

"Now, Mr. Roberts, you say you were just appointed to this position a few months back?" Already knowing the answer.

"That's right. Like you, I'm a replacement."

"Oh, I didn't realize you were replacing someone. How long was he up there?"

Brett turned to the window and stared at Mars, "Too long."

3

The weeks went by and Brett's long voyage was coming to an end. By the end of the day they would dock on Phobos, the smaller of Mars' two moons. Brett was drinking a mug of coffee in the cafeteria when he heard a familiar voice.

"Do you mind if I join you?" said McGregor who proceeded to take a seat next to Roberts.

"Of course not. Are you ready for Mars?"

"Oh, yes. I've been reviewing some information about Mars." He held up his personal computer. "I didn't realize how similar the days on Earth and Mars really are. I didn't even know that a Martian day is called a Sol. Did you know that a Sol is 24 hours and 37 minutes? They use military time on Mars and midnight is actually 24:37:00!", continued McGregor reading from his personal computer. "The days are similar, but a Martian year is almost twice as long. The Martian year is, lets see, here it is." He hit a few pads, "668 Sols long." Brett could sense the excitement in McGregor.

"Brett did you know the average temperature on Mars is –63 Celsius, that's – 81 Fahrenheit, with ranges from 20 Celsius to –140 Celsius. It sure is cold."

"Yes, Mars definitely is a harsh and cold planet, although one day they hope to Terra form Mars into a planet that will be a little more kind to us."

"I've heard about the terra forming, but when I was reading about the atmosphere it seems like a large task." McGregor again hit a few pads, "Right here it says that Mars atmosphere is composed of 95% carbon dioxide and small amounts of other gases such as Nitrogen, Argon and oxygen? I don't know the exact percentages of Earth, but it's sure not that!"

"Yes, the two planets have very different atmospheres, but there are quite a few groups that feel they can terra form Mars. I personally haven't read too much on it, but there are a few people on Mars who are working on it right now."

Just then an announcement was made on the intercom.

"We will be docking on Phobos in approximately three hours. From there you will be able to take a shuttle down to your final destination."

"I was just reading something about Phobos," said McGregor as he scrolled through his computer. "Yes, here it is, Mars has two moons, Diemos and Phobos. Both are irregularly shaped and pitted with craters. Phobos has become the hub for all traffic to and from Mars. It says here that Diemos orbits Mars every 31 hours, while Phobos speeds through the Martians sky three times a day. Pretty convenient, Mr. Roberts, don't you think?"

"Mr. McGregor, you're full of information today aren't you. Yes, from what I understand using Phobos eliminated the need to build a space station orbiting Mars. Almost all freighters and ships use Phobos as their port."

"Well, I'm looking forward to getting my feet planted on Mars."

McGregor said as he stood up from the table. At the same time the air brakes on the Novelette could be felt and McGregor almost lost his balance.

"Well, Terry, I couldn't agree more" he responded, catching him from falling. "I think it's time to gather our things so we'll be able to expedite our trip down to Roman."

"I'm all for that." And with that McGregor made his way to his quarters.

Brett also went to his quarters wanting to make sure he had packed everything. He sat down at the terminal at his desk and brought up a picture of Kathleen, Alex and himself. His heart was pumping, so many emotions pulling at him. Sitting there, he could feel the engines of Novelette braking, and he knew the journey to Mars was coming to a close with a new journey beginning. He thought of life as a series of journeys, as one ended a new one was always there.

The computer broke in as he looked at the picture, "You have a message from Roman. Would you like to take it?"

"Of course"

On the monitor was an older man in his late fifties. "Hello, Mr. Roberts. Jonathan Conners here."

Brett knew, from the files, all about Mr. Conners. He was the assistant to Mendez.

"Hello, Conners. Call me Brett please."

"Sir, hope your trip was pleasant, as pleasant as one can be," he said nervously.

"A bit long. I'll be happy when I'm on the ground."

"Well, sir, that's the problem. We have a major storm coming quickly upon us. I suggest that you may want to ride out the storm on Phobos. I'm not sure they can land a shuttle in this." Brett could see the sweat on Conners.

"What are the conditions now?"

Conners look down of his notes. "Sir, getting high winds, storm should be here in about an hour or two." Brett could see the picture was breaking up.

"Within a few hours I'll be on Phobos. From there I will find transportation down and I'll see you on Mars," Brett replied. The screen went blank.

* * *

This was one of those days Troy Smitts was wondering what he was doing on Mars. He had been an Assistant Professor at Princeton less than a year back coordinating the weather models for Mars. His team had beat out other groups to send a scientist to Mars to set up small satellite stations on the surface in order to gather and hopefully forecast the storms that were causing havoc in the colonies on Mars. The team leader Barb Jefferson broke her leg a month before launch, and Troy had been named her replacement.

Although Troy loved his work, he really hadn't been interested in going to Mars, but he had not been in a position to decline. He could return from Mars after his assignment and get a position at any University or weather station. He also felt it didn't help that he was having an affair with Professor Svoria's wife. He wasn't sure if Svorias knew, but he had a feeling that Svoria's was suspicious and wanted him away from his wife.

Troy had predicted a small storm moving northeast at 70 kilometers per hour about 90 kilometers north of Roman. But as the storm approached, it appeared much more severe and heading directly toward Roman.

"What the frig is going on?" he muttered to himself. "The computer model shows this should be farther North." He plugged in the numbers into the computer, but still no change. He ran his hands through his wavy brown hair.

"Something isn't right. Let me see the specks," he shouted to Corey Davis.

Corey Davis sat at the computer going over all the weather stations. "Here it is, Troy!" he said nervously, not wanting Troy's temper to get any worse.

"Station 185. None of the readings have changed in the last 5 days?"

"What? That's impossible. Damn, they said they would fix that station. It's the third time it went down. Frig!" He slammed his fist down on the desk.

"Corey take out all of 185's reading and lets see the forecast," Troy asked as he gained his composure.

"Storm grade 5 headed right into Roman with a margin of error of 26%."

Troy looked at the monitor of the sky to the North of Roman. "26% or not, we're gonna get hit, and bad. Keep 185 out of the equation until we get up there to take a look at it. I'll let everyone know to buckle down. You keep an eye on it."

*   *   *

Brett entered through the airlock connecting the freighter to the hub on Phobos. He could smell the stale, musty air of the moon as he made his way through the corridor. A female attendant was at the end of the corridor.

"Excuse me. Who do I see about the shuttle to the surface?" he asked as he looked for a monitor.

"If you proceed, you will see that farther down all flights are posted. Where is your final destination?"

"Roman, the city of Roman."

"Oh, no. You won't be going there anytime soon. There is a major storm raging there. The last flight just came in from Roman. It will be some time before anyone will be able to fly into Roman. "

Brett didn't even want to waste his breath on her. It wasn't worth the time. He needed to catch a shuttle or flyer down there. He proceeded to the postings.

"Cancelled"

"Damn." He found his way to the information desk.

"May I help you?"

"Yes, I was wondering if there might be any flights to Roman that aren't posted."

"If there are and aren't posted on here, I'll have their ass! These would be all of them and not one is going to Roman," said the large man from the other side of the counter. Brett could tell that hygiene was not of importance to this man. The man looked at his monitor in front of him, "Looks like one hell of a storm coming in. Might be weeks till it blows over. Next!" He looked over Brett's shoulder.

"Excuse me," Brett piped in "I'm not done yet. Are there any private flights? Any independent flyers?" The man was a bit surprised at Brett's tone.

"Yeah, we do have independent flyers in airlock 15, but no one is allowed to have a flight path to Roman. So sit it out, Earth boy. Next!"

Brett found a diagram of the terminal to figure out where he was. Airlock 15 was a bit off from everything else, but it wouldn't take him to long to get there. He walked quickly on the moving walkways. As he proceeded, he quickly noticed that the people on Phobos were very different from the people he had spent time with on the moon. On the moon there was a feeling of adventure and excitement, a pride in work and the surroundings.

Phobos seemed old and rundown. Very few people seemed to have any type of uniform. Although water was extremely valuable, it appeared that bathing and hygiene were not the norm. After numerous corridors and walkways Brett came to an area just outside Airlock 15. There was an old man at a desk checking over invoices on manifests.

"Excuse me, can you tell me where I might find someone to take me to Roman?"

The man raised his eyes from the electronic clipboard "Should be numerous transport and flyboys down at the main hanger. But don't think anything is going to Roman for some time."

"Yes, I understand. But I'm looking to go down now!"

"We'll, I can't imagine anyone dumb enough to try that, but there are a few pilots at the lounge over there." He pointed to the far side of the corridor.

"That's your best shot."

"Thanks." Brett turned and made his way down to the lounge. There he found the lounge filled with many pilots who were either between flights or celebrating on the break resulting from the storm. Brett approached the bartender. "Hello, I was wondering if you might be able to help me. I'm looking for someone to take me down to Roman,... now!" The older man behind the bar raised his eye on Brett's last word.

"Well, that's a problem, Mister. You're not gonna find anyone who would risk that." He walked towards the other end to serve a customer. Brett followed him to the other end.

"Surely someone is willing to go down, someone's willing to make some extra credits?"

"Sorry, I'm just a bartender. Maybe he can help you." He pointed to a man sitting at a table by the entrance. "The one with the dark blue jacket. He's a supervisor for the union flyers."

"Thanks."

Brett tried to size him up as he walked over to the table. He looked like the typical ex military flyer, flying supplies to Mars and making a lifetime of credits in a few years.

Brett put out his hand "Hello. The gentleman at the bar said you might be able to help me?"

The man looked up, looked at Brett's hand and reclined back in his seat.

"That's no gentleman, and I don't help anyone, at least for free," he said. The group at the table laughed as Brett put his hand down.

"Well let me rephrase it then. Do you know of anyone looking to make some extra credits?"

"How many credits? What do you need?" He chewed a swivel stick between his teeth.

"I need to get to Roman immediately."

The man sat upright in his chair and laughed. "None of my boys would go down into that. We get 200,000 credits for bringing supplies down and another 400,000 credits for bringing raw material back up. I don't think you have enough credits to get anyone's interest."

Again the men at the table laughed. "Really, I was hoping a million credits would spark someone's interest?" the table became quiet.

"A million credits? You have that much? Bullshit. You're trying to yank my chain! I don't think you have that and like I said, I wouldn't have any of my people fly into that!"

"I'll do it," came a rough voice from the next table. "Sure, good a day to die as any," he chuckled. "But I'll want the credits ahead of time."

Brett walked over to the man. "I can transfer them right now. When can we leave?"

The man stood up. He was a large man, over two meters. He had straight brown hair that went passed his shoulders, with his hairline receding in the front. He had a large flat nose and a goatee that was peppered with gray hair.

"I need about an hour to draw up a flight plan and get the paperwork done. Meet me at gate 27." He jotted down something and handed it to Brett. "Here is my account, I'll check the balance before we leave."

Brett went to an automated credit machine and transferred the credits and within the hour was at gate 27. Brett walked up to the large man. "We really didn't get to introduce ourselves. Brett Roberts" He put out his hand. The man put out his large hand and shook Brett's.

"Tom Doughet. I've plotted in a bogey flight path. Otherwise they wouldn't let us take off. Any fines from this and I'll expect you to pay."

"Of course. Did you look at the storm? Get any data. Is it really that bad?" Brett said as the two walked to the flier.

"It's hard to tell. May look worse than it really is. It will be one hell of a ride. It'll be totally cool! You can sit in cockpit of you want. It's the least I can do for what you're paying. The passenger area might be a bit quiet." He chuckled.

Brett sat next to the pilot and placed the large harness from above him over his shoulders and locked it in. The adrenaline raced through Brett as the pilot hit a few switches and the engines were turned on. The flier slowly accelerated out of the hanger into the darkness of space. The sky was totally black and filled with bright stars. The ship rolled into a descent and the view drastically changed to a brilliant red. The shades of red, pink and brown were so rich, so engulfing. He felt like a young boy, as the excitement levels increased when he could pick out objects. He thought how Alex would love this. A new adventure, a New World. Brett could make out the storm as the small ship descended quickly onto the planet.

It was a slow decent towards the surface of Mars. He could see the storm on their first path as they headed closer to Mars.

"First time to Mars? It's totally cool," said the pilot

"Yes, it is. It was a long trip, and I'm anxious to get to Roman"

"Well, it's a busy place. The cargos to and from Roman keep a lot of us busy."

"You have a cargo on the way back from Roman?" Brett said surprised.

"Yeah. Not sure what it is. But the money they pay, who cares?"

The flyer entered the Martian atmosphere and encountered some slight turbulence. Brett closed his eyes as the flyer bumped through the Martian sky. As he got older, he disliked flying. But there wasn't much one could do about it if you wanted to explore the universe.

"Well, it's going to be getting a bit bumpy when we're in the storm," said the pilot. "Should be entering it in about fifteen minutes. It's that dark area ahead. We'll try to fly above it as long as possible."

"I probably should have asked before we took off. What's the biggest challenge, staying level?"

"Well, that will be the trick. These flyers have a large wingspan, so I'm not too worried about losing control. We might be able to ride the wind. It would be cool. My biggest concern is that the vents to the engines might get clogged with the dust."

Brett continued to look out over the majestic beauty of Mars. The shuttle COM link went on, "Flight 1848, you've gone off your flight path and are headed for a storm. Please resume flight plan. Do you read?"

The message repeated two more times before the pilot replied.

David Czaplicki

The pilot hit his COM link, "I've lost my stabilizers and am having difficultly keeping this piece of crap up. I would like nothing more than to get back on course." There was silence as they headed into the red dust.

"Flight 1848, we still don't know how you got so off course?"

The pilot leaned forward and turned off the link. "I'll swing around and try to get in from the north side of Roman. Maybe not as much turbulence there. They usually have us fly south of Roman, so I'm not familiar with the path. But might be the smartest way to attack this storm."

Brett looked out as they slowly descended into the storm. He looked down upon the swirling floor of red dust. "It looks like a blanket of clouds"

"Yeah, it does. But it's five thousand meters of swirling sand down to the surface. It will be a wild ride." He turned the flier down into the storm and they descended on Mars. "Hang on."

As almost in cue the flier began to rock. The noise magnified as the flier entered the storm, which made it almost impossible to communicate. The flier dropped a hundred meters as if it were falling out of control. Was it a good day to die? Maybe, but Brett never feared death. He almost welcomed it. As the ship was tossed around like a rag doll Brett thought of Alex and Kathleen. Whatever happened was in Gods hands. He would just have to play it out.

Brett could barely hear the pilot, "It feels worse than it is...shit!" As the flier took another sharp drop, he could hear Tom once again, "Totally cool!"

Brett could feel sweat rolling down his legs. Nothing could be seen as the dust hit the windshield.

Another sharp drop, as Brett could feel is stomach jump.

The pilot glanced at Brett, "Sorry about that. Don't know when we'll hit an air pocket. Some strong gusts in here. Hell, the visibility is so bad, not sure where here is!"

An alarm went off along accompanied by a bright red blinking light. The pilot hit a few switches between the drops. The alarm finally turned off. All Brett could see was the red sand hitting the windshield. He noticed that he was clenching onto the armrests. With every drop or roll he wondered if he had made a mistake.

Brett looked over the control panel but couldn't make out any of the readings because of the bouncing.

The pilot glanced again at Brett, "You look a little pale," he said "I'm sorry about this. I didn't think it would be this bad. Do you want to try to make it back to Phobos?"

27

"No. No, keep going. We've gone this far." The flyer took a sharp drop and Brett held the armrests tightly. "Guess I just don't enjoy wild rides. Never was one for roller coasters." He could feel his back wet with sweat.

"Well it is a wild ride. Problem is we can't stop this one to just get off. Don't worry I have some living to do myself."

The pilot looked at his instruments, realizing that they weren't far from landing. He turned his COM link back on. "Roman, this is flight 1848, requesting clearance to land." He chuckled to himself, like the answer mattered.

"1848, you are way off your flight path. Do you read?"

"Roman, this is 1848, we got a bit bumped off course in the storm. Stabilizers went off line and must have gotten lost. Can we please land?"

There was a long pause as the flyer took another sharp drop, "Head ten degrees north and begin to descend."

As the flyer turned with the wind, the mountains of Mars could be made out. Through the red dust Brett could make out some type of lights. Another strong gust took the flyer into a small roll. The pilot took evasive action and had control of the flyer within seconds. Another few more pockets of turbulence and they could make out the blinking lights of the runway. The flyer seemed to roll back and forth and at the last minute straighten out as the wheels rolled onto the runway.

"Good God! We did it. Totally cool!" yelled the pilot "I just made a boat load of money on this."

4

The flyer taxied into a hanger, and Brett could make out his reception party that consisted of Jonathan Conners and a few others. Jon Conners seemed nervous as Brett walked up to him. He was an older man who had lied and cheated his way in order to get to Mars. Yet he was ideal for his position. He had kept all the administrative side of things moving smoothly. Jon Conners had always dreamed of adventure but didn't have the necessary determination or courage. Being the paper shuffler was his only chance of getting to Mars.

"Well, you said a few hours. Guess you meant it. You couldn't get me in one of those on a sol like today," he said as he fixed his eyes on the storm outside. "Mr. Roberts, you're either the craziest person I've met or the bravest."

"Neither. Probably the stupidest," laughed Brett.

"I have a breakdown, Mr. Roberts on the storm forecast as well as the current conditions on Roman," Conners said as he handed him an electronic clipboard.

Brett replied as he continued to walk through the hanger, "No, thank you, Conners. Lets get everyone together to make sure we have everything under control. Why don't you show me to my office?"

* * *

Troy Smitts walked into Ivory's office. He didn't need any crap from him. After all, it was Ivory who promised to get station 185 working. Troy didn't know if he and Ivory were like oil and water or if they were so much alike that it led them to despise each other.

"Smitts, another great job!" Ivory sneered at Troy. "Do you realize your inaccurate forecast has cost us more precious time? Time is money!"

"Listen, Ivory, if you would've had Station 185 up and running correctly we wouldn't be having this conversation," Smitts responded as he leaned over Ivory's desk.

"185? What's wrong with it, Smitts? I don't need excuses, I need results. 185 is up and functioning. What the hell is the problem?" said Ivory raising his voice.

"The problem is you, Ivory!"

The door opened, and Brett Roberts walked in. Gary Ivory had seen a picture of Roberts but was still surprised by the sight of him. He was tall, had broad shoulders and a strong face. He carried himself with confidence and appeared in control.

"Gentlemen, Brett Roberts. Glad to meet you. I was told that you were in your office. Hope you don't mind me stopping in unannounced?" Brett said holding out his hand.

Ivory walked from around the desk. "Roberts." Ivory acknowledged him and put out his hand "Gary Ivory. Glad to have you aboard, and of course there is never a problem stopping in," he said in a very monotone voice. "This is Troy Smitts, our local weatherman." Ivory grinned.

Troy turned to Roberts. "Yes, I was just talking to Ivory about our problem. Seems some of his men didn't install a weather station correctly, and it threw off the forecast considerably."

"Considerably! This is going to cost us time and money," snickered Ivory.

Brett tried to size up Smitts. "Well, whether the forecast was accurate or not the storm still would have come. What are we looking at and what are we doing to minimize damage?"

Troy tapped a keypad on his wrist, and a three-dimensional view of the storm came up.

"As you can see, the front is coming down from the north and has slowed down. We are looking at winds of 300 kilometers an hour with gusts over 500. Should move out of the area within a week."

Ivory pointed to the three dimensional images on the far wall. "The last sector was closed down, and most of the people are in the main interior of the city. Problem is without the proper warning about this storm, a lot of heavy machinery will be left out in it. The Martian sand is a killer to these vehicles. Going to be a lot of unnecessary maintenance." He glared at Troy.

Brett pointed to the image, "Any chance of getting any of the machines into dock 47?"

Ivory was taken back. It was apparent to Ivory that Roberts was familiar with the layout of Roman. It was going to be difficult to keep Robert's nose out of his business.

"We have some heavy machinery there, but visibility is down to zero," replied Ivory. "We'll have to dig them out when it's all over."

Roberts listened as the two discussed the storm. These were two men that definitely didn't care for each other. Roberts looked over toward Troy, "Well, Troy, keep me posted on the storm. Ivory, I want to meet with all the foremen and supervisors in two hours. We'll set up a game plan so that when the storm does clear we're ready to go." Brett turned and walked toward the door.

Ivory nodded and replied, "I'll see you in a couple hours. You might want to start looking through the files. I haven't had time to get to some of them. Sorry. Probably last thing you're interested in are the forms and requisitions, but we've been busy." He said with a half smile as Brett walked out.

Troy walked over to Brett and held out his hand "Glad you're here." He proceeded then down an adjacent corridor.

*   *   *

The conference room was filled with questions and concerns. Roberts entered the room and approached the far end of the table. "Thank you, everyone, for getting here so quickly. I know some of you had a difficult time getting here. For anyone who doesn't know who I am, I'm Brett Roberts, the new administrator of Roman." Everyone in the room viewed Roberts with mixed feelings. To some he was just another Calprex puppet, to some just another person to report to, to a few, those who knew him, respect. To another select group Roberts represented another obstacle.

"First thing I'd like to do is have Troy Smitts update us on the storm. Troy?"

Troy walked over the screen on one side of the room. He took the remote control and with a click, a three-dimensional view of Roman appeared on the wall.

"Thanks. This is Roman about five hours ago. This mass to the north is the approaching storm. As we forward the view you can see that Roman is smack in the path of it." He hit another button and the projection was an aerial view from a satellite. "You can see this is just the beginning. The storm could last for at least a week. The winds will stay at a constant 300 kilometers per hour with some strong gusts, but the winds won't diminish until the storm has completely passed." He hit another series of buttons and Roman appeared again. The view swung to the Aquarius.

"You can see," he went on "that there's almost a meter of sand piled up along the perimeter of the dome. This corridor is almost covered on the North side. The inner city won't be as bad due to the structure of the domes acting like snow fences, holding out some of the sand. At this rate though we will see anywhere from two to six meters of sand across the entire city. Almost like a major snowstorm, but like a snowstorm with a magnitude Earth has never seen. The other difference is that sand doesn't melt." Troy went back to his chair.

Brett went around the room asking for feedback from all of the supervisors. "Marylou, what's the status on the monorail?"

Marylou Brown was an up and coming engineer who had grown up in the inner city of Philadelphia. Hard work and studying had paid off for her. She jumped at the opportunity to be the first black female supervisor.

"Well, we're in the process of shutting down the monorail system. The sand on the track is too much for the system. If we shut it down now and clear when the storm is over, we'll have minimal damage."

"Mr. Chang, how does the integrity of the Domes look?"

Ho Chang was Japan's finest architect, combined with his hunger for adventure. Mars was an ideal place for him.

"Well, this will be a real test. These domes were constructed to keep in the pressure, and not to withstand the pressure and weight of the sand. We should be okay, but we will monitor the structure as the storm progresses. The northside corridor is already buried. At this time no one is permitted to use those corridors until we've evaluated the situation more carefully."

Brett turned his eyes to the other side of the table. "Ali, what about the machinery that's outside?"

"It's getting tossed around like matchboxes, Brett. We're getting buried. The entire city."

Gary Ivory took notice as Brett went from one person to the other, calling them by name and asking them specific questions. Brett Roberts had definitely done his homework.

By the time the meeting was over they had a plan installed for the cleanup and the attempt to get back on schedule. "Mr. Conners, I believe you've got this all down. Make sure everyone has a copy of what is expected of them. If anyone has any questions or wants to discuss anything, my door is always open."

Brett stood up and briefly talked with everyone as they left the conference room.

Ivory looked around the room to get a feel of what the others thought. Too hard to tell now with the storm going on. They're all worked up like rats in a cage. That was fine with him. The storm bought him some more time.

* * *

Brett finally made it to his quarters. His personal items were still not in. His room was larger than he had expected. He had a bedroom, bathroom and a large room that contained two large desks, and a couch with a couple of chairs flanked by end tables. The main room had a large window, while a breakfast bar divided the far part of the room. The kitchen contained a heating unit, sink and refrigeration unit. He opened the refrigeration unit and happily found it stocked with freeze-dried fruit, concentrated beef bars, carbo-bars and bottles of water. The room was dimly lit with the lighting coming from the ceiling. The lights above the desk were shining on the terminal. He sat down in the chair, in front of his terminal, wondering if it were tapped into the one in his office. He turned it on.

"Computer, am I able to get files from my office?"

"Yes, but you must submit your employee number as well as your password."

Brett plugged in his number, but before he could go any farther...

"You have two personal messages. Would you like to read them?"

"Yes"

The first message appeared on the screen

"Brett,
Welcome to Mars, your new home. Give me a call when you have time.
Rebecca"

A warm smile went over Brett's face. He had remembered the good times he had shared with Rebecca on Moon Base. It was going to be nice to have an old friend to talk with.

"Computer, next message."

The screen appeared blank for a moment and then a message appeared.

TRUST YOUR FEELINGS, NOTHING ELSE!
A FRIEND

"Computer who is the message from?"
"Unknown"
"Can I respond?"
"No."

"Can this message be traced?"

"No."

Brett looked at the message, wondering whom it was from.

"You may continue with your password."

Brett turned away as he watched the sand fall and whip against his window. He walked up to the windows. He could hear the wind and sand hitting against the window. The red sand turned to white in Brett's mind as Brett recalled an earlier time. A time when life seemed uncomplicated and free. A time when he was with Kathleen and Alex.

"Dad, can I help you shovel?" said a young boy of five.

"Maybe sometime soon Alex, but not today. The wind and cold would freeze your fingers."

"But, Dad, I want…"

"Now Alex, you heard your father" came a voice from the next room. Kathleen walked into the room with two mugs of hot chocolate.

"Here you go. One for each of the two men in my life." She handed them each a mug. The boy noticed that his mug was not like his fathers. It had a lid and was a bright red.

"Mom, I want a cup like Dad's."

"Don't give your mother a hard time Alex." Brett interjected. The three looked out the window at the snowstorm. The snow was piling up in front of the house. They could barely see across the street.

Kathleen looked out the window, "I hate this weather. We should move down south."

"I know you do, but I love this. Mans last frontier on this planet, the weather. Can't do much about it except take it."

"Daddy, I like it too," said Alex. "When can we go out and play in it again?"

"Soon, Alex. Maybe tomorrow."

"Is there snow on the moon?"

"No Alex. No snow, no water, no life." Brett's eyes meet Kathleen's.

"Brett, when do you leave for the moon?" she asked with a more serious tone in her voice.

Brett grabbed her hand "'Next month, on the fifth."

"Well, we should think about moving somewhere warm when you get back. I was thinking about applying for a position at the University of Southern California."

Brett loved the winters in the Northeast. But he was going up to the moon for four months. It was tough to expect Kathleen to live here, with this weather, when he wasn't around. They had talked about moving for almost a year, and with him leaving it was something he wouldn't be able to control.

"I know you hate this weather Kathleen. With my work we can live anywhere. If moving is something you really want, I understand. Just don't sell this place. We could always rent it out."

Kathleen put her arms around Brett, "I know you love this place, but moving to California will be great. It will keep Alex and me busy while you're having adventures on the moon!"

Alex had overheard their discussion. "Dad, do you have to go to the moon?"

"Well, no, son, but it's what I've been trained to do. It's my job. I thought you were okay with everything."

"The kids in school are saying you won't come back. You'll die up on the moon."

Brett picked up Alex and sat him on his lap "I'll be coming home, don't worry. It is dangerous up there, but I've trained for a long time to handle any situations. Don't worry."

"But what if you did die Dad, I'd want to die, too, to be with you."

"Oh, you wouldn't want to do that. Always remember that when someone you love dies, you have to continue and carry on with your life. You can keep alive those you love in your heart. So as long as you are alive, your mother and I will be alive in your heart."

The little boy hugged his father as they looked out at the snow. Kathleen walked up from behind and wrapped her arm around Brett. She kissed his cheek and whispered, "I expect you home as well. Don't do anything stupid." That night the two made love for the last time.

* * *

Nick walked into his office overlooking downtown Houston. He sat down at his desk and turned on his monitor. "Any messages?"

"You have sixteen. Would you like them listed." came the voice from his computer.

"Yes, please." Nick wondered why he was always saying please and thank you to his terminal. He read the list. A few of the messages were from one of the manufacturing plants. One was from Brett, another from Ed, and the rest appeared to be copies of orders.

"Let me see the one from Brett Roberts."

"Nick

Landed on Phobos safely. We seem to have a large storm heading for Roman. Will assess situation and take care of it appropriately. If you

have any additional information for me, address it to my Mars address. I
hope to be there by the end of the Sol.
Take care,

Brett"

"Computer, show me the one from Ed Brocton"

"Sir would you like me to save the last message?" The mechanical voice asked.

"No, delete it please."

Nick went through a few other messages. The message from Ed was just to call him when he got in. Nick signed off on a few things and then picked up the telephone and called Arizona.

"Hi, Betty, is Ed in? He left a message for me. I don't know if it's important, but I also wanted to call to see what's up," he said warmly.

"Hello, Nick. Yes Ed's here. Just hang on and I'll patch you through to him. He's in the control room."

Nick waited a minute and then heard Ed's voice.

"Nick, we have a few problems. Roman is being bombarded with a storm, a size we've never recorded. Haven't been able to make contact with them for over an hour. Have you heard from Brett?"

"Yes, just got a message that he arrived at Phobos and is headed down to Roman. He did mention a storm was on the way. How bad is it?"

"Appears to have winds of 300 kilometers with gusts close to 500. Looks like at least a week to go. The main reason I called is I have to fly to Washington. We're getting a lot of pressure to complete Roman. The Arab Republic wants lands to the North if they're not able to occupy the living quarters and offices according to the contracted arrangements."

"Why would the Arab Republic want to claim land to the North? They have more land claims on Mars then they know what to do with?" Nick responded.

"I know. I think it's an empty threat. I'm going there to stall for some time. Make sure you keep Brett updated on what's going on. Have him put a rush on completing Capricorn. That's where the Arab Republic have their contracts, and they want to be in there within four months. Have him complete Capricorn, so they can move in, even if the rest of Roman needs work. Keep an eye on Brett and keep me posted. I have to catch my flight. If you need anything let me now."

Nick heard the click before he could respond. Ed was trying to do everything himself. Flying here and there, trusting no one to do anything for him.

5

The next morning Brett got to his office early to review the reports. He went directly to Troy's report on the storm. It didn't look good. The storm could last for weeks. The doorcom chimed.

"It's open."

In walked a tall woman. She had short dark hair, which was layered around her face. She had a light complexion and radiant blue eyes. The woman looked at Brett and a warm smile appeared. "Well, Mr. Brett Roberts you're looking as dashing as ever."

Brett stood up from behind his desk and walked towards the woman, "Rebecca, how are you? And you're still as stunning as ever." The two embraced. Brett had forgotten how beautiful she was. She had natural beauty, was the type of woman who looked as good in a pair of sweats as in an evening gown.

He looked into her big eyes, "No one makes these jump suits look as sexy as you."

"Still have a great sense of humor I see. How was your first Sol on Mars?"

"Wow, anything but dull would work. But it feels good to finally be here. It was a long trip."

"I want to know about that trip. Buy a woman breakfast?" she chuckled.

Brett smiled back as the two left his office. Rebecca led him to a small café where they ordered two cups of Martian java and high protein bars.

"I saw, Rebecca, that you're heading up one of the geology units."

"Yes, and it's wonderful. I mean the moon is great, but there is so much history on Mars. We can get some great readings and get some pretty specific dates. Within a year we hope to publish a theory called 'the Rivers of Mars'. We have some mind-blowing data." She took a sip of her java. "This storm is slowing us down a bit, but we have enough in the laboratories to look at." She sat back and crossed her legs "So you, you're back, back in space." She smiled.

"Yeah, I guess I am. Ed and Nick wanted someone they've worked with in the past. They want me to see what I can find out about Carlos' death."

Rebecca looked puzzled. "What do you mean? Wasn't it an accident?"

"I don't know. I hope to find out. I have a long meeting this afternoon with Gary Ivory to review his death. We'll see what turns up."

"I hear he's a warm fuzzy guy. Enjoy," she said sarcastically.

The two smiled, laughed, and chatted the morning away.

*   *   *

That afternoon Brett went to Gary Ivory's office. His assistant said he had stepped out, but that Brett could have a seat and when Ivory returned he would let him know. Brett sat for a few minutes outside of Ivory's office and after a few minutes thought he heard voices coming from Ivory's office. Brett thought he must have a second entrance to his office and he would call Brett in any minute.

A good ten minutes passed and still he hadn't been called in. Maybe Brett was mistaken and the noise was coming from somewhere else. Brett stood up to examine a few items on the walls. Most of them were an assortment of pictures of Mars. Brett was examining one of the photos when he heard a thump from the next room. Brett looked over at Ivory's assistant, who had also heard the noise and was looking over at Brett.

Brett didn't mind waiting but really wasn't interested in playing games. He quickly walked over to the door and, opening it, entered Ivory's office. Ivory was sitting behind his desk arranging a few items. "Good timing, Brett. I was just finishing up." He stood up and placed a CD into a cabinet on the far wall.

"What was it you wanted to review again?" he said smugly.

"I wanted to see what information you have on Mendez's death."

"You have it all. I sent it to you when you were in transient. It was a pretty open and shut case. He fell off the cliff and punctured his suit."

"Can I see the suit? Must have been some pretty sharp rocks to rip a space suit."

"I'd love to accommodate you, but we no longer have it. I had three of my men examine the information, take some pictures, and analyze the area, and they came to a logical conclusion. As for the suit, it was pretty messy, as I'm sure you can imagine. We used some of the gauges for backups and destroyed the suit."

'Well, Mr. Ivory, I'm sure you and your staff did everything you mentioned. But the file I received was awfully small. Doesn't look like a lot of work was put into it."

"Accidents do happen. Read the reports. A lot of shit occurs here. It's not as safe as back home. If you aren't careful you might find yourself having an accident!"

"Is that a threat, Mr. Ivory? I was on the Moon for a total of fifteen months in a three-year period and we never had the number of accidents you have here at Roman. I want to meet with the three men who did the investigation."

Ivory looked a bit startled over the request. "What do you want with them? They answer to me. If you have any questions, ask me."

"That's not the way it works with me, Mr. Ivory. I'll have Connors call you later in the day and arrange times to meet with all of them tomorrow." Brett turned and left the office.

*   *   *

Troy Smitts looked at the model of the storm. If the wind changed just a few degrees, it could bypass Roman and cut the storms effect on Roman by Sols.

"Corey, show me the reading of station 131 and 145," Troy barked.

Corey Davis hit a few keys on his terminal, and the 3-D reading of the two stations came up.

"Damn, just too much guess work! Without the reading from 185 there really is no way to predict the storm."

"Troy, both 131 and 145 are also in the northern area. I think 131 is near Baron's Pass, and 145 is about twenty kilometers west. You should be able to make an accurate estimate." He was looking at the numbers with Troy.

"It sounds like we should. But with those mountains and the canyon lying here," he pointed to the area, "the winds can take some drastic changes. The winds could whistle down this canyon and hit the ridge here and diminish. If they take this path they can actually accelerate and head in a more southerly flow."

"Wow, I never noticed that. When did you come up with that information?" Corey asked.

"A while back. God knows how long we've been without station 185's input. I don't understand why the computer didn't show that the readings were not coming in."

"I'll have someone look into that Troy. The IT people should have the answer to that."

"Screw them. I don't trust their work. I have a friend who's good with computers. I'll have him take a look at it. When this storm subsides, I'm going out to 185 to fix it personally."

"Well, since the storm we've had about six stations needing some maintenance. So we'll be busy."

* * *

The last man left Brett Robert's office. All their stories were the same. They sounded rehearsed and all seemed to have a clear recollection of the events. Almost four months ago and still they didn't waiver in their stories at all. The only one who seemed the slightest dazed was Ivory the day before, when he was told that Brett planned on meeting with the three men.

No suit, no creditable witnesses. He wondered if he would ever find out what happened to Mendez. He pulled up Mendez' personnel files to look for clues in the notes. After hours, he rubbed his eyes and wondered if this was a waste of time. Surely Ivory had reviewed and manipulated the information in the files. Ed and Nick were counting on him to find something, but it appeared that everything was cleaned up and disposed of. If Mendez had come across something, surely he would have had a coded message in his personnel file. Something that Ivory couldn't figure out. But what?

Brett needed to get a break. He closed the files and decided to take a walk through Roman.

Gary Ivory went down to the fourteenth level under Gemini, to near where the waste facility was located. He had a quick jump in his step as the door opened to the local security office.

"Where is Adam Delillo?" he barked at the guard at the desk.

"He's in the back. Just got here a few minutes ago."

Ivory walked down the hallway and entered the far room. Sitting at the table were four men. A fifth man was getting a cup of Martian java at the counter. He was a large man of European descent. He had jet-black hair slicked back. His face was covered with dark stubble, and he had a large scar on his right cheek. He stirred his drink and looked up, calmly glared at Ivory. "Well, that didn't take you long to get here."

"Don't be a friggin smart ass. What does Roberts know? Did he believe you?"

Delillo took a gulp of his drink. "Relax man. I stuck to the story. No deviation, no problems. He has nothing but hunches. He has no evidence. The only thing he has is you panicking about every move he makes."

Ivory glared at him. "Panic? Are you an asshole? If he finds out before we're ready, this entire operation is in jeopardy. One slip by any of us and he might be looking for answers and then stumble across something important. Just stay out of sight, and if he wants to talk with you again, let me know. Do you understand?"

Delillo grabbed a chair at the table and sat down. "Yeah, man. Relax, I'm not going to say anything. Chill."

Ivory stormed toward the table and slammed Delillo's face into it. "Chill! You better stay away from me as well or you'll be in a body bag!"

Delillo lifted his head from the table with blood running from his nose. Ivory turned and left.

* * *

The storm raged for another two sols with no end in sight. Brett decided to survey Aquarius one morning. He always took his communicator and a small locator that would help him find his way around Roman. He was always in touch should something come up. He had visited Gemini, Capricorn and Virgo. A lot of work needed to be done and the deadline had come and gone about five months ago. This storm was not going to help the situation either. He packed a few power bars and a bottle of water. Brett clicked on his communicator.

"Hello, this is Brett Roberts. I'm going to be surveying Aquarius today. If you need to get hold of me, I have my portable with me." An affirmative answer was followed over the communicator.

He walked through a maze of corridors that led to the center of Aquarius. As the hallway passed through the center area, Brett looked up at the top of the dome. Although he had seen the pictures and blueprints, the sight was breathtaking. The center of Aquarius, like all the domes, had a center area in which were a park, a number of small shops and a food court. It would give one a feeling of Earth. Although not complete, it was an incredible job of engineering. Above him were still another six levels, all meeting in the center.

He walked toward the center and looked out through the reddish glass of the dome. He could see the sand racing across, piling up in the grooves of the glass. The mountains to the North of the city could not be seen, visibility was only a few meters. It felt good to stretch his legs, he thought, much better than riding the stationary bike on the Novelette.

Brett reached for his communicator as it chimed.

"Hello. Brett Roberts here."

"Mr. Roberts, how are you? More importantly, where are you?" It was Rebecca's voice.

"Actually, I'm just stretching my legs. I'm walking through Center Park in Aquarius."

"Really? My quarters are on the bottom level of Aquarius. I'm only a few minutes away. Would you like some company?"

"Sure thing." Brett replied. "I'm where the fountains are to be installed. Do you know where that is?"

"Hey, I'm the local here. I know where it is. Be there in a few." Brett could almost feel her smile over the communicator.

The storm outside of Roman intensified. Outdoor equipment was being thrown around like children's toys. The weather tower outside of Gemini came crashing down. Almost all outside cameras were disintegrated piece by piece. A small funnel picked up one of the trackers and carried it into the side of Aquarius. The thick glass held, but a small hairline crack developed near the base.

Within a few minutes Rebecca joined Brett near the fountains. Walking up to him, she gave him a hug, then grabbed his hand. "Let me take you to my favorite part of Aquarius."

The two talked as they began walking through Roman. It was minutes before Brett realized that he was still holding her hand. "Rebecca, why didn't we stay in touch? I forgot how great your company is."

Rebecca smiled and glanced away, a little embarrassed. "Well, we both left the moon and had some issues we had to resolve. We were in a bubble up there, figuratively. We all got close with each other. Then reality hit us all when we got back Earthside."

Brett knew she was right as he thought of his first year back. Brett's mind raced back to those years following his return home. He could feel his heart race and began to sweat. Rebecca clutched his hand harder.

"I wrote to you, Brett when I heard. You never responded." She looked into his eyes and could still see the pain.

"I know, and I appreciated it. I just couldn't face anyone, face anything" tightening his grip on her hand.

She took a deep breath and tried to alter the mood as her voice changed it's inflection. "Well, Mars is a lot different from the moon. No one seems to be close. Maybe there are too many people here already."

Brett wanted to change the subject as well. "What kind of work are you doing here?"

"We're studying some of the early geologic sites here, trying to establish the age and formation of some of the land formations."

The two continued to walk in the corridors of Aquarius, unaware the hairline crack in the glass was increasing as the wind and sand crashed against the dome.

In Gemini a crew of a dozen people looked over monitors and checked for possible damage in the structure. Readings were showing damage to Aries, which was not sealed yet. Another monitor confirmed the weather tower was down. An alarm went off. Reading on the monitor showed that the pressure in Aquarius was decreasing. "Sir, we have a possible leak in Aquarius," the engineer at the monitor yelled into his headset. "Doing a diagnostic to pin it down."

Rebecca took Brett by the hand "Look at this..." The noise was incredible as if a bomb went off next to them. The seal in Aquarius broke, and anything loose was being sucked out into the storm. A bench became a projectile as it blew by the two who had fallen to the ground in reaction to the seal breaking.

"What's going on?" she yelled, as she held on to a corner with one hand and Brett with the other.

"I'm not sure. Must be a break somewhere. We have to get out of here before they seal the doors."

The noise was deafening as the air was being sucked out of the dome. Anything not bolted to it was flying across Aquarius. The alarms went off.

"Yes, it's a break in the seal," Rebecca screamed in response to the alarm. "We need to get to the far corridor. The hatch door will close in five minutes. How are we going to get there? If we let go, we'll get sucked out."

The engineer had set off the alarm and put the emergency protocol in action. "We are evacuating Aquarius. This is not a drill. Evacuating Aquarius," he cried as his palms were wet with sweat. The room quickly filled with people.

"Any idea how many people are in there?"

"Can they get out?"

The engineer looked up to the group "I would estimate at least a few hundred people, and at the rate that the dome is depressurizing I'm not sure how many can get out."

Jon Conners step forward. "I can't reach Roberts. He's not answering his communicator. Does anyone know where he is?"

The engineer turned towards Conners "I just talked to him about thirty minutes ago. He was in Aquarius."

In the back of the room Ivory chuckled to himself. "That didn't take long."

"There has to be something we can do." Someone yelled from the back.

The engineer looked at a series of diagrams on his monitor. "I can close off and seal the leak by closing storm doors in quadrant 8, 9 and 10." A few other people looked over his shoulder to confirm. "The problem is, it will only last for a few minutes till there is structural damage."

"What kind of damage?" asked Conners.

"The pressure at that location," replied the engineer pointing on the monitor, "will blow a hole in the wall about 100 meters in diameter. Aquarius will be uninhabitable until the hole is repaired along with, and of course, any damage to the seal."

"And if we don't close the storm doors?" asked Ivory as he walked toward the group huddled group.

"If we do nothing? If we leave the doors open, minimal structure damage, but, but everyone inside will die."

Jon Conners stared in amazement. "You can't be serious?"

Ivory snarled at Conners, "I am serious, very serious. Structural damage will cost us millions and put us back months."

"There are people in there!" Conners exclaimed.

"Mr. Conners, you will do as you're told or I'll put you in your place. What the hell are you so concerned about?" Ivory raising his voice and, walking over to Conners, and sticking his chest in his face.

Conners was quiet, the engineer nervously breaking in. "Its not a choice."

"Not yours, Mister. It's mine!" Ivory declared.

The engineer made a few adjustments at his terminal. "No, it's mine. I'm in charge of engineering. I'll close the doors for a few minutes. They'll have about five minutes to get out."

They all looked at the monitors and watched the storm doors close.

Brett was becoming lightheaded as he hung on to a railing with one arm, the other, was around Rebecca. Almost as soon as it began, it stopped. The noise ceased, and the wind died down.

"YOU HAVE ONLY A FEW MINUTES TO EVACUATE" came the announcement over the public communicators. "QUICKLY EXIT TO ANY OF THE WEST SIDE EXITS OR TUNNELS TO THE UNDERGROUND. WE HAVE ONLY TEMPORARILY STOPPED THE LEAK. YOU HAVE APPROXIMATELY FIVE MINUTES."

Brett and Rebecca could see that they were not alone as other people were getting to their feet and beginning to run to the West Side of

Aquarius. Brett grabbed Rebecca's hand and started to run. People were pushing each other to get to the exits. Rebecca and Brett gathered around the first exit where a man who had a large cut on his head was trying to keep an orderly exit.

"Please. One at a time. Please don't push."

Brett could see there were too many people at the exit and that he had to get Rebecca out.

"Look, isn't there another floor hatch around the corner?" he asked Rebecca

"Brett, I have no idea."

He grabbed her hand. "Look, you people in the back of the line, follow me."

The group of approximately twelve followed Brett around the corner. As he ran, he looked for a hatch along the floor. The floor was made of red and brown bricks. The area was damaged, and there was considerable debris lying on the floor. He stopped and looked around. "It's got to be here, somewhere."

A woman voice yelled, "Here. I think this is it!"

An uprooted tree had fallen on the hatch, its upper branches and leaves concealing it from view. Brett and another man cleared off the branches and opened up the hatch.

"Lets move it," Brett yelled as he was on one knee helping a woman down. "Let's keep order and get everyone out of here." He looked up at Rebecca. "Let's go. You're next."

She looked around and let a few people pass "No I'll wait for you."

The people continued to go down the hatch. "Look Rebecca go down, now" as he held her hand. She hesitated before starting down the ladder in the hatch. "Hurry, Brett. Hurry!"

There were two more who had begun down, Brett, not being one of them when the seal gave in. Brett could feel the power of the suction as he quickly grabbed the hatch. He reached out to hold onto one of the other men. The third man was gone.

"LET ME GO! SAVE YOURSELF," the man yelled. Brett pulled him closer until the man was able to grab the railing on the inside of the hatch. The man had maneuvered his legs into the hatch when a piece of debris came hurling toward the two of them. It crashed into Brett's hand, holding onto the door. His reflex to the pain caused him to release his grip. Pain shot up his arm as his legs went flying skyward. The man still held Brett's arm and was attempting to pull him in.

Everything was in slow motion for Brett. He could see objects being blown across and crashing into each other. He no longer heard the deafening noise and could not feel his arm on the other man. The only thing he felt was the intense pain in his other arm. The man was yelling something at him. Brett couldn't hear him but he could sense he was slipping. This wasn't the way he imagined dying. He was no longer afraid of death, however the man yelled but Brett could no longer hold him.

In a split instant the noise came back, and Brett became a human projectile and flew across the park of Aquarius.

* * *

Rebecca heard the hatch closing behind her. Yet it was hard to make anyone or anything out in the auxiliary light. The hatch closed and the air got thicker. Rebecca took a deep breath. "Brett, are you over there?" she said as she made her way past people moving toward the hatch. "Brett! Brett! Where's Brett?" She asked the man still holding onto the latch.

She looked into his eyes and knew the answer. Yet she needed to hear it. "Where is Brett? Where is he?" she screamed.

"I'm sorry. We tried to bring him in, but the force was just too great. I couldn't hold on!" the man answered as he began to shake. "He saved my life."

"Well we have to get him." She pushed him aside and pulled on the latch.

A tall redheaded man pulled her away, "Miss, nothing we can do, nothing from here."

She knew he was right.

* * *

The control room was full as Aquarius split open. A large crack, almost a hundred meters long at the foundation was expanding as Mars was sucking the inner pressure out.

"Did anyone get out? Was it really worth it?" Ivory asked. "Aquarius has structural damaged that will cost us valuable time and money."

"We're getting reports from the emergency exits. There've been numerous injuries, and people are still trapped in Aquarius."

Conners wiped the sweat from his brow, "Well, at least we saved some people. Anyone have any idea if Brett Roberts made it out?"

Ivory perked up at the name. Wouldn't it be perfect if Roberts were already out of the picture?

A few communications checks were made at the emergency.

"I think we have Roberts, Mr. Conners," said a communication technician at the control panel.

"Please put him on the audio speaker." The room became quiet as they listened to the speakers crackling through the static. "Roberts, are you all right?" Conners said loudly.

"Hello, this is Rebecca Marceau. I was with Brett Roberts. He helped many of us get to the emergency exits, but he's still in Aquarius. Can you find him?" She sounded frantic.

"I don't know if there is anything we can do." Conners said as he looked around the room for an answer. "What is your location?"

Through the static they could barely make out her reply, "AQ-2479."

He glanced around the room once more with a look of terror in his eyes.

* * *

Brett Roberts became a human projectile. He was flying towards the hole in Aquarius. He could see debris from the park flying by him. Trees were uprooted, walls collapsed. With a sudden jerk his body got caught in netting that was strung between two beams. More debris crashed into the net. His leg was caught in the net and he couldn't move. The pain shooting through his arm was intense. Part of him wanted it to all end, yet another instinctively wanted to survive.

A piece of twisted metal flew by his face and into the net. He knew he wouldn't last if he didn't get untangled. He felt like he was stuck to a target in a shooting gallery. He tried to reach his twisted leg, but his left arm was numb and he couldn't get hold of the netting. He looked up and saw a large object heading right for him. The object ripped right through the netting above him, leaving a large hole.

He wasn't going to wait for the next object to crush him. He reached over and grabbed some of the metal that was intertwined in the netting and began to cut the net. He slowly began to fall as the net was ripping. He hit the floor and slid towards the break, but his leg caught in the net stopped him from going much farther. He was getting light-headed and tasted blood in his mouth. There wasn't much time left before the oxygen had escaped. He lay on the floor trying to clear his mind. His view was becoming fuzzy, and the noise appeared to be fading.

He rolled over and saw a handle a few meters away. He pressed his fingers against the floor and pulled himself over. It was a hatch leading below. He attempted to turn the latch, but it wouldn't budge. He didn't know if it was locked or that he didn't have the strength to open it. He read the number on the hatch, AQ-2744. He put his communicator up to his mouth, "This is Brett Roberts. Is anyone there? Can you hear me? I am at hatch AQ-2744. Is anyone there?"

There was no answer.

* * *

They were still arguing in the control room when Troy Smitts walked in.   Jon Conners looked at the engineers, "Is there anyway to tract him down?"

"No, not really. There's a lot of interference with this storm. By the time we'd find him it'll be too late."

Smitts noticed that Ivory had a smirk on his face. He appeared not at all concerned.

Troy walked up to Conners "What's going on? I heard an explosion?"

Conners turned toward Smitts, sweat rolling down his forehead "Aquarius seal has been compromised. Roberts is still in there, along with many others. Not much we can do."

Still trying to comprehend the news, said Smitts, "You have no idea what part of Aquarius he's in?"   Not waiting for a response he turned on him communicator. "Brett. Brett Roberts, can you hear me?"

Ivory chuckled under his breath, "Don't even waste your time"

"Brett, can you hear me?" Nothing but static. Troy turned up his communicator. Still nothing.

Ivory walked up to him and grabbed his wrist, "Turn that thing off. We have enough commotion in here. Don't you have a storm to watch?"

Troy pulled his arm back "Don't you ever touch me again, or..."

"Or what? I'll have you put away so fast."

The anger in Troy was starting to boil. He knew he shouldn't do it, but doing the right thing wasn't one of his strong points. He pulled back him arm, and clenched his fist and punched Ivory in the jaw. Ivory fell back into the monitors, and the room went quiet. Ivory got up, placing his hand on his jaw.

"You're finished Smitts," snapped Ivory. "You're done." The room remained still.

Conners spoke up excitedly "Listen do you hear that? Is that coming from Troy?"

"Hear what?"

The room went quiet as they listened to Smitts communicator. "Hatch AQ-2744, can you hear me?"

Smitts turned it up. "It's Roberts!" then, speaking into the communicator, "Brett we hear you. Can you hear us?"

But all that was audible was static. "Hatch AQ-2744. Where is that? Get someone over there now," Conners bellowed.

Brett knew this was the end. The pain in his arm was intense, and he was becoming very light headed, with everything around him seeming fuzzy. He closed his eyes and waited for the end to come.

"Dad, hold on. Don't give up." Brett opened his eyes "Alex, is that you?" He could make out a figure approaching him. "Alex, is that really you?"

Brett had no strength left as he raised his arms and closed his eyes.

6

Ten Sols later the storm came to a sudden halt. The sun came out through a pink sky. Dunes of sand covered Roman and its terrain. Construction vehicles were making their way out across the sand. The storm had seemed to move mountains. The landscape had changed as entire dunes had been moved from one place to the other.

Aquarius was severely damaged. Aries had also suffered serious damage, and the entire northern side of Roman was buried. The monorail track had to be cleaned and cleared away, as well as the roads out of Roman.

Troy Smitts wasn't too happy about what had happened. Although most people didn't comment, it was believed he hadn't given them much of a warning of the storm. He knew it was Station 185 that corrupted his computer model. The station had gone down before, and when he reported it, Ivory had told him he would have it repaired. It seemed to be operational until the storm.

He wasn't going to trust anyone to do something he could do for himself. When the clean up was complete, he was going to sign out a MultiVec and take a trip out to Station 185 and get it full-functioning himself. But tonight he was going to have a few drinks and get laid.

Troy made sure everything was working as he checked the monitor one more time. Corey Davis was still at his terminal "Corey, you all set for the night? I've got to get away from here for awhile."

Corey turned around and looked at Troy. He hadn't gotten any sleep and was taking a lot of this personally.

"Man, everything is cool. Take off. I'll see you sometime tomorrow."

Troy raised his hand and headed out the door to Olympus. Olympus was one of the larger drinking establishments in Roman. It was located on one of the lower levels near many of the workers' barracks. It had everything one would need to forget about reality, which included women, drugs, and Martian moonshine.

Alcohol was much too expensive to import from Earth and it didn't take long for the first colonist on Mars to find a way to make a strong, cheap drink. Martian moonshine had become a big business. Many of the workers had more money than they knew what to do with, and Olympus was the place to spend it.

Troy walked up to the bar and ordered a drink. He looked over the crowd. It was a busy night, he thought, considering the entire cleanup that was taking place, but hell everyone needs to unwind. He quickly gulped the drink down. The first swig was always the toughest. He ordered another and then picked out a redhead at the end of the bar.

*   *   *

Rebecca walked away from the beverage dispenser with a cup of Martian java. She hadn't gotten much sleep in the last few days. After finding Brett in Aquarius, they took him to the clinic where she stayed with him until he was in stable condition. Brett was badly bruised and had lost some blood. He was put on oxygen and given a blood infusion. Within 24 hours he was stable, but remained in a coma for several days.

Brett awoke with a pounding headache. He wanted to rub his eyes, but as he tried lifting his arms he could feel the pain. Now he remembered what had happened. He had been in Aquarius by the hatch. Someone had called for him. Was it Alex? He turned his head toward the door and saw Rebecca sitting by his side.

"Rebecca, what happened? How did they find me? Was it Alex?" She looked at him, puzzled, "No, your communicator. You told them the hatch numbers. Don't you remember?" She rubbed his forehead with her hand.

"It's kind of blurry right now. Are you okay?" he said as he felt her soft hand take the pain away.

"I'm fine, fine now. You gave me some scare. Don't do that again." Brett looked into her warm smile and fell back to sleep.

*   *   *

Nick sat at his desk wondering if it was all worth it. His stomach was all in knots. He knew that Ed was doing too much and that in his shape he needed a break. Carlos was dead, and now Brett was injured and laid up in the infirmary for a couple weeks. What was this all about? It had started as a dream to colonize mans' next frontier, space. When he was young, he had joined Calprex and became involved in the colonization of the moon. Calprex had helped construct many of the numerous space stations orbiting Earth. Mars was the next logical move, but the most costly. As Nick looked back on the last year, he wondered if it was worth it. It became larger than life. It became too much of a business of who owned what, who had rights to this or that. It was no longer a dream. It was a nightmare.

Nick clicked on his monitor to check for messages. Nothing new, only updates on equipment headed for Mars, and notes from the last stockholders' meeting, also two messages from yesterday that he had saved. One was from Ed, and the other from Brett. Nick leaned back, not sure why he didn't file these two messages away.

The message from Ed was bothering him and he didn't know why. It was nothing out of the ordinary. Ed had sent him his itinerary for the following week and mentioned a few things about his meeting in Washington. The Arab Republic wanted their facility on Mars ready to go within two months. They had contracted out a considerable amount of suites, laboratories, and barracks within Capricorn. If the work couldn't be completed on time, they wanted compensation, lands to the north. That's what was bothering Nick. What the hell do they want with more land on Mars?

"Computer, let me see the message from Brett Roberts." The screen flashed on Brett's message sent yesterday.

Nick,

I'm back on my feet after three weeks. Storm was a bit of a surprise to Roman as it came out of across the Northern Ridge. Cleanup of Roman is continuing and I have also sent you a copy of latest updates. Will keep you posted. Seems we underestimated the magnitude of the storm. Have not had time to talk with anyone else about Carlos. Hope that as things progress on the cleanup, I'll be able to find out more. Received a message from Ed stating that the completion of Capricorn is the number one priority. Will keep you abreast of its completion.
Brett

Something just didn't add up. Nick couldn't figure out what it was as he reread the messages from Ed and Brett over and over. He turned off the monitor and turned his chair to look out at the star-filled sky.

* * *

Jon Conners monitored the cleanup. He knew that Brett had talked with all the managers and supervisors before the storm had ended. All he had to do was to keep everyone on task. Seemed simple enough, except within no time he found that cleanup was behind schedule and falling further behind with each passing hour.

He had sent reports to Roberts, but it was becoming more difficult to conceal that within three weeks they were already four days behind.

Conners looked out the monitors to view Aquarius. He saw numerous and various machinery at work, and everyone seemed to be busy. The amount of sand was underestimated, and its removal was a slow and tedious job.

Brett had enough of doctors the last few weeks. He was feeling much better and decided to check out the cleanup himself. It was already taking too long. He checked to make sure a buggy was available and was headed out the door when Rebecca walked in.

"I'm sorry. Are you leaving?" she said with a warm smile.

"Well, yes. I'm going to check on the progress of the cleanup. It appears that we're falling behind schedule, and we need to get working on completing Capricorn."

She looked at him sternly. "Look, you really aren't ready to go out on the surface."

"Rebecca, I know you mean well. But I can't be patient forever. You don't know what it has meant to me that you were here with me these last few weeks, but I have things to do. You can come along if that would make you feel better," he said with a wink at her. "I'll need a guide anyway. I've really only seen Roman on holograms and blueprints."

"Well, this storm has put a hold on my work. I'm actually looking for something to do. Do they have extra suits here?"

The two walked to the corridor.

"I hope, Rebecca, we're headed in the right direction. The buggy is in garage A17," he said with a smirk.

"Wise guy, huh? Yes, you are headed in the right direction."

The two walked a bit farther, dressed into their suits and went over the garage to pick up the buggy. As the doors opened, Brett drove the buggy onto a cleared area.

"Looks like they've cleared a road for us, kind of reminds me of trenches," Rebecca said through her COM link.

"Yeah, I don't think you can appreciate the magnitude of this until you're in it. I need to find a path to get me above this. I want to survey from higher up."

The two looked along the road for a path that would get them to elevated ground. Rebecca was a bit surprised that Brett seemed to know exactly where he was going. The buggy with its four oversized wheels ripped through the sand. They came to a drift that seemed to be gradually rising.

"Hang on Rebecca."

He turned the buggy up the incline and accelerated. It appeared that they were going to get stuck a few times, but they were able to maneuver themselves up a ridge. They had actually driven away from Roman and had a perfect view of the storm beaten city. Aquarius seemed to have taken the brunt of the sand. It was the farthest north part of Roman. The corridor from Gemini, which was headed southwest to Sagittarius, was completely buried.

"It doesn't seem they've made a lot of progress over the last few days. Damn!" Brett said as he surveyed the area with a special pair of binoculars designed to work with the visor in his helmet.

"There was a lot of sand, Brett . They can only transport it out of here so fast. This could take a couple of weeks."

"We don't have a couple of weeks. Capricorn has to be completed within the next six weeks," he said with some disgust.

"The Arab Republic is forcing completion or they want to be compensated. Calprex needs the money from the lease to continue construction. Let's go get a closer look."

The two made a trek to the group working on Aquarius. The distance seemed closer than it actually was. Every time they cleared a dune, another one was just ahead of them.

"Brett, I remember the first time I saw you. It was on the Moonbase. There you were, walking into the meeting with a dark blue jumpsuit. You sat next to Anna Biskstein. Do you remember her?"

"Yes, I do. Boy, that seems like yesterday. We had some great times back then."

The two continued to reminisce about their time on the moon. As they got closer to Aquarius, a man walked over to them, raising his hand.

"Hey, you two, you better get out of the way. We got a lot of work to do."

"Yes, you do. I'm Brett Roberts. I wanted to find out what the problem is here? We have a schedule to keep and it doesn't seem that you're close to it. What's the problem?"

"Sorry, Mr. Roberts. Didn't know it was you. I'll tell you what the friggin problem is. Half the equipment we need isn't here!"

"Isn't here? What's missing?" said Brett, getting a bit annoyed. 'We had everything arranged on where everything is going. That was weeks ago."

"Yes, sir, but we don't have our WORM here! Can't do much without it."

Brett looked over at four large vehicles to his left "What about those. Can't they be put to use?"

The man chuckled. "You're kidding. Those are Laser Blasters. They're great for blasting rock into sand, which we have enough of already. We need the WORMs to take them away,"

Brett was loosing his patience. Capricorn needed to be completed. The clean up was going nowhere. "The WORM, what's that?"

"Sir, its what removes and transports large amounts of sand, rocks, you name it."

"Do you know where it is?" Brett asked.

"What I was told, it's in for maintenance. The groups working around Capricorn and Aries have the same problem. They told us we'd have them by the end of the day. That was two weeks ago."

Brett and Rebecca drove around from sight to sight. The same story, missing equipment, even some of the men weren't there. The sun was setting as the pink sky took on a blue hue. "Thanks for the company, Rebecca, I know I was probably a bear today. It's just so frustrating."

"No, I enjoyed it. We've really been able to catch up on each other's lives. I'm glad you're here. I'll buy you dinner tonight."

Brett could almost imagine her smile, since the face masks of the helmets were too dark to see into.

"You're buying? Sounds like an offer I can't refuse," he chuckled as he turned the buggy back toward the hanger.

"I have some things to check on, but you have a date for later tonight" he said as they entered the garage.

7

Corey Davis felt a bit excited going out to repair one of the weather stations south of Roman. Troy was taking the surprise storm personal, and it was difficult working with him. Corey and two others had taken a MultiVec and gone out three days ago to repair Station 27. The storm had knocked out reception and buried a good part of the dish.

It was a hard and tedious job, making repairs and clearing away the sand from the station. A plow was on the front of the MultiVec, and it also had a mechanical arm, which helped dig out some areas.

It had taken a sol to get there, a sol to repair it and clear it out, and now another sol to get back. As the MultiVec was heading home towards Roman Corey was thinking about switching assignments and going out on the next repair. He felt like one of the explorers he had read about as a small boy. The MultiVec climbed dunes, went up mountains and across a valley. The red planet was getting in his blood.

The weather unit was only allowed one transport due to the cleanup of Roman. They had repaired six stations since the storm and had three more to go. As they approached Roman, the sun was setting and they could make out the lights of machinery at work. He knew Troy wouldn't be in the office when he got back, but he had a good idea where he would find him.

* * *

Brett Roberts was just about to leave to pick up Rebecca when his monitor chimed in,

"You have an urgent message"

Brett walked over to the monitor "Lets see it"

"WHERE ARE THE WORMS?

A FRIEND"

Brett was thinking the same thing. "Message is from who?" Already knowing the answer.

56

"Unknown"

"Can I reply?" Again knowing the answer,

"Negative"

The question was eating away at him even before his message. Why were all the Worms being worked on? He walked through the maze of corridors to Rebecca's quarters. He hit the bell, and she let him in. He was surprised at how small her quarters were. The room had a small sofa and a desk with a large bookshelf behind it, and on which Rebecca had put rock specimens. The bed was folded up into the wall and pulled down when needed.

"Not exactly what you were expecting?" she said as she read Brett's face.

"Um, no, it's nice," he responded with a smile.

"Well, Brett, we can't all have the large quarters like yours!" she countered in a teasing tone. She walked into the lavatory and brushed her hair. "Brett, what are you in the mood for tonight?"

"Worms," he said, not really listening to what she asked.

She took a step out. "What!"

"Sorry, I've just been thinking about these WORMS. Why are they all being repaired at the same time? What happened to them?"

"Why don't you call maintenance and see what they say."

"I did, after I dropped you off. The controller was gone for the night. I called his quarters, and he's not there either. His personal communicator is taking messages."

"Well, we could go find him. Not many places he could be in Roman."

Brett stood up. "Really? Have a hunch?"

"Yes, most of the construction and maintenance guys hang out at Olympus. It's a bit too much of a hole for me, but I'll take you there."

Rebecca and Brett took the elevators to the lower levels of Roman. As they stepped of the elevator, they noticed a pungent odor.

"I told you it's not a place I frequently visit!" she declared putting her hand up over her nose. As they walked off the elevator, they came to a large directory that listed the location of everything. The level was mainly made up of sleeping barracks for the construction workers.

There wasn't much in the barracks except beds and lavatories so that most spent their free time elsewhere. The main place was Olympus. As they followed the yellow tags on the ceiling, leading to Olympus, they could hear the noise. Brett turned the corner to enter Olympus.

It was more than a bar. It was a playroom. In front were small circular tables at which people were eating and drinking. Farther back was a large bar with fluorescent lights. Patrons were gathered in front drinking and laughing. There were many smaller rooms off the room. One had a large blinking light on the entrance "Computer World." It was set up with cubicles each having a computer. Another room had exotic dancers.

Rebecca looked around the room as they walked through Olympus "Some things will never change."

"No, probably not. Earth, Mars, no matter. Men will always be the same," Brett said with a smirk.

"Brett, how are we going find this guy? There must be five hundred people in here." They walked up to the bar and waited for the bartender. Brett looked at the people around the room. They looked tired, dirty and either intoxicated or high.

The bartender finally got around to them. "What can I get you?" He said impatiently.

"I'm looking for the controller of the maintenance garage."

"Are you kidding me, mister. Take out an ad, I serve drinks not find people." He turned away to ask the next person for their order.

Brett leaned over, picked up a stool and threw it into the mirrors and bottles along the bar. "Maybe you don't understand. You help me or I'll have this place closed down within the hour."

The bartender pulled back as two men in clean overalls walked up. "Can we help you, Mr. Roberts?"

"Yes, I'm looking for someone from the main garage in maintenance," he said as Rebecca stood behind him wondering how they knew who he was.

"Well, we can't help you out with any specifics, but those tables over there in the far corner have a few of the workers." The man pointed over his shoulder.

"Thanks a lot." The other man leaned toward Brett "If I can make one suggestion. Don't come back. This is a dangerous place. Now, if you'll follow me."

Brett grinned, "Oh, I can see that. But I will be back, and frequently!"

He headed toward the corner tables. Brett and Rebecca walked over to the tables.

Brett introduced himself. "Hello. I'm looking for one of the controllers of the maintenance garage. Any idea where I could find him?"

No one answered as they looked at each other. Brett noticed the apprehension among them. A waitress walked by and Brett called her over.

"Give this table a round." Brett placed his credits on her tray. "If any of you know where I can find him, I'll be in the lounge."

Still no one spoke as both Brett and Rebecca left.. They walked into the lounge, which was much quieter, and got a drink.

"Brett," said Rebecca, "I've never seen this side of you. You're going to get hurt, or worse, killed. Those are some mean people in there."

He placed his hand upon hers, "Listen, most people don't want any problems and will back off. Besides, after what I've encountered I'm not afraid of much."

She still look bewildered, "What are you looking forward to? Death?" He simply smiled at her, wondering if she was right.

"Excuse me," came a harsh voice. It was one of the men from the corner. "I'm Charlie McBride. I'm one of the controllers. What can I help you with?"

Brett stood up and gestured to the empty seat, "Please sit down."

"No. Thank you. I figured since you bought us a drink I can answer one question, and only one. I don't want too many people seeing me getting cozy here with you."

Rebecca was feeling uncomfortable about everything. She looked around the room, and it appeared that everyone was watching the three of them.

"Well, Mr. McBride, I really have only one question. Why are all the WORMS being worked on now, when we need them?" Brett noticed one of the men who had come over to the bar earlier, was watching the two of them.

"WORMS? We haven't had the WORMS in for maintenance in months. They're actually overdue on scheduled service."

"Well, where are they then?"

The man scratched his arm, "Damn if I know. They aren't in my garage though. Well, thanks for the drinks." He walked away.

At the other end of the lounge sat Troy Smitts. He was holding a glass in one hand and a redhead in the other. A small man with a cane walked up to the table.

"Mr. Smitts, I'm Harvey Greenberg. Your friend told me you need my help."

Troy couldn't help but stare at his leg. Most people with serious injuries were sent back to Earth. "Please sit down, I appreciate you coming."

Harvey Greenberg put down his cane and slid into the booth. The redhead at Troy's side took a gulp of her drink, "Excuse me, what's with your stick," she giggled.

Troy felt embarrassed, knowing she was half out of her mind on Martian alcohol.

Harvey Greenberg remembered it like it was yesterday. After making modifications to a program, Gary Ivory's thugs broke his leg while giving him a beating. He remained in the hospital for five weeks. When he was able to return to work, he found he had been replaced and demoted to doing diagnostics on systems throughout Roman.

"A few of Mars finest security decided to play with me. I can't bend my right leg any more. So my duties are confined to working and programming the computers. Not exactly as exciting as being up on the surface exploring."

"I apologize she's drunk," said Troy.

She giggled and kissed Troy on the neck.

Harvey was anxious to change the subject and leave Olympus. "You are having problems with Station 185 and you wanted me to run some diagnostics?"

"Yes, that's correct. They are telling me it's working. But readings don't show anything. It's the farthest station we have in the North, and it's quite a trek to get there."

"Well, I've done some preliminary readings and I'm afraid it's something you'll have to care take of in person." He handed him a disk. "If you install this program into the mainframe, you shouldn't have any more problems."

"This is great! I'll send someone out tomorrow," Troy said with relief. Station 185 had been a thorn in his side.

Harvey Greenberg reached for his cane, "I'm afraid you'll have to go and install it personally. It's programmed so that you must personally be there."

Troy's smile quickly faded.

"What the hell are you pulling? Why would you do that?" responded Troy raising his voice.

"Because I trust you, Mr. Smitts. Your problem will not be resolved if others are involved."

Troy looked into his eyes, and a calm went over him. This little man had him at his mercy, and Troy knew he could knock the living crap out of him. But he felt that Greenberg was right. He would have to do it himself.

"Well, any other bombshells you want to drop?" he said sarcastically.

"Yes, one more thing. Tell as few people as possible that you're going." He walked away then.

Troy took a swig of his drink, not knowing whether he should feel relieved or more irritated.

* * *

Rebecca pushed her drink to the middle of the table. "Brett, can we leave this place?"

"Sure, I'm sorry. Just that something's not right and I have a bad feeling," he said as he slid his chair away from the table.

"Well, none of those John Wayne heroics. You're not that big a guy."

Brett put his hand on her shoulder, "And I'm not carrying a gun!"

She turned quickly "You don't get it. They'll kill you! Get in their way and they'll get rid of you." She shook in disgust as she looked around the room. The two started to walk to the door.

"Rebecca, who? Who is going to kill me? Ivory?" Before she could answer Brett bumped into a small man. The man's cane dropped, and his bag fell to the floor, multiple disks falling out. "I'm sorry I didn't see you," Brett said as he picked up the cane.

The man just looked into his eyes "No excuse me, I should look where I'm going. I'm sorry Mr. Roberts."

Their eyes meet, "Do I know you?"

The man remained silent then grabbed his bag and headed for the door.

Troy Smitts had seen the collision but by the time he walked over, Harvey Greenberg was gone.

"Hey, Brett. Not the kind of place I'd think you'd be in," Troy said as he looked over Rebecca.

Brett noticed his scrutinizing of Rebecca. "I could say the same thing about you," Brett replied.

"Yeah, but I don't have a title or reputation to worry about. I don't believe we've met," he was still looking at Rebecca.

"I'm sorry, Troy. This is Rebecca Marceau. Guess I thought everyone knew everyone here."

She was uncomfortable and felt as if he was undressing her with his eyes. She put her arm on Brett's, "We were just leaving."

"Well, you two have a wonderful evening. I plan on it." Troy said and headed back to his table where his companion was waiting for him.

"Brett, can we have dinner in your quarters tonight?" she said remaining uncomfortable.

"Of course."

"I'm scared of this place, I'm scared of Roman."

* * *

Charlie McBride had a little too much to drink and was feeling the effects of Martian moonshine as he staggered to his room. He had only two things on his mind, to sleep and to empty his bladder. He headed for the lavatories just outside the barracks. He walked up to one of the urinals, almost falling on his face. He undid his pants and started to relieve himself when he felt a sharp thud on his head. His head hit the wall with force, cutting his temple. As he fell to the ground, he felt a fist ram into his back.

"McBride you can't keep your friggin' mouth closed, can you?", he heard as he fell to the floor, a boot then kicking him in his stomach.

"What did you tell Roberts," came a second voice.

"Nothing. I swear nothing," McBride moaned, trying to catch his breath.

"What did he want to know? What did you tell him?"

McBride could taste the blood in his mouth, his head pounding as he lay on the floor in his own urine. "He wanted to know about the WORMS. How the repairs on them were going. I told him we hadn't made any." McBride looked up and he saw a pipe descending toward his head.

Brett sat next to Rebecca on the couch, "What did you mean you're scared of Roman, Rebecca?"

She put her hand on his, "I don't feel safe here. I feel like I'm being watched. I came here to explore Mars and they won't even let me do my job. Places are off limits or quarantined. Ivory was running this place with thugs and I think they're trying to get rid of anyone who gets in their way. Maybe they want to get you the way they got rid of Carlos." Her eyes got watery.

"Listen, I'm not going to let anything happen to me, or to you for that matter. I'm not even sure Ivory had anything to do with Carlos's death." Brett brushed away a tear from her cheek.

"But the way you acted in Olympus today. They'll kill you Brett!" She wiped away the flow of tears.

"I'm sorry. I won't do anything like that again. Ivory is up to something, I don't know what. And I still haven't found anything that points to him as being responsible for Carlo's death."

Rebecca stood up and began pacing the floor. "I'm sorry. You must think I'm a bumbling idiot. Maybe it's my hormones, she said with a smile. "I'm scared. Can I stay here tonight with you?"

Brett stood up and held and kissed her, "You can stay here as long as you want."

The two walked toward the bedroom.

8

The following morning Troy Smitts sat up in bed, noticing his redheaded friend beside him was still sound asleep. He felt bad. He didn't even remember her name. He wished she'd wake up and leave. He went to wash up and grabbed a protein bar. He figured Corey would be back from completing repairs on Station 27 and would be doing a diagnostic this morning.

Troy glanced at his clock. 10:16 a.m. Corey was probably already working. Troy quickly got dressed and went to work. If Station 27's reading were fine, he was going to head out to Station 185 by the end of the day. Troy walked over to the table by the bed and picked up the disk that Harvey Greenberg had given him last night.

Troy looked at his watch as he walked into his office. 11:04 a.m. Hopefully, Corey was finishing up the diagnostic on 27, and he could get started on Station 185.

"Corey, you around?" He glanced around the corner expecting to see Corey at the terminal. The chair was empty, and the computer monitor was blank. He walked over to his screen. As he approached the desk he saw that his screen was blinking, "One Message."

"Computer, first message."

"Troy,

We got in last night from Station 27 and ran a diagnostic. Everything looked great. We decided to get a head start on station 30. Rogers and Oakanoie went with me. Should be back in about three days.
Corey."

"Damn it!" he exclaimed as he struck the table with his fist. He needed the MultiVec to head out to Station 185. It wasn't going to be easy getting another vehicle, what with all the cleanup going on. He thought better about calling up and asking for one. Maybe if he went down and found something not in use, he would have a better argument.

About 11 a.m. Brett Roberts got the news that McBride was dead. McBride had been caught without a suit on when one of the garage doors had opened. Brett headed for the maintenance garage where his body had been found, or what was left of it. Roberts entered the huge garage and saw Ivory talking to a few other men. With a nod Ivory directed them to leave as Roberts approached.

"What happened? Any idea?" Roberts asked.

"Went through the first set of doors without a suit." Ivory pointed to the large garage door behind him. "Operator had a vehicle coming in and wasn't aware that McBride was there when he opened the second set of doors. As a matter of fact, they didn't even notice his body till about six this morning."

"Six! Why wasn't I told earlier?" he said in a louder voice.

"Look, you may be in charge of Roman, but I'm still am in charge of Security and I had a job to do. I'm not going to stop doing my job so you can watch over my shoulder. I had a job to do. The body had to be examined and we had to go over the area to learn what happened."

"And what was McBride doing between the doors without a suit on?" Roberts asked in disgust.

"No idea. He definitely knew better. I understand he was drinking heavily last night. Must have been disoriented."

"So that's it. No marks on the body? Nothing?"

Ivory looked at him with a smirk. "You know as well as anyone, what happens to your body in this atmosphere. We're lucky we could figure out who it was. There was nothing much to go on. But looks like a drunk making a mistake. I'll send you a copy of my report." Ivory turned and walked away.

Roberts knew it was no accident. He was talking with McBride last night, and apparently McBride had said too much to him. He looked at the door, knowing you don't accidentally go through one even if you've had too much to drink.

Brett heard yelling coming from the far side of the garage. It was Ivory and Smitts.

"Who put you in charge of transportation and vehicles?" Smitts was screaming.

"Look, you little piss ant. We've had an accident here. No ones taking anything out without my authorization," Ivory snapped back.

"Well, I don't care what happened here. I have work to do and I need a MultiVec."

Ivory's mouth turned to a smart mouth grin "Listen Mr. Weatherman, we had a storm here! I'm not sure if you knew and that we need every vehicle for cleanup."

"Well, I have some cleanup myself. Clean up the mess your people did, or should I say, didn't do, at Station 185."

Ivory's grin was wiped away, "Look, I told you the North region is restricted. My people will make the necessary repairs."

"I'm going and you can't stop me!" Smitts screamed. He wanted to hit Ivory but knew it wouldn't get him anywhere but the slammer.

"I'm afraid you can't." Seeing the frustration in Smitts eyes, Ivory's grin reappeared.

* * *

Nick Gambino was reading the reports sent from Mars. It appeared the cleanup was taking longer than expected. The progress on Capricorn was also falling behind. The storm had caused structural damage, and work inside was hampered by the use of manpower needed in the cleanup of Roman.

Less than six weeks left and the Arab Republic would want compensation for the uncompleted Capricorn. They would take additional lands north of Roman. Bert's last message said that all additional manpower would be used for Capricorn once storm was cleaned up. But at this rate it might take two more weeks alone to complete the job.

Brett Roberts had never let him down in the past, but was this the same man he knew a half of a dozen years ago? Nick felt helpless in the situation. He turned on the hologram of Roman and scanned out. He viewed the lands around Roman. The lands to the North were mountainous and for the most part unexplored. What did the Arab Republic want with this area? Had another diamond mine been found? There were no reports on minerals or anything else in that area. Maybe it was time for him to get some of his eyes out there.

* * *

Brett just made it to his afternoon appointment with Mr. McGregor of Relin Incorporated. He was still upset about this morning. McBride must have told him something he shouldn't have. But what? He said he hadn't seen the WORMS. Records showed they were at the job sites, and the foremen say they had been informed the WORMS were in for repair in the garage.

The backtracking kept coming up with dead ends. Someone was going through a lot of effort to cover his or her tracks. By the time he had gotten to Roman, Carlo's death was all cleaned up and swept under the carpet. The messages he was receiving on his computer were untraceable.

And now McBride's death. Roberts walked through the corridors to his office, wondering where the missing pieces to this puzzle were.

The door opened, and McGregor was sitting at the end of table on one chair while Jon Conners sat at the other.

"Hello, Mr. McGregor, I appreciate you making time for me."

"Please, Terry. Call me Terry," McGregor said as he stood up to shake his hand.

"Terry, I know you've been extremely busy since you've gotten to Mars."

"Oh, very busy. We are staying on schedule, even with the storm and all." He boasted.

"Yes, Mr. Conners showed me. Relin Incorporated is by far the most productive subcontractor in Roman and that's why we need your help." Brett walked over to Conners who handed him a small hand recorder used for reading documents.

"We need your help with Capricorn."

"Capricorn? We've completed all our jobs there. Was there something wrong with the work? Did the storm damage our work?" said McGregor, somewhat flustered.

"No, your work is fine. We need some additional services from Relin." Conners interjected.

Roberts handed him the recorder, "This is a copy of what we've sent to Relin. It's a request to switch gears and work on Capricorn."

"Well, what did they say? I can't make those types of decisions," McGregor said.

"We understand that. They said it was fine as long as you felt the men could handle it. Each man will be compensated handsomely with a bonus if all the work is completed within seven weeks." McGregor was scrolling through the recorder. "This is a lot of work! I'm not sure we could get it done."

"Terry, I need your help. We need to complete Capricorn in six weeks."

"Why six weeks? What's the hurry?"

Conners stood up. "We have contractual obligations with a client. If they're not filled, they want some compensation." Brett leaned over McGregor's chair. "Compensation we're not willing to give up."

McGregor swallowed hard. "I understand. I think we can get it done for you."

"Great!" Brett slapped McGregor's shoulder.

Brett Roberts made some arrangements with other subcontractors and by the end of the day it looked like, at least on paper, that Capricorn would be completed in six weeks. He still had one major problem, Gary

Ivory. Somehow he was behind some of this. Something didn't add up. He was going to have to keep Ivory busy or preoccupied. But how?

Roberts's screen flashed on, "New Message"

"Computer, please show me the new message."

Brett,

Something is going on to the North of Roman. Not sure what, just a hunch. The Arab Republic is playing hardball without a good reason. I have a feeling there might be a diamond mine, possibly nickel or copper. I'm not sure. I need you to find a geologist and to get out there and take a look. I think answers might be to the north of Roman.
Good hunting.
Nick

Brett leaned back in his chair. The Northern region. Was this the answer? Rebecca had told him she wasn't allowed to do research there. He knew he could trust Rebecca to help him, but he couldn't let her go out there alone. If he went with her, Conners would have to oversee Capricorn. He knew he could handle that, but could he handle Ivory? Well, if Nick was right about the northern region, and he went with Rebecca, that would definitely get Ivory's attention, hopefully getting Ivory to forget about Capricorn.

* * *

Brett sat at the table in the cafeteria, with Rebecca, discussing his plan. She was anxious to get outside of Roman after being confined to the city for weeks.

"Brett, we're just going to ride out of here, just like that? We have to log in a plan, and you know Ivory will see it," she said getting caught up in the whole thing.

"Well, he can't stop us. Ivory reports to me, but if there's something there, he'll try to stop us before we get there."

"Yeah, when he sees it's you and a geologist, he'll know we've figured out they found a mine of some type. He'll stop us before we ever get close." Brett felt a hand on his shoulder. He turned. It was Troy Smitts.

"How are you two doing? I don't mean to interrupt anything, but, Brett, I'd like to talk to you about Ivory."

"What about him? I know you guys are close buddies." Brett replied sarcastically.

"I'm trying to get a transport of some type to repair my station and he won't let me have one. Seems all the transports are being used, either for work or evidence!"

"I thought you had a MultiVec?"

"We do, but one of my guys took it out early this morning to fix another station. Didn't realize I needed it to get to Station 185." Smitts said, swinging a chair around and straddling it.

"I'll have Conners take a look to see if he can find you something. What do you need? How far out?

"I'll take anything. It's about fours sols out. Station 185 is the farthest north of Roman."

Brett and Rebecca looked at each other.

Troy remarked, "What? What's with the looks to each other?"

Rebecca grinned and turned towards Troy, "I think we have a proposition for you!"

The three sat at the table discussing what they would need and when to leave. They would use Troy as a cover to look around the northern area.

"So you're going to tell Ivory you're going with Troy to help him with the weather station?" Rebecca asked in amazement.

"Exactly, I'm going to ask him for a route." Brett laughed.

"But he'll send us on some wild goose chase. It'll take twice as long," Troy said.

"Who said we're going stick to the route. We'll see where he detours our route and take it from there."

"Well, if we're leaving tomorrow morning, I have to pack," Rebecca said as she stood up. The three all rose to their feet.

Brett turned to Troy. "Troy get whatever you need, then take the list of provisions and send them to Conners. I'm going to talk to him now about a MultiVec, so he'll be expecting you. Then I'm going to get a hold of Ivory and spring it on him."

Troy knew he had everything he needed in the disk from Greenberg. He'd check the reading, pick up a few personal items, and then go to see Conners.

Gary Ivory was a bit surprised to see Brett Roberts at this hour, and even more surprised on finding out why. "You mean you're going to go out with Smitts and fix his weather station?"

"Yeah, I've been trapped in here and I thought that everything seems under control. So I might as well see Mars." Roberts needed Ivory to buy this. He was trying to read his face, but was having a tough time doing it.

"In the northern area there are a few restricted areas." Ivory wished he could have taken that back as soon as he said it. "Of course, Brett you can go wherever you please, but we had a radiation leak there," Ivory said, hoping Roberts would buy it.

"I know Smitts told me that's why he wasn't allowed to go to Station 185," Brett replied.

Ivory was concerned. Why had Smitts been talking about Station 185 with Roberts?

"Yes. Unfortunately, that's where the leak took place."

"Well, that's why I came here. I thought you could figure out a route to get us out to about here, keeping us away from the radiation." Brett pointed to a spot on the map. "That's if there is one."

"I still don't understand why you're coming to me. It's not like you need my permission. You can do whatever you want," Ivory said sarcastically.

"True, but if I go out in some area that's contaminated and die from the radiation using a route you gave me, they'll figure you're responsible. So in my notes I'll include the route you suggested." Brett said with a smile.

"So you think I'm going to try to dispose of you? You're out of your mind."

"No, but if I wandered around aimlessly out there, I don't think you'd care?"

"You must think I'm a friggin idiot. I'll get you a safe route. I'll have it to you within the hour."

Brett walked out of the room while Ivory turned on his monitor to send a message to Afidan.

9

Tom Afidan wished he had more information. He couldn't get a read on Roberts and wasn't sure if Ivory was getting a good read on him either. It was a cat and mouse game, and the stakes were high. It could be that Roberts was concerned for his well-being and really wanted Ivory to take the fall if something were to happen. He must know that McBride's death was no accident and he's covering his ass.

If that were the case, they had Roberts right where they wanted him, looking over his shoulder every move he made. It would be a gamble to let him go up north, but if Roberts was concerned about his safety, he must stay on the route Ivory gave him. Roberts would be away from Roman and there would be no one to get in the way of any unforeseen delays in the completion of Capricorn.

Afidan didn't know much about Roberts, only what the history books revealed. Roberts was a national hero, but his personal life was filled with tragedy and had turned him into a hermit. If Afidan were wrong and Roberts went exploring off the route, it could be disaster. They had come so far and he wasn't going to let one man destroy all the work they had accomplished.

He couldn't exactly have Ivory tell Roberts not to go north. It would lead to suspicion and a convoy of people. Afidan thought about having Ivory take care of Roberts as they had so many others who had gotten in their way. But this time it would be difficult to hide.

In the end he decided to send a message to Ivory telling him to give him a route that would keep him away from the restricted area. He also gave Ivory instructions on using surveillance from the satellites orbiting Mars, so that every move Roberts made could be followed. If Roberts went into the restricted areas, have him killed.

Ivory downloaded a route for Roberts, which would keep him kilometers away from the restricted areas. He also warned against getting to close due to radiation in the area. Ivory chuckled to himself. That should keep him away, he thought. He would have a vehicle going parallel with them once Roberts was within 50 kilometers of the restricted area, which would be at least three sols out. Any deviation, and a crew would be sent out to take matters into their own hands.

Rebecca met Brett and Troy at the garage as Troy was checking in all the supplies. "Good morning. How are things looking?" She said with a bit of excitement in her voice.

"Morning," Troy said as he continued to check off supplies

"Good Morning, Rebecca," Brett chimed in. "We should be ready to leave within the hour. Troy is checking everything in. Then he'll have someone to check over the vehicle, and we're out of here!" Brett he tossed in a duffel bag into the hatch.

"Any problems with Ivory?"

"No, but I'm not sure he bought my story. He seems to be going along with it for now. We'll have to see what happens."

"How many sols does his route take?" she asked.

"Well, he has us taking an extra two around this group of mountains," He pointed out the route to her on the map.

"Can I take a closer look at that?"

"Sure." He handed it over to her.

Rebecca didn't know what she was looking for, but something didn't seem right. If that area was similar to others of that type, there shouldn't be any diamonds or copper.

Brett turned toward the MultiVec as he saw a small man enter the vehicle. It was the same man he saw with Troy the other night at Olympus. He walked up to Troy, "Your buddy in there. Don't tell me he's a mechanic," Brett said with some disbelief.

"No. Computer whiz. He's checking it out for bugs and monitoring devices. I don't trust Ivory, the bastard."

"Good idea."

Harvey Greenberg stepped out of the MultiVec and walked up to the three of them. "It looks like someone is going to be watching you closely. You're outgoing and incoming communications will be monitored, and a tracking device has been attached to the vehicle. It looks like your conversation within the MultiVec should be safe. The MultiVec can also be monitored by the satellites if you're thinking about deactivating the tracking device, so take that into consideration." He handed Troy a disk. "Download this if you get into any kind of trouble, but I suggest you stay on the route as long as possible and complete what you need to at Station 185."

"What do you mean trouble?" Rebecca asked.

"Let's just say you need to make it hard to find you," Greenberg said as looked around the garage nervously. He turned towards Troy, "This is very important," He reached into his pocket and pulled out a disk. "When you get to Station 185, take this memory cube and replace the one in the main units hard drive. It will look just like this, except it will be red. This is very important."

Troy looked at him, puzzled " Harvey what the hell is this? I just want my station to work properly. What about the other disk you gave me?"

Greenberg looked at the three, remaining a bit nervous, "Listen, this will solve all the stations problems, everyone's problems. I also have a back-up cube stored under the dashboard. I really need to be going. If you need anything, send me a scrambled message."

Harvey Greenberg looked over his shoulder to make sure no one was watching as he quickly exited through a back door.

"Nervous little fellow you have there, Troy," Rebecca laughed.

A smirk came over Troy's face, "Yeah, but one of a few on this planet I can trust."

Brett carried the last of the supplies into the MultiVec. "Looks like we have enough supplies for a month!" he said as he popped his head out of the side door.

"Not exactly a month, but we could stretch it out if we had to." Troy replied.

Brett closed the hatch behind him. "Troy, take us out of here!"

"Will do." Troy said as he sat in the large seat and started up the engines.

The three rode the MultiVec out of the main hanger as Gary Ivory watched the MultiVec ride over the dunes North of Roman. He wasn't going to let anyone get in his way. He had worked too hard and long to get where he was. If things got sticky, he would have Roberts killed, with or without Afidan's blessing.

The MultiVec climbed toward the mountains lying North of Roman. It was an incredible piece of machinery. It had four independent oversized tires in the front of the vehicle. There were additional tires in the middle and back of the vehicle. It also had a wheeled track between the tires, which could be lowered down for additional traction when needed.

The MultiVec had two large windshields forming a sharp point. The MultiVec was over six meters in height and almost twenty meters long. It was built to take anything Mars could throw at it. The top was comprised of solar panels, which on five hours of daylight could run the MultiVec the entire sol. The earlier vehicles on Mars had encountered problems with the sand and radiation, but this vehicle had a strong shell and was tested in rollovers in which it had received very little if any damage.

The vehicle could carry up to eight men comfortably for over a month, but as many as twelve men had made journeys in the past. The main cockpit could hold two men. Just outside the cockpit was a communication station. This section had multiple screens that had a variety of things on it, from maps to temperature gauges. Further down the vehicle were sleeping quarters comprised of four enclosed bunks. As large as the MultiVec was, it was a very smooth ride.

Troy had taken the first shift at the wheel as Rebecca did some geology analysis on one of the computers. Brett took the seat in the cockpit and looked out over this beautiful planet. The shadows that lay upon the mountains and across the canyons made for countless shades of reds, oranges and pinks. It was a breath-taking voyage, sights that only a few men had seen. As the hours went by, the pink sky was slowly changing to a deep blue as the sun set.

They arrived at a large canyon, and Troy came to a stop. "Looks like some winding roads down through the canyon. I don't think it's something we should attempt maneuvering through in the dark," he said as he unbuckled his harness.

"No, you're probably right. We can get an early start tomorrow," Brett responded, his eyes still surveying the landscape outside.

Rebecca was analyzing some data from her reading as the two walked back.

"Well, this canyon was definitely formed from running water. Look at these pictures. I've found no evidence or traces of any unusual elements. I'm going to take some soil samples since we've stopped, see if anything shows up."

Brett fixed his eyes on the video pictures of the canyon and the mountains they had driven through. Rebecca began to discuss some geologic details of the mountains, and although Brett heard her, he focused in on the breath-taking pictures she had captured while they had climbed the mountains. It brought back memories of climbing the mountains in Colorado with Alex.

Troy stretched and opened up one of the compartments along the top, "I don't know about the two of you, but I'm starved. I've got to eat something."

The three of them ate as Rebecca went into more details about the makeup of the soil samples. Troy reviewed the weather data he had taken, while Brett looked over Rebecca and Troy's shoulders, and out the window, watching the sun set in the canyon.

* * *

Terry McGregor sat down at his desk in total exhaustion. Having spent the entire day on his feet, the oversized chair felt good. He turned on his monitor and pulled up the work schedules. He had reviewed additional projects in Capricorn with all the Relin employees. Most of them were less than ecstatic until they saw the bonus credits they could get. Word traveled quickly, and McGregor was juggling schedules so that the regular contracts would still be completed on time as well as the work in Capricorn. Many of the workers were interested in only the Capricorn assignment, but McGregor knew Relin wouldn't have any of that.

McGregor carefully matched assignments with technicians and made sure that there wouldn't be any conflicts with the original work details. He knew that Roberts had asked other contractors to see if they could get anyone to work on Capricorn, but he felt that he had to prove himself to Brett. McGregor had come to Mars questioning his ability and wanted to prove to himself and everyone else that he was the best man for the job. He reviewed the assignments and projected that the work could be completed in five weeks with the Relin employees alone, giving him a few days cushion. Brett Roberts believed in him, and he would not let him down.

Brett walked up the red cliffs as the morning sun was coming up over the horizon. He felt his heart race as he continued to climb the steep slope. The visor on his helmet was steaming up with perspiration. He reached up and grabbed a boulder to pull himself to the peak of the cliff. As he looked down into the canyon, he couldn't believe his eyes. He tried to clear his visor, but was unable to. He looked down into the canyon and saw a large river running through it. This couldn't be possible, flowing water on Mars! He took a few more steps to the top of the cliff. He heard someone coming up from behind him.

"Dad, wait up. I want to take a look!" came a young man's voice.

Brett turned around and gazed in amazement "Alex, what are you...?" He looked at his hand in front of him and realized he was no longer wearing his suit. He turned to the river and saw that the sky was a majestic blue. "Alex, am I dreaming?"

"No, but it's a beautiful sight isn't it? The Colorado River. I want to take a tour down those rapids some day. It has to be awesome to do that."

Brett turned back toward the canyon and knew he was dreaming. Yet he replied, "It looks awfully dangerous to me Alex. I don't think it would be a wise thing to do."

Alex went to his fathers' side and put his hand on his father's shoulder "Dad, you're such a worry wart. With all the time you've been in space and on the moon, you're going to tell me a river is dangerous."

Brett looked at Alex. What a stunning young man he had turned out to be. Large blue eyes with a chiseled nose and full lips that young women would die to have. Although still trim, his body had become more toned and muscular.

"Alex, please don't go on those rapids, I have a bad feeling about it." He turned toward the white rapids below and felt the perspiration running down his forehead. He turned back to Alex, but his son was gone.

"Alex! Alex where are you? Come back. Don't go on the rapids!" He turned around, looking for Alex. He started to go back down the cliff quickly. "Alex, where are you?"

He moved more quickly, yet his feet seemed to stay glued to the cliff. The harder he tried to race down the more his feet were stuck to the ground. He looked below and thought he saw Alex. Brett took a leap to a boulder below and lost his footing and began to fall down the cliff.

Brett sat up from his bed, "ALEX!"

Rebecca raced over to his cot. "Brett, are you alright?" She saw the sweat on his face, and his clothing appeared soaking wet.

"I'm fine, just a dream," he said wiping his face with his hands.

Troy rushed into the back cabin. "Everything okay?"

Brett stood up. "Yes. Sorry just a bad dream." He stood up with a glazed look in his eyes. "Troy, am I able to send a message from here to Earth?"

"Yeah, it's no problem. It'll be monitored by Ivory, but we can send it out. We're still on the route he gave us, so giving our location away isn't a problem," Troy further explained following Brett toward the front cockpit.

"If Ivory wants to listen to my personnel message, let the bastard. Can you set it up? I want to send a message to my ex-wife Kathleen Roberts, living in San Diego."

Troy sat at the console, made a few adjustments and rose from the chair, "It's all yours, Brett."

"Thanks, Troy," Brett took Troy's place at the console. Troy walked into the back cabin where Rebecca was making some Martian java. "What is that about?" she asked.

"He wanted to send a message to his ex-wife. What a hell of a time to think about your ex!"

Rebecca turned to the pot of Martian Java, wondering why she felt hurt that he needed to send a message to his ex. She was fully aware of Brett's history and knew he would always have a bond with Kathleen, but with all that had happened the last few weeks, it still hurt.

"Kathleen, I'm out here on Mars, riding over its mountains and across its canyons. It's breathtaking. Even the smallest mountains dwarf the largest on Earth. There are so many beautiful shades of red, pink, orange and brown. We passed through a large canyon yesterday." Brett's voice started to get choked up.

"It reminded me of the Colorado River," he went on. "It made me realize how much I miss you, you and Alex. If only we could all go back in time. I'd sell my soul in a heartbeat." Brett wiped away a tear. "We still have a long voyage ahead of us. Just wanted to let you know I was thinking of you. Take care of yourself. You know I love you and always will."

Rebecca went over the soil samples but found nothing out of the ordinary.

Troy walked up to her and said. "Brett seems to think you'll find something in the soil up here. Anything in particular you're looking for?"

Rebecca turned the screen down.

"We're not sure, maybe Diamonds, Nickel or Copper. We just don't know. Ivory doesn't let any of the geologists up here. He doesn't want you going to Station 185, and then you've got the Arab Republic interested in the North region. There's something there. What it is, I have no idea."

Brett walked into the back where Troy was reviewing the map.

"Brett, this is where Ivory has us going out of the way," said Troy. "I hope we're staying on Ivory's course."

Brett walked up and glanced at the route.

"Yeah, let's stay on the route for now, if we don't find anything in the next sol or two, we'll deviate then."

Troy looked at both of them. "Look, I know the two of you think that there's something there, but can we stay on Ivory's route as long as possible? Get out to Station 185. Once we get there and fix it, I don't give a rat's ass what route we take."

"I know what you're saying, Troy, but if our hunch is right and he expects us to enter the North zone, it would be somewhere here." Brett pointed on the map. "We can do it on the way or heading back from Station 185. My thoughts are to just wait and see what the next few sols show us."

Troy and Brett went to the cockpit.

"Brett, I'll take the wheel for the first few hours, then you can have it."

"Fine with me," Brett replied, then taking a gulp of the Martian java.

Brett went back to check on Rebecca's work. She was marking the samples she had taken before they had started off this morning. He fixed his eyes at her and thought how beautiful she looked. Her hair was back in a short ponytail, and she had on an orange jumpsuit. No makeup, yet she was absolutely gorgeous.

She glanced up as Brett entered the room. Smiling at him, "Troy driving again? I think he feels like a little kid driving a truck."

Brett chuckled. "Yeah, he won't let me have a turn at the wheel."

Rebecca's face formed a more serious expression. "Brett, is everything okay? I mean your dream? Your message to Kathleen? Is there anything you want to tell me?"

Brett took her hand. He looked into her eyes, realizing no matter what he said she wouldn't understand. "Rebecca, look nothing has changed. I think we have something special here. You have to remember that Kathleen and I produced one special boy. We shared a lot of history together, history that doesn't go away. It's nothing to be worried about."

She did feel that they had something blossoming, but also knew she would never have Brett completely.

Brett walked back up front and sat down next to Troy. "Notice anything in the weather pattern this morning, Troy."

Troy glanced over, keeping an eye on the trail down the canyon. "Well, nothing out of the ordinary. Low front is coming in from the east. Looks like a few dust devils to the northwest, but besides that, not much. Should be a quiet sol."

Brett slugged down the last of his cold Martian java. "Quiet is good, very good!"

* * *

Ivory sent his report to Afidan.

"MultiVec is staying on course with no deviations. Very little communication. Roberts contacted his ex wife but nothing important. Have my people looking for a coded message within the transmission. Cleanup from storm is slowing down completion of Roman. Relin workers are being paid overtime to work on Capricorn on their own time. At this pace they may have Capricorn complete within five weeks. Should we take measures into our own hands? Advise."

Afidan deleted the message. Idiot, he thought. Ivory needs everything spoon-fed to him. He knew the accidents were becoming too numerous and that too many people were getting suspicious. He swung his chair to the left and picked up the phone, "Margie, please get me George Schumaker from Relin Incorporated and let me know when you have him on the line."

They were too close to have everything fall apart now. Roberts didn't seem to be any closer than Mendez was, but what caused Roberts to go up North? One wrong move and everything could come undone. Ivory's constant messages seemed to sense fear. Was it actually Roberts causing this fear or was it that they were so close to completion? In truth, what could Roberts do? Even if they were found out, it would be too late. He had covered his tracks here on Earth and if necessary, was ready for a quick exit.

The intercom buzzed in, " Mr. Afidan, Mr. Schumaker is on the line."

"Thank you, Margie." He heard the line disconnect and then reconnect. "George, we have a problem, a problem on Mars."

10

Brett was driving the MultiVec down a canyon trail and looking at the majestic scenery. At times, as they climbed steep inclines it felt like they were barely moving. As they reached the top of one mountain, another lay just ahead.

The route had them circling exceptionally high mountains. The vehicle had much more power than Brett was accustomed to. When he was on the moon, the buggies and transports were very stiff and slow. This vehicle had a complex series of gauges and panels across the dashboard as well as a series of instrumentation above the windshield. Once Brett got over the cluster of controls, he found driving it quite easy to operate.

Over the last few hours they passed through Baron's Pass and were headed into a valley. Brett noticed on the horizon some of the dust devils that Troy had mentioned. The wind had picked up and he could hear the grains of sand hitting the windshield.

Troy had gone in the back a few minutes ago to get some updated weather reports. He returned soon, walking into the cockpit with a small device and spouting out statistics, "It dropped five degrees in the last hour. Winds have picked up and looks like we'll being seeing more of those dust devils."

Rebecca followed him into the cockpit, handing Brett some Martian java, "Those dust devils, are they anything we need to be worried about?" she asked.

"No, we can drive right through them and with the number of them out there, odds are we eventually will have to. What we have to worry about in regard to them is the visibility, could go down to zero. The ride might be a bit rough. Otherwise, it shouldn't be a problem."

Brett scanned the horizon "There's one at two o'clock. Looks like a big one."

"Yeah, some of them are several kilometers in diameter. The wind just picks up the sand and whips it around. They are more common in the Northern Hemisphere. I'm really not sure why."

Rebecca looked out to get a better view of the dust devil, "Well, if we can stay clear of them, I wouldn't mind."

Brett turned around, "Anything interesting from the samples you took this afternoon?"

"Not a thing. Mostly oxide iron. I really don't think we'll find anything on this route Ivory gave us."

"So you think we need to go east? Head into the restricted area?"

"If you want to find out what's going on, it may be the only way."

Troy looked at his readings again. "Look, I think Ivory is up to something, too. But can we fix Station 185 first? We're less than two sols away."

Brett watched the dust devil move slowly east. "Troy, can you get me a course on that dust devil?"

"Yeah, but don't tell me what I think you're going to."

"We'll get a estimated course and then I'll tell you," Brett chuckled.

Troy got up from his seat and walked past Rebecca to get some additional readings.

Rebecca's eyes turned on Brett. "Tell him what?"

"That we're going to hide in one of those dust devils and go east along with it."

"Are you crazy? It could be zero visibility. How will we see? Ivory can still track us, can't he?"

Brett continued to accelerate the MultiVec. "Actually, Troys friend, Mr. Greenberg, told us Ivory would be tracking us two ways. One is by the satellites in orbit. Once were inside a dust devil he can forget about that. The second is the device Greenberg pointed out. We'll place it on top of the MultiVec as we get closer and strap a small parachute on it. Let the wind take it for a ride."

"Sooner or later, Brett, we'll have to leave the dust devil, then what?"

"Well, if we're right, we'll take some samples and hopefully find what we're looking for before they spot us. By that time it will be too late."

Troy came back up front, "Well, good news for you. Nine out of ten models show it headed northeast for over ten kilometers."

Brett stopped the MultiVec and walked towards the middle of the vehicle.

"Perfect. Rebecca, I'll need you to make some type of parachute for this." He ripped the tracking device from the ceiling. "Troy, run some simulations on what will happen to this if we place it on the top of the vehicle and entered the dust devil."

Troy and Rebecca turned to each other and smirked. "Troy, if you haven't figured it out, Brett likes things his way!" said Rebecca.

Within an hour Troy had run numerous simulations and worked with Rebecca on making a few adjustments to the parachute to help keep the tracking device airborne. Brett had been driving the MultiVec at top speed to gain ground on the dust devil.

Troy and Rebecca walked into the cockpit. Troy held up the device with Rebecca's homemade parachute and said, "This baby will blow halfway across Mars. I've run numerous simulations. Since the dust devil is rotating clockwise, if we ejected it when we're at the bottom of the dust devil, it should carry North for some time. It should blow around for 20 to 30 minutes. After that, it will hit the sand and wait for one of the other little devils to send it elsewhere. Sixty percent of the models keep the device within respectable distance to Ivory's course."

"What's respectable?" asked Rebecca

"Few kilometers."

Brett looked up "Wow, sixty percent. That's a large area. Let's hope luck is on our side!"

Troy glanced down at his notes, "The odds seem to be better if we're moving at top speed and release it when we are approximately here." He pointed to a location on the chart.

The sky appeared smaller as the winds increased and they entered the dust devil. Brett turned on the infrared scope, but it wasn't much better. The MultiVec hit something large, but continued on.

Rebecca looked out of the window, wondering how they could continue riding through this. "God, Brett, how do you know where you're going?"

"I can make out a little bit better with the infrared. Don't worry. A bit more and we'll release the tracking device and we can slow down a bit."

The MultiVec continued to race across the Martian sand, hitting numerous bumps along the way. Rebecca looked out the window, hoping to see something, anything. She thought it was less than an hour when they were driving in sunshine watching the dust devils from a distance.

The MultiVec hit something large and veered to the side.

Rebecca fell to her knee. "Brett, we can't continue this. We'll drive down a canyon or into a boulder!" she exclaimed pulling herself up.

"Troy, is the tracking device loaded?"

"We're almost there" as he looked at the chart on the dash.

"Yeah, just let me know when we get to the coordinates and I'll eject it."

The sand was pounding the windshield. Brett thought he could make out the terrain in front of him, but as soon as the view came it was gone.

"We're almost there, Troy. Steady, steady, okay release."

With Brett's command Troy hit the eject button, and Gary Ivory's tracking device became airborne.

"Troy, can you monitor where we are within the dust devil?"

"No, we can't get any readings. Just head northeast and we should be able to ride in it for a few hours."

Rebecca was holding tightly onto a support rail. "All right, gentlemen, what's the plan when we finally ride out of here?"

Troy looked at Rebecca and then to Brett. "My question exactly."

Brett continued to hold onto the steering wheel as her tried to keep the vehicle from bouncing around. "Look, we'll end up about 10 kilometers northeast of here. We should be able to get a few more kilometers farther before they pick us up on the satellites. At that point we'll take some soil samples and find out why they didn't want us here. We can forward our information on, continue to Station 185, then head back to Roman and get the work on Capricorn complete."

"Well, that sounds easy, too easy," Troy replied looking at his calculations again.

* * *

Gary Ivory had just finished listening to his message from Afidan when his COM alerted him to get to the Control room. He rushed through the corridors knowing that it had to do with Roberts. Afidan had told him no more accidents, though he was to stop Roberts at any cost, but only if Roberts interfered. Ivory almost ran over two technicians as he entered the control room,

"What do we have? What's the problem?" He knew it could be one of numerous things, but felt Roberts would have something to do with it.

"Sir, it's the MultiVec we've been monitoring," the technician said, hoping Ivory wouldn't take the bad news out on him.

"Yes, what about it?" Ivory screamed

"We've lost visual with it on the satellites. Looks like a storm overtook them and we can't get a visual on them."

Ivory's fist slammed down on the counter, "What about the tracking device? Are we getting a reading?"

"Yes, sir. Reading is a bit odd, but I'm sure it's due to the storm."

"Well then what's the problem? I don't have time for this. Keep me posted, but send the information. Don't call me down here for every little detail."

Ivory stormed out of the control room. He could feel his heart racing. For over two years he'd been able to keep everything quiet, for the most part with ease, and now with less than two months to go he felt like it could all crumble at any minute. Maybe it was just the pressure he was putting on himself. He knew Brett Roberts was looking around for answers, yet he left himself easy to monitor. Ivory knew if Roberts was getting too close to the answers, he would be taken care of, just like the others before him.

The MultiVec was slowly working its way out of the dust devil. The visibility was increasing and the winds were dying down.

Troy was sitting in the cockpit with Brett "Well, we're almost out of this," Remarked Troy. "Are we going to continue until they radio us?"

"Yeah, that sounds about right," replied Brett. "If they don't try to contact us within the hour, we'll stop and Rebecca can take some readings. Hopefully, we'll find our answers in the samples."

Rebecca walked forward. "I heard my name. Good things, I hope?" she said with a big smile.

"Well, someone's in a better mood. Have anything to do with us leaving this dust devil?" Troy laughed.

"Could be. I think I can almost see pink sky through the dust."

"I was just telling Troy," said Brett, "that we'll try to get some distance from this devil and take some samples within the hour. If they try to contact us, we'll take the samples sooner. So get everything together and be ready."

"Already done. I've got a few other things I want to test this time. I want to do some carbon dating on some of the samples. Few other things as well."

Brett slowed the MultiVec down and put it in park. "Good. Troy I'll let you drive for a bit. I need to stretch my legs in the back."

The MultiVec continued northeast leaving behind the dust devil. A large mountain range lay straight ahead of them. The sky was a soft pink, and the MultiVec sped across the Martian terrain.

Troy couldn't help but look at this majestic view and think of how incredible this planet was. It seemed like it was so long ago that he was forced to take this assignment on Mars. His thoughts had always been, to do a solid job, do a few experiments and hopefully get back to Earth in one piece. His time on Mars should help him land a great position at one of the prestigious universities. But as he looked out at Mars, those dreams appeared so far away.

He scanned the horizon and thought he saw a flicker of light, then it having suddenly disappeared.

Rebecca was sitting at the workstation running some diagnostics. Her suit was lying on the bench, all ready for her to get into on a moments notice. Brett walked up behind her.

"I apologize," he said, "I'm not sure if this is what you expected."

"Are you kidding? It's one adventure after another with you. I'd have to say things got more interesting since you came." Brett placed his hand on her shoulder as she reached up and placed her hand over his. "And," she added "I wouldn't want it any other way."

"You guys come here, take a look at his!" Troy called from the front.

Troy was pointing to the north at about one o'clock. "Over there, that flickering light. I noticed the light a while ago, but thought it was just a reflection of some ice. But whatever it is, it's definitely moving."

Brett looked at it through the scope. He couldn't make out much except that Troy was right, that it was moving, moving directly towards them. "Troy's right. It's headed directly towards us. Rebecca get your suit on, and let's get some samples. Troy stop this thing and help Rebecca with her suit. I'll get another one ready and go out with her."

Within fifteen minutes Rebecca was taking soil samples. She set up a long cylinder that would take a punch sample over three meters deep. Brett helped her unload a few other devices needed for taking additional samples. He glanced out over the horizon. He could see the object was getting closer as it kicked up Martian sand in speeding toward them.

Brett hit his COM link. "Any idea what it is, Troy?"

"No idea, but it's moving fast." Troy replied as he tried to gather data in the MultiVec. "Doesn't look that big. Readings showing it's smaller than our vehicle."

"Any idea how many minutes we have?" Brett asked looking as Rebecca worked quickly to gather data.

"Should be here with in ten minutes." Replied Troy on the COM link.

Brett still keeping an eye on Rebecca "How much time do you need? What can I do to help?"

"I need at least ten minutes, maybe more. The first punch sample is still only halfway complete. It collects the samples, sorts and then analyzes." She glanced at the reading of her first sample. "I should be able to take this one apart in about five minutes. Then I can move to the next one."

"And how much time will that take? Do we need to retrieve all the data?"

"It will take more time than we've got, and I need all the data to get the accurate comparisons. Without all the samples, the predictability values will be too low and probability values will be too high."

Brett turned to look at the horizon as the object came closer. He could almost make it out. It did seem smaller, yet seemed to be higher off the ground than their vehicle. The red sand flew up as the large tires raced toward the three of them.

"Troy, have they tried to make any contact, any communications?"

"Not a peep. You two better get in here. It's only a few minutes away."

Brett saw that Rebecca was placing the first sample in a large cylinder. He went over to take it from her and place it on the ramp. She turned to him as she began to work on the second sample. "We need more time," she said.

"How much more time do you need?"

"Ten minutes. At least five."

"Okay, keep working. Don't stop, no matter what happens. These samples might give all the answers." Brett placed his glove encouragingly on her shoulder.

"Brett, what are you doing? Don't do anything stupid," she cried as she worked on the second sample.

Brett started to walk toward the oncoming vehicle. "Troy do you read me?"

"Yes, loud and clear. What are you doing?"

"Buying some time. Keep the engines going. If we have any trouble get Rebecca and the samples loaded and take off."

"Look, Brett, that's no good. We'll all be leaving together. Do you understand?"

Rebecca still working, chimed in, "Listen, I agree these samples are important, but not enough to take any unnecessary chances."

Brett continued to walk towards the vehicle. "Look, you two, I'm not going to argue. Those samples may have the answer to a lot of questions."

Rebecca looked out and could see that Brett had already walked fifty meters towards the oncoming vehicle. "Listen," she said "Whatever these samples show, gold, copper, whatever, it's not worth it!"

Brett's eyes were fixed on the vehicle. He could make it out more clearly. It was a newer version of the CT-X buggy that was used on the moon. He waved his hands over his head as the buggy got closer.

"Those samples might have the answers, Rebecca. The answers that people have killed for. Maybe they show something we haven't even thought of. Maybe they show that there was life on Mars!"

* * *

Nick had always found a round of golf would clear his head and distract him long enough to forget about reality. Beside his passion for his family and the space program, golf was up there around the top of the list. Nick found that he usually could combine one of his other passions with golf. Both his sons played golf, and he spent many weekends on the fairways with them. He also found that this relaxing atmosphere was ideal for business deals. Many of his biggest moves were made between the 9th and 18th hole.

Nick made his way that morning to the links by 7 am. It had been a warm September in Phoenix, and he wanted to get a round in before the hot sun began to bake the desert. He had found a few old timers at the clubhouse who were more than delighted to let Nick play a round with them. The old timers at the club always wanted to find out the latest in the space program from Nick.

Nick was having an incredible back nine, paring the first three holes, a bogie followed by a birdie, two more pars and another birdie. His drive out off the box on the eighteenth went a good 250 yards with the green off to the left, about 130 yards away. He set up for his second shot, pulling out an eight iron.

He hit the ball cleanly and looked up at the ball as it traveled through the deep blue sky. His eyes followed the ball to the green that stopped about a foot from the pin.

"Nick, one hell of a shot," said one of the old timers.

"Thanks. That felt good. Real good."

Nick placed his club in the bag and took a seat in the cart as they drove to the green. His mind was clear, and he was relaxed. He looked out over the beautiful course that lay in the orange desert of Arizona. Then as he watch his partner's shot, his pager went off. Who was paging him this early? He glanced down to check the text on the pager. He sat in disbelief. He didn't need any more bad news. This was sure the last thing he needed. Nick got out of the cart and walked to the clubhouse without taking his last shot. He kept thinking, how was he going to break the news to Brett?

11

Rebecca franticly rushed to the final probe. All she needed was five minutes. She glanced at the electronic gauge on the top of the first cylinder. "Sample complete." She looked over at Brett. The vehicle had come to a complete stop within five meters of him. "Brett, I'm just wrapping it up here, five minutes and I'll have the samples loaded."

"No problem, Rebecca. Troy, any communication?" Brett responded as he raised his hand in the air.

"Nothing," said Troy, "I've been scanning all bands."

The vehicle door was slowly raised open as Brett stood in front of it. Out walked someone that was wearing a gray space suit that appeared to be an older issue that had been used with some of the early explorers. The individual walked towards Brett. Brett unable to make out a face through the visor was glancing over the suit for any patches or insignias seeing only a Mars patch on the right shoulder. The stranger took a few steps closer. He wasn't carrying anything, and Brett didn't notice any weapon. The individual finally raised his hand and held three fingers up.

Troy watched closely on the monitor. "Brett, what is he doing?"

"I'm not sure yet. He's holding three fingers up. Just help Rebecca get those samples in."

"Brett, turn to band three on your communicator"

Brett held out his arm and turned his personal communicator to band three, then raised his hand in the air holding up three fingers.

"Hello, I am Ali Samad" came a voice over Brett's communicator. "I live in a small modular unit about 20 kilometers from here. I picked up a visual on you and thought you might have some problems. Could I be of any assistance?"

"Hello, I'm Brett Roberts. I work for Calprex and am overlooking the completion of Roman. We've just come out here to run some tests. Nothing of any significance."

"You're a bit off the track. Most of the vehicles that come from the new city take the road along the canyon," Ali Samad replied in his broken English.

"I'm not sure what road you're talking about, but this was the route given to us. Maybe you could tell us how to get to the other road?"

"It's about a half a sol from here. You could follow me back to my modular unit and you're two-thirds the way there."

"You live in a modular unit? Is it self-supporting?" Brett asked, remembering reading about the hundreds of modular units scattered across the terrain of Mars.

Troy opened the back hatch and was helping Rebecca load the samples. Troy closed the hatch and quickly equalized the pressure as he and Rebecca took off her suit. Troy went to the monitor then to observe Brett and this new stranger. He had been listening to the conversation as he had helped load the samples.

Rebecca walked up behind Troy, "Is there any way to get a reading from inside that vehicle? Anyone else in there?"

"No, nothing we have would be able to pick up additional life signs. That thing is pretty small, couldn't hold more than a few people." Troy buzzed Brett who then changed frequency.

"Brett, this is Troy. We're all set here. All the samples are loaded. We are good to go as soon as you're ready."

"I understand, Troy. We can follow this Mr. Samad to the main road he's talking about. Says it's half a sol from here. See if you can find it on any maps."

Brett hit his link and continued his conversation with Ali Samad. "So it's self-supporting. What do you do for supplies?"

"We have to make a trek out to Marrilles Trading Post every few months. So far no problems except that I seem to spend most of my credits on battery cells. My unit is in desperate need of recharging."

"You say this road is on the way? Maybe you could show us the way and we can recharge your cells with our battery? It's worth a look."

Brett could sense the appreciation in Samad's voice, "Oh, yes, thank you. That would be very helpful. Thank you, thank you."

"We'll follow you. Give me a few minutes to get back in. Stay on this frequency."

Ali Samad raised his hand. "Yes, thank you. Band three is the one we are on."

Samad turned back toward his vehicle, and Brett retreated back to his.

* * *

McGregor walked throughout Capricorn reviewing the work. As he added the data in his link, the projections were even better than he had anticipated. His people were completing more work than any of the other sub-contractors. He had spent the entire morning making sure things were going smoothly in Capricorn. He knew he would have to spend the remainder of the day, and probably work late into the night to catch up on his official duties. It would be a long day. One of many, McGregor thought, but he didn't mind. He felt a sense of urgency and the adrenaline pumping throughout every square inch of him. He felt more alive on Mars in the last few weeks than he had ever felt on Earth.

He was going to link his data into the mainframe in his office, pick up the Relin assignments and head back out. He had a spring in his step as he entered the office. He pulled out his data, and linked it up. As it was downloading he noticed the blinking message on his monitor.

"Urgent Message... Relin Corp."

McGregor sat in front of the monitor. What was so urgent? Maybe Relin heard about the extra work, maybe they want to see the work schedules. Well everything is in order. It shouldn't be a problem. He watched the blue bar streak across the bottom of the screen as the message downloaded.

"T. McGregor... Stop all additional work in Capricorn. Relin has contracts only on certain work and will negotiate any additional work, additional fees and payments. Stop all work IMMEDIATELY."

McGregor gazed at the message. This couldn't be happening. The Relin work was being completed ahead of schedule. The workers were getting paid well, and Roberts had planned on compensating Relin as well. He sat in disbelief, wondering what he would say to Roberts. It occurred to him that maybe he should have gone through the home office on the additional work rather than set it up himself. Maybe all he needed to do was to send the terms of the work and get their stamp of approval. A control issue. Yes that was it. Procedures and rules. Step A before B.

He quickly scanned his database for the information and transmitted it to the home office. They should receive the information within fifteen minutes, and it would be another fifteen minutes before he would get their reply. McGregor sat up and went to get some water. He started to feel better. A small problem, and he had taken care of it. Another reason, he thought, why he was the right man for the job. Others may have panicked, but he remained cool and collected.

Although he was feeling good about his quick thinking, he kept looking at the clock and waiting for a reply. He spent the next hour going over work schedules and cost analysis, keeping one eye on the clock. Surely, they had received his message and would send an acknowledgment back. He knew he had work to complete in Aries, but he didn't want to leave till he heard back from Corporate. Another hour went by and still no response. He started to wonder if his link was working? Just then the monitor blinked.

"One new message"

He hit the read button, but it was just a cost analysis report from one of the technicians. He hit the return key and sat back, pondering over what he should do. He noticed the monitor still read, "One new message." He clicked the read button one more time in desperation.

"Stop all work on Capricorn. Any further work will lead to your dismissal. Repeat, stop all work immediately."

* * *

The three of them followed the buggy across the rugged, hilly terrain of Mars for over three hours. Troy kept a good distance from the buggy in case he needed to pull away for any reason. He turned to Brett and said, "Tell me again why are we doing this?" He half chuckled.

"Curiosity, I guess! He said something about vehicles from the "New City" that were taking a road by the canyon."

Still keeping he eyes on the buggy in front of him, Troy said, "What you think, Roman is that new city?"

"Exactly! And my other question is where does this road lead to?" He turned his head and called back to the lab area "Rebecca how are the samples coming? Anything I can help with?"

"No, I have everything under control. The analysis will take some time. Really we can't do anything to speed the process. We should get some initial reading in a few hours. If anything particular comes up, we'll be able to take more precise tests when we take the samples back at Roman."

"Great, let me know if there's anything I can do."

A blue flashing light went off on the front dash. "Brett, looks like your friend is calling us. He's hailing us on COM 3."

"Hello, this is Roberts." Brett sat in one of the large bucket seats in the cockpit.

"Yes, this is Samad." He said in his broken English. "We are almost there. Please follow me into my home. When we arrive you are all welcome."

"Thank you for your invitation. We will talk to you when we arrive."

Troy reached over to flick the COM link off, "We're not all going in there, are we? Who knows who he is? Could be a trap? One of us should stay with the MultiVec and near the COM link."

Brett smiled, "Alex, my son, would have called you a worry wart! Usually, I was the worry wart though. This is a switch. Look, let's scan the area when we get there and then we'll decide who's going inside."

Rebecca called to them from the lab area. "Hey, guys, no reason to decide when we get there, I'll be staying in here to work on these samples. You two can explore!"

Troy looked at Brett. "Leave it to a woman to tell us what to do!"

All three laughed.

The two vehicles climbed a small incline, and Troy could make out the modular unit. It was much larger than he had expected. He had heard numerous stories about how small these units were. It was a cylinder shape, appearing to be about two stories high. The entire unit was raised above the surface of Mars on four metal pillars that were approximately five meters.

Samad's small vehicle parked under the modular unit. Troy used the scanners to view the area around the unit. "I don't see anything unusual," he said. "Looks like it's just him and us. No other tracks."

Brett looked over Troy's shoulder at the monitor. "Looks clear all the way up to the far mountain range to the West. Great view he has here."

Troy parked the MultiVec up to the unit and turned off the engine. "Well," he said. "I guess it's time to suit up and take a look." He stood up and started through the lab. "Rebecca, I have the cameras scanning the area. If it picks anything up, make sure you contact us."

"This guy seems pretty harmless, Troy," said Brett. "This isn't a bad neighborhood you know."

He smirked and went to help Brett with the suits. It took them a good ten minutes to get into their suits and crosscheck them. "Seems like a lot of work for a two-minute walk!" Laughed Troy as they left the MultiVec and then headed toward the modular unit. The two walked to the far cylinder, which had a ladder.

Brett and Troy climbed up the ladder, closing the hatch after them. They could then feel the decompression, a green light going on.

They finally heard Samad's voice. "All clear. You can take your suits off."

Troy took a quick look at the monitor before he took his helmet off.

The decompression area was small and circular, large enough for only two adults. The large door swung open, and a small man of middle-eastern descent smiled. "Welcome," he said. "Welcome to my home."

Brett and Troy walked into the unit, entering a hallway that led to a large room. A small counter divided the room into two areas. The near side appeared to be the kitchen, which contained a small table, with the far wall containing a small oven, a refrigeration unit, and a waste removal/ water unit. The other side contained a large desk with multiple monitors. The room had a few chairs and a sofa, and surrounding a small table. All the outside walls had shelves and storage units and every few meters a porthole. The lavatory was off to the side, and a small flight of stairs led up to the sleeping quarters and a small green house.

Brett visually scanned the unit. "A very impressive setup. All the comforts of home. Very compact."

A smile appeared on Samad's face, "Yes, I am self- sufficient for the most part."

Troy was busy looking over the instrumentation. "Looks like you have your own weather station here."

"Ah, yes. We didn't want to get caught out there in a storm."

"We?" questioned Troy.

"Yes, my wife and I. We had come here almost two years ago. Earth years, that is. We did work on mapping this area."

Brett walked over to the two. "Is she here?"

Samad's expression changed. "She went out one morning, almost four months now, and never returned. I have been searching for her ever since. She was actually mapping the area where I saw you."

"Did you find anything, any clues?" Troy pursued.

"No. When she did not return that evening, I thought that she may have had trouble with her buggy. But I never found the buggy or any of her supplies." He pulled out a picture of her. "She is my life."

Brett walked up to him and put his hand on his shoulder. "We'll keep our eyes open, when we go out there. Now you said you had some problems with your batteries?"

"Hmm, yes. The leads have just about burned out. I will show you."

Samad left the main room.

Troy walked up to Brett. "Sounds like a lonely place to me. You think he might want to go back to Roman with us on the way back?"

Brett was holding the picture of Samad's wife. "No, if he stays here he'll still feel there is hope. Once he's gone, so is all hope."

Samad returned in with his battery. It was charred on top, looking like it had been in a fire. "It's in bad shape, but I can still get it working."

Troy walked over. "Well, it does look a bit rough but I believe we have a few things in the MultiVec and can give it a shot."

"Thank you, thank you. I will fix something for us to eat. You will stay the night, won't you?"

Troy looked over at Brett, "Sure, we'll be glad to," Troy said before Brett could reply.

Samad came back with three small plates of salad, three protein bars and an assortment of packaged drinks. "I hope you enjoy. The lettuce is home grown. I am very proud of it."

"Looks really good!" said Troy as he took a forkful. "That is really good! What's your secret, or don't I want to know?"

Brett smiled, "I bet we probably don't, at least not until we're done."

The three continued to share stories. Troy talked about his work at the University and the Mars weather. Brett told a few of his experiences on the Moon, while Samad discussed his last few years on Mars.

Troy finally glanced at the clock. "Why don't I get suited up and take your battery with me and see what I can do."

"Oh, but it is so late my friend. Why not stay and sleep here tonight and enjoy my hospitality?"

"Thank you, but I'd love to get moving in the morning. What do you think, Brett?"

"Yeah, I agree. Troy, see what you can do. Samad, I'll spend the evening here if that's okay? Then we can get an early start tomorrow."

"Very well. Let me help you with your suit," replied Samad smiling warmly.

The following morning Troy came back with the battery. He was able to salvage some materials as well as repair Samad's batteries and give him a small backup system from the MultiVec. In return Samad would take the three of them to the road he had mentioned the sol before.

Samad's buggy took off over the dunes of Mars while the MultiVec followed.

"Well, boys, sounds like you had a nice evening. Troy was telling me a few things last night," said Rebecca, putting an arm on Brett's shoulder.

"Yeah, I guess so. Some good male bonding. How are the samples looking?"

"Actually, it's frustrating. Nothing out of the ordinary. A few samples had higher concentrations of radiation, but nothing beyond the norm. The composite is what you would expect. No rare elements. Sorry."

"Nothing to be sorry about. Just wondering what's going on up here."

A few hours had passed when Samad radioed them. "We will be at the road on the next bend. I will be heading east to look for my wife. You will want to turn left and head north. So let me thank you once again, and please stop by anytime you are in the area."

Brett hit the communicator. "Thank you, Samad, for all of your help. We'll keep our eyes open for your wife."

Glanced at Brett, Troy said, "Samad, when I get back to Roman I'll see if we can find you a new charger. When I come back to work on the weather stations, I'll bring it by.'

"Well, thank you both again. Good luck."

With the final words, the buggy and MultiVec turned around a bend as the buggy headed east. To the surprise to the three of them, there actually was a road.

Rebecca reached over to magnify the cameras. "Look at that. Who built this and why don't we know about this?"

"Good question. Lets see where it leads, the answer will probably be there," Brett answered.

Troy turned the MultiVec north "I thought you were going to say that!"

12

The technician knew it was a no-win situation. Be the one to report to Ivory what they had found, and be the one held responsible. Not tell Ivory and pay for that consequence as well. He could wait a few days, maybe? But what kind of days would those be, wondering what was waiting for him. There really was only one thing he could do, and that was to tell Ivory.

Ivory walked into the control room and took out a seat. "Mr. Lucinie, I received a message that you have some information on Robert's coordinates."

"Well, I do have some information, but it doesn't look good."

Ivory stood up from his seat, "What doesn't look good? Where is he? Has he moved into the Northern area?"

Jack Lucinie tried to keep a calm and level tone in his voice. "We're not sure where he is."

"What? You friggin idiots! What do you mean you don't know where he is? We have a tracking device in his vehicle as well as the monitoring from satellites above! Explain yourself!"

"Sir, the reading from the device had not moved for over twelve hours. We zoomed in a satellite picture and found the device lying on the sand."

Ivory threw his fist down on the armrest. "Have you started scanning the area from the satellites for his vehicle?"

"Yes, sir. So far nothing. We haven't even been able to find any tracks!"

"You fools! If they're already in the Northern area, we won't be able to find them with the satellites. We've blocked all sensors so that no one can see what's going on. They may be there already!" They may already be close, he thought, but how close?

Lucinie stood as Ivory made his way over to him.

"Listen, Lucinie, you have one more chance before I dock a entire month's wages. I want you to send a message to Roberts. How long does the message have to be in order to track their location?"

"A few minutes, maybe two or three."

"All right. Send something out to them and get a fix. Do you understand me? I want them found. I also want scouts working their way out from P - Base looking for Roberts. Can you handle that?"

"Yes, sir, I'll get to it right away." ·

Ivory thought about hitting Lucinie to make an example of him, but he knew it wasn't really Lucinie's fault and he needed Lucinie to help him find and stop Roberts. He knew he needed to find Roberts quickly before Afidan would ask for reports on their tracking.

As he was walking back to his office, he knew he couldn't just sit here and wait for Roberts. He had to go out and do what he wanted to do from the start, get out there and take care of Roberts personally. He clicked on his COM link. "This is Ivory. I want a transport, a G-11 model ready in thirty minutes. I want a crew of three, with supplies for five sols."

There was an affirmative response.

Ivory knew that Afidan didn't want any more accidents, but this one was needed. By the time Robert's death would be disclosed, it would be too late. Ivory went to his quarters and packed a few things. He grabbed a duffel bag, threw in a few CD's for his reports, some clothes and personal effects, and a Martian handgun.

In the control room Jack Lucinie had just finished sending a message to P - Base and informing them to start searching for Robert's MultiVec. Not an easy chore. Without satellites it would be like looking for a needle in a haystack. He was now busy trying to compose a message that would be sent to Roberts. He knew it had to have some substance or they might not listen to the entire message and Lucinie would lose their trace. If this didn't work, Ivory wouldn't be as forgiving as he appeared today.

"Jack, you might be interested in this," said someone from across the room. "It's a message to Brett Roberts from Earth. It's scrambled, but classified as both urgent and personal. It looks like it's a good five minutes."

Lucinie hit the delete key on his bogus message. "Perfect. Encode a tracer on the message and send it out immediately!"

Lucinie watched the monitor as the screen blinked "Sent." He flipped on an incoming message from Ivory.

"Lucinie... I am going to the P - Base to take care of matters personally. As soon as you get a fix on their location, forward it to me and I don't want any excuses...Ivory"

Lucinie sat back in his chair, a little more relaxed now knowing Ivory would be away from Roman for a week, hopefully two. He knew that

Ivory was going to take care of Roberts, but inside he was hoping that Roberts might also take care of Ivory.

Lucinie was sitting in his chair when an old colleague he hadn't seen caught his eye. Lucine looked up. "Greenberg, what are you doing here? Good timing. Ivory just left!"

* * *

Troy drove the vehicle for a few kilometers up the road when he saw an oncoming vehicle. "You two see that? It's headed down the road towards us."

"Yep, stay on the road and keep a steady speed, let's see what happens."

Rebecca's voice came from the control room. "I'll monitor all the communications. See if they try to make any contact."

As the vehicle approached, other vehicles could be seen farther down the road.

"Rebecca, anything?"

"I don't hear anything. It's all quiet."

The oncoming vehicle was closing in fast. It was a large cargo truck used to haul large material. It was almost twice the height of the MultiVec and it continued on the left side of the road without deviating or slowing down. The three looked out the window as the vehicle drove past them. Over the course of the next few minutes numerous vehicles passed by. A majority of them were also Cargo transports, but there were a few MultiVecs and some smaller vehicles.

"Looks like we're blending in. Part of the normal traffic!"

The three were looking out the window when the flashing light from the communicator started to blink.

Rebecca jumped back, "Oh that startled me," she exclaimed. "Looks like someone out there wants to talk to us."

Troy hit a key and looked to see what channel it was on. "Not out there. It's a message from Roman, actually two messages. They're both addressed to you, Brett. One is marked personal, the other marked urgent. The urgent one is from "a friend" and, get this, the topic says, "Open before any other messages!."" Troy looked over at Brett.

"Well, you read the topic. Open that one first."

Do not open or communicate with Roman or any messages outside of your general vicinity. They are being traced. As long as you are in the Northern Region you can not be seen from satellites. Do not reply and do not accept anything!
A Friend

Troy finished reading the message and turned to Brett. "Who is this from? It could be a trick. Someone may not want us to find out what's happening in Roman."

"That's a possibility, but I've received messages from "a friend" before and so far he hasn't led me astray."

"Are you sure? Maybe I should call the weather station in Roman to find out if everything is ok."

Rebecca watched the message fade as Brett leaned over and hit the delete key. "We can monitor the broadcasts and news from Phobos," she said. "We'd lose the signal for a few hours every Sol, but if there was an emergency or anything we needed to know about, it'd be on their broadcast."

Troy nodded in agreement. "She's right. They carry weather reports and news so that any remote outposts or settlements can keep in touch."

"Sounds like a plan. Lets forget about that second message for now. We'll monitor the signal from Phobos. Keep driving down this highway and see where it takes us."

Troy hit the accelerator, and the three continued down the road.

* * *

Everything was in place. Yet everything was so close to falling apart. Harvey Greenberg had worked many long and hard years to get to Mars and to make his knowledge of computers and his love for space a lifetime quest. Harvey had worked with Carlos Mendez for years in Arizona, both planning their dreams and making their ideas a reality.

He was a small man and scored poorly on the physical testing. He was much older than other candidates and had no flying or space experience. The harder Greenberg tried to show he was durable the more he failed. He spent numerous hours in zero gravity and in different flight simulators, but in the end he would always end up sick to his stomach. He was sure he would never make it to Mars. When Carlos Mendez had been told he could hand pick twelve essential people, Greenberg had been one of them.

Greenberg had worked behind the scenes programming networks and files to help run Roman. Over the course of the first year Greenberg had found that the security, led by Gary Ivory, could not be trusted. Unfortunately, he had found out the hard way. Greenberg came across programming that was trying to hide cargo shipments.

He went to Ivory to report the information. At the time Ivory seemed receptive and asked Greenberg to show him how he found out about it. Greenberg explained in details how he had come about this information.

When all had been said and done, Ivory had taken this information and arrested Greenberg for helping smugglers, then had beaten him in what Ivory called an "interrogation."

Mendez knew Greenberg had been framed but had been helpless against the evidence and a so-called admission to guilt. A deal was cut, and the charges were dropped, Ivory didn't want Greenberg going back to Earth and informing authorities of the activities. It was much safer to keep an eye on Greenberg if he were with him on Mars. Greenberg was able to remain on Mars but his job responsibilities were reduced to routine checks and maintenance on mainframes and checking basic programs.

Over the next six months Greenberg became paranoid in the conviction that he was being watched and followed. Every evening he would return to his quarters and look for bugging and monitoring devices. The following morning he would return to his cubical early to search for the same thing.

One morning, to his horror, Greenberg did find a bug under his desk. Unsure what to do, he left the device and continued with his work and made sure that any and all correspondence and discussion were positive on Roman and referred only to his job. Three days later Greenberg returned to his cubical to find the bug was no longer there, although he still continued to check every day.

The mind game was becoming too much for Greenberg. He decided he needed to turn the tables. For the next few months, as Greenberg did his routine diagnostics on the programming, he placed tracers, log files and decoding programs throughout the entire system. Within three months there wasn't anything that went on in Roman that Greenberg didn't know about.

At first it was all bits and pieces. He quickly uncovered numerous romances, employees cutting hours off their shifts, a few small drug operations and even a subcontractor over-billing Calprex. But it took a few weeks until he came across his target, Ivory.

All of Ivory's correspondence went under the name, "Beatle." Once Greenberg had uncovered this, everything started to fall into place. Most of the information was in code, but as more and more messages were intercepted the computer was able to break the code.

What Greenberg didn't know is what to do with this information. Who could he turn to and who could he trust? He knew he could trust Mendez, but before he would get Carlos involved he wanted to gather enough information. Greenberg also knew more people were needed to stand up to Ivory and his people.

Greenberg began to make a list of people who had problems with Ivory, along with list of people Ivory had under surveillance. This was cross-referenced with numerous lists from things ranging from common employer, educational institutions, etc. A multiplier was used to rank the list. The number two person was not a surprise, Carlos Mendez. The number one person was someone Greenberg had never met. Troy Smitts.

Greenberg made a point of meeting the top ten people on the list and getting a feeling if they could be trusted and how they felt about Ivory. It was a pretty uniform group with all feeling that Ivory was up to no good. But for the most part they were not looking for trouble and wanted to do their work without interference.

The only two people on that list that Greenberg felt he could trust were Mendez and Smitts. Mendez knew that Ivory was up to something but was so busy, he couldn't figure out what it was. Smitts plain hated Ivory and would do anything to piss him off.

Greenberg had come to the conclusion that the information he collected would have to be sent back to Earth as well, but to whom? If he sent it to the wrong people, they would cover it up and take care of those who knew about it. This led Greenberg back to wondering if he should tell Mendez and Smitts about his findings.

Greenberg had enjoyed many drinks with Smitts over the course of several weeks and thought he was trustworthy. But what could a meteorologist really do to help. So Greenberg decided not to get him involved. Greenberg thought then that he would send his findings to Mendez. Greenberg downloaded all the information and burned a disk and left it on Mendez's private desk.

The next day Mendez was killed. Now almost four months later Greenberg's plan of letting all of Earth know of what was in the North Area would fall apart if the three didn't make it to Station 185 and download the information.

* * *

The three continued north on this red, baked highway created by the large amount of traffic. The farther north they drove the more it resembled an old highway on Earth. They had passed vehicles of all types and had come across numerous intersections along the way.

The sun was slowly setting, and the Martian sky took on a purple hue. The silhouettes of the large mountains looked even larger against the sky. The high beam lights from the multiple vehicles gave the rocks a dark red color. They were going with the flow of traffic, and it was noticed that there was congestion ahead of them.

"What do you think that's all about?" Rebecca said, leaning against Brett's seat.

"Not sure, Troy, what do you make of it?"

"I'm not certain. Do you think they know we're here? Or maybe it's a checkpoint? Either way it probably isn't good for us."

"Troy, direct a spot light over to the side of the highway. Any chance of us slipping out?"

With a couple moves, Troy had a few high beams shining along the side of the highway.

The area seemed to be somewhat drivable though with only a few shattered boulders. As the light moved closer to the congested area, they could make out a small, steep ridge. The ridge was forcing all the traffic into the bottleneck.

"Maybe I was wrong. Maybe it's just everyone is merging," Troy said.

"Well, I don't want to find out. Let's pull off to the side. After a few minutes kill the lights, then we'll slowly head east. We can find a place to park and start again in the morning."

"Does this MultiVec have an infrared viewer, Troy?" Rebecca asked.

"I think it has one of those IR-16 types. It should help us from driving off a cliff or into a boulder, but we'll have to take it slow."

Rebecca turned to Troy. "Well, if you two don't drive us into anything, I'll make something for us to eat."

"Thanks," Brett said, feeling a bit tired.

* * *

Terry McGregor was still trying to come to grips with the message he received yesterday morning. It was pretty clear that Relin was not interested in subcontracting any additional jobs in Roman. The men had been eager to earn extra money and most important Terry gave his word to Roberts that he could get it done.

McGregor couldn't get any sleep that evening and had sent a message out to Roberts but hadn't heard anything yet. He wasn't sure how far Roberts had gone out and if they could even receive the message. By the time Roberts got the message, would it be too late?

He had to make some type of decision. He needed to get men working on Capricorn, get those men paid, and have no ties to Relin. If he wanted to save his job, he couldn't have any ties to them. The only person that came to mind who might be able to help would be Jon Conners. He seemed like a guy who could be trusted, but McGregor was finding out that it was a different world here on Mars.

McGregor had caught up with Conners later that morning and went over the situation. "I can be behind the scenes," he said, "organizing the shifts. All you need to do is be the front man for this. You're working for Roberts and Calprex, so no one can tell you to stop your job."

Conners appeared a little uneasy. "I wish it was as easy as that. There are numerous factors going on here in Roman. The bottom line is, I have to save my ass first. I have a good job and don't want screw that up. In the last seven months I've had to report to three different supervisors. I don't know what tomorrow will bring."

"Mr. Conners, your job is to assist Brett Roberts. You can't be worried about who will eventually replace him. If the job is not done, he may replace you."

"What you don't understand, is that if I do this, I might not be alive to see another supervisor!"

"Will you talk to Roberts about this?" McGregor asked in disbelief.

"He's already got a full plate. If he makes it back to Roman from his little trek out to the Northern area without having problems I'd be surprised."

"Isn't there anything I can do, Mr. Conners? Please help me."

"Possibly, but it will cost you."

"What are we talking about?" McGregor replied, almost enjoying the haggling.

"Look, McGregor, I can make a fictitious supervisor. One who authorizes and signs the work orders. But for putting my neck out, I'll want a five percent cut on the entire payroll for the entire project."

"I can't authorize that! It's not my money. It's Calprex's!"

"Well, it's my neck and I say you can do it, if you wanted to."

"How?"

"This fictitious supervisor will get hourly pay. His pay will indirectly be transferred to an account that I'll set up. You're doing all the work, you decide."

"Damn! I was hoping Mars would be different than back home. Give me a name and I'll have the work order out to you in a few hours. Damn it." McGregor walked out the door. He was angry about all the greed and deception in business. Yet, as he walked down the corridor, he felt happy that he would keep his word to Roberts and get Capricorn completed.

13

Troy woke up and looked over at the clock. It was 5:50 am. He just couldn't sleep on the small cot in the MultiVec. He would wake up every morning with a backache and feeling exhausted. He knew this journey was getting to Brett as well. Although Troy didn't know him very well, Brett seemed more distant as the voyage went on.

Well, no sense pretending I can fall back asleep, he thought. He went into the galley and made a quick cup of Martian java and rode a stationary bike for thirty minutes, then got into the cockpit and sat down. He looked out the front windshield and saw what looked like a ridge in front of them. It was more difficult than he thought, driving in total darkness, with an outdated infrared system. He gulped down the java and looked at the scanner to attempt getting a fix. Nothing, however seemed to match.

Well, he could hang around in here and end up waking up everyone, or take a nice stroll up the ridge. Within ten minutes he was suited up and out, headed for the ridge. As he took his first step, he could hear his boot crush against the small red stones.

He looked up at the incline. From inside, it didn't look so steep, but from where he was now he asked himself what he was doing. Well, he definitely wasn't going to go through all the trouble of suiting up just to be outside for five minutes. He began to climb the ridge. His boots slid down with each step, but he slowly made progress.

He gradually made his way up and was a few meters from the top when a voice chimed in on his COM link.

"Bored this morning? You know that was an awful chance you took by not waking us up and letting us know what you were doing," Brett said, though knowing he might have done the same thing.

"Well, it was a spur of the moment kind of thing. If you check, you'd see that I did set the volume on the distress signal all the way up if I needed to call you," Troy replied as he continued to climb to the top.

Brett glanced at the monitor and set the volume back to normal. "I guess there is nothing wrong with a morning walk," he said then glancing at the scanner as Troy had done earlier to check on the location. "You know, you could have made us a three course breakfast. Some powdered eggs, dry toast, and a bag a juice. I could have gone for that." He chuckled, but there was no reply from Troy. He quickly stood up and looked at the horizon to get a fix on Troy.

It didn't take Brett more than a few seconds as Troy was standing to the left on the MultiVec on top of the ridge. "Troy, are you okay? Can your hear me?" There was nothing. "Rebecca get up and get my suit ready!" He cried to the back of the MultiVec.

Rebecca's training and years in the space program had her spring from her cot to quickly do as requested. She was pulling out Brett's suit within thirty seconds.

"Troy, can you hear me? Are you alright?" Brett asked again.

"Yes," said a bewildered voice over the COM link. "Yes, I hear you."

"Are you all right? Did you get cut off?"

"No, I heard you, I think. You'd better come out here... both of you."

"Troy, what is it?"

"You'd better get out here! Now."

Rebecca was still getting Brett's suit ready when she had overheard the conversation. She began to pull her suit out as well. "Brett, yours is all set and ready to go."

"Thanks. I don't know what's going on, but he doesn't seem right. Be alert out there."

Rebecca nodded as she slipped out of her overalls and into the suit. Within a few minutes they were both racing up the ridge to join Troy at the top.

"Troy, is your gas mix fine?" Brett asked as he climbed up to meet him at the top of the ridge. But no answer. Troy just stood looking out over the ridge.

"Troy, are you okay?" Rebecca tried but still no answer.

The two were losing their footing as they continued hurrying upwards, but within a few minutes they would be at the crest of the ridge.

Troy turned to them as if he knew when they were only a few steps away. He extended his arm and helped Brett up to the top, then assisted Rebecca who had been right behind Brett. Brett couldn't see his face through his visor so didn't know if Troy was okay.

"Buddy you're scaring us," said Brett. "What's going on?"

Troy pointed to the other side of the ridge. "Take a look."

Brett turned and saw what Troy was looking at and what had made him speechless. Below them was a quarry dug out over 750 meters deep with a radius of almost 2 kilometers. The size of the quarry was impressive, but it was what was in the middle of it that left them speechless.

The three of them looked down and couldn't believe what they saw. What were the implications that went with this? What did this mean for mankind?

In the middle of what may have been the largest dig in the history of mankind were two massive Pyramids. Hundreds of vehicles were loading and unloading material as they excavated the area. The three looked down at the largest quarry known to man, two massive Pyramids in the center of it.

* * *

Nick Gambino was in his office all day. Almost two days since he had sent the message and still no response. It was times like these he hated the delay in sending a message. He missed the face-to-face conversations, even if they were over a cam.

He realized it would be news that would be difficult for Brett to take, but he thought he would have heard back by now. Time was important, and a decision had to be made. He scrolled through the personnel list. He came across Jon Conner's name. He knew he would get a quick answer from Jon. He quickly typed a text message to Jon, asking him to have Brett contact him as soon as possible.

He hit the send key and leaned back in his chair. His dream of exploring Mars and making it habitable for humans no longer seemed as important as it did years ago. He had lost many friends and seen lives destroyed. Roman had become a power struggle and a political tool.

In order to obtain funds for the building of Roman, many backroom deals had been made with the wrong people. They had had alternative motives but they had been the only ones who would fund the project. At the time Ed and Nick knew there would be problems down the road, but they were too focused on getting Roman built.

Now years later as completion was in sight, it was time to pay for those deals. The Arab Republic and Japan, that which now were unrealistic. The Corporations were actually easier to deal with. For the most part they increased the length of the loans, though were compensated for extending the loan.

It was the countries that were more demanding. Japan wanted to increase the interest rate of their loan, and the Arab Republic wanted land rights to the North. He had truly become a businessman now, negotiating, giving and taking while hoping he and Calprex could live with the results.

Looking back over his career, he felt he was not exactly where he thought he would be. He was one of the pioneers in space engineering. He had developed and supervised numerous space stations. He was one of NASA's most decorated astronauts and the Director on U.S. Moon Base 16.

As the major corporations spent more money on space development, they became the leaders in research and design. The bureaucracy that went along with government projects slowly took them out of the running. Within a short five years any government funds used in space were contracted out.

In order to remain in the space industry Nick had taken a job with Frontiers, the leading company in manufacturing space station. He hadn't been happy there and in less than a year had taken a position with one of his old friends from NASA, Ed Brocton. Nicks innovative designs made Calprex a profitable company. He was responsible for designing some of the greatest structures built on the Moon.

He became Ed Brocton's right hand man and supervised all new projects. That is where he was introduced to Carlos Mendez. While Nick had been on the Moon building magnificent structures, and forging relationships with people like Brett Roberts, Carlos Mendez was on Earth lobbying Ed Brocton, trying to get him to move on to the new frontier, Mars.

It was almost fifteen years ago when Nick was heading back from the Moon and he had had a heart attack on reentry of Earth's atmosphere. He had full recovery, although the Doctors thought it best that space travel be left to the younger and healthier. At first, it had been a tough blow to Nick, but he threw himself more into his design work. His ideas were years ahead of others, although the price tags of these projects were also years ahead.

The Moon was profitable, and although travel to Mars was becoming routine, Calprex was putting most of its resources into the Moon. Carlos had blueprints of a large multi-corporation, multi-national city. To make Mars a profitable expenditure for investment, corporations needed to establish habitats, just as they had on the Moon.

The short distance from the Moon to Earth made investing safer, but millions were lost on Mars. If a large structure was in place, explorers, scientists, religions and corporations could expand their reach. When Nick was based in Calprex's home office, Carlos began to sell his city to Nick.

Nick was caught up in the concept and talked Ed into starting up a small project, having him begin drafts and designs for this future city. As the weeks, months went by, Nick came to spend more time on the Mars project than those on the Moon. Also, during this period small contractors became more aggressive and commenced specializing in certain aspects of space engineering. The cash cow, the business of building on the Moon, was coming to an end. With the revenues declining, Ed turned to Nick and Carlos to learn what they thought about the prospects of Mars.

Ed was surprised by the amount of work that had been done. It looked like a no-brainer, except for one problem. The cost was like nothing they had ever had before. It would be a difficult sell to the shareholders.

Nick and Carlos crunched the numbers numerous times and were able to cut a few million here and there, but it was peanuts compared to the final price tag.

The following month Ed presented the project at the shareholders meeting. The shareholders felt the same way Ed had when Nick and Carlos had presented the idea. They loved it, but the expense was unacceptable.

"Mr. Brocton, with these numbers how would Calprex be profitable?" someone said in an old scratchy voice from across the board table.

"Mr. Jacobs, I understand this may be one of the largest undertakings we've ever had, but the profits for decades will make up for a few lean years," Ed said.

"Mr. Brocton I may only have a few years left," came the scratchy voice.

"Ed have you looked at different loans that might reduce the interests?" asked another member of the board.

"We're still looking into some of the financing," replied Ed. "But the bottom line is many of our holdings on the Moon would be our collateral."

"And this project, what is it called anyways?" asked one of the board members.

"Ummm, Roman," he replied, not wondering why he came up with that name.

"Well, this Project Roman, how long would it take to complete?"

"Our estimates are three to four years depending on what type of problems we encounter," Ed replied.

"Do we have a location picked out yet? What is the price tag on the land rights?

The questions continued, but in the end they wanted to play it safe and build what they could on the Moon and space stations. To them a small profit was better than gambling it on Mars. They did concede to use necessary funds in purchasing the rights to the future sight of Roman.

So Nick continued splitting his time between small Moon projects and with Roman. As the next few years went by Calprex was losing bids to small contractors. At a future meeting, consequently, Roman was readdressed by the board members. This time they agreed to it with a few concessions. Tom Afidan, who was hired a few years earlier, would help to oversee the building of Roman. There were also numerous deals made with certain corporations and countries on rights and contracts. These deals now were the ones Nick was dealing with.

* * *

The three returned to the MultiVec to try comprehending what they had just seen. Rebecca pulled out three mugs that she placed on the table in the control room. "Maybe they're building them?" she suggested knowing immediately it wasn't the truth.

"And maybe they're going to run the Nile River across the Martian Desert," quipped Troy as he pulled a pot of Martian java from the food processor and began pouring into the three mugs. "I'm sure we could all use something to spike this java with, but I didn't bring anything."

Brett pulled his mug up and took a sip. "That does sound good, but I think we're going to have to be on our toes. Now we know why they didn't want us here."

"Those appear twice the size of the Pyramids on Earth. They should be visible from Diemos and Phobos or even from any large ship in orbit, shouldn't they?" Rebecca asked.

Troy drew up one of the chairs "It appears they are somehow controlling the satellites."

"Yes. I'm not sure how, but they're either manipulating the feed or jamming signals," said Brett pulling up a chart of the northern area. "I think we're somewhere about here," he said pointing to the map.

"The question isn't how they're doing it, it's why are they doing it? What does this all mean?" Rebecca said looking into Brett's eyes.

"I'm not sure. We're not alone, though." Brett stood up and put his hand on her shoulder. "Or at least at one time there was someone else out there."

Troy glanced to both of them, "It could mean many things. Maybe humans came from Mars and we're just now beginning to return home. Maybe Earth and Mars were two colonies from a distant civilization."

"So why keep this a secret? Eventually this is all going to come out regardless of the type of security or who has rights to this land," Rebecca, appearing to be calming down.

"Well, think about it. Whoever controls this becomes very powerful and wealthy." Troy said.

Brett nodded, "Yes, also think of the ramifications it has on science, religion and our history. There will be many who won't want this to come out. There will be those who will pay to hold things back."

"Like what, hold what?" Rebecca asked.

"It's hard to say," Brett answered. "But the information will change the way we look at things. Of course, all of us on Mars know that this will be the jumpstart for new investments into anything dealing with space. Depending on what they find, this could put major holes in every religion back home. The possibilities of what will happen could equal the number of speculations on what this all means."

"Brett, did Calprex mention anything about excavations or anything about work being done here?" said Troy.

"No, my job was to get to Mars and get Roman on schedule. If Ed or Nick had known about this, they would have told me. It wouldn't add up if they didn't."

"Well, maybe they used you as a cover," Rebecca suggested.

"I would hope that with all I went through for Calprex, they would have found someone else for that. I know those guys like brothers. They don't know about this."

"How are we going to tell them? I'm betting that any communication through Roman wouldn't make it to Earth," Troy said.

Rebecca looked with concern at Brett. "Well, if Phobos, or the people on it, are blocking radar, visuals and other communications, any message we send will never make it past them."

"They must have some type of jamming device that works both ways. That's why they can't tract us down," Troy remarked.

"But how come no one has seen the Pyramids while flying over them?" Rebecca asked.

"Brett, she has a point. My guess is there are several people on Phobos in on this. Whoever comes up with the flight paths could keep any ships from a direct fly over. And let's face it, with all the mountains, canyons and valleys, if you're not looking for this, you wouldn't see it."

"Let's get back to Roman. We can let everyone know," Rebecca suggested.

"If they figure out that we've seen this, we'll never make it back alive." Troy responded.

"Troy's probably right," Brett said. "They've lost their trace of us and they'll have to assume the worst. I think we need to figure out how they're blocking transmissions from this area. Once we find out I think all of Earth will see what we just saw."

Troy glanced across the table at his scattered charts and printouts. "That's it!" he suddenly cried, standing up. "Of course, that's it. Station 185 is somehow jamming the reception."

A smile went over Brett's face. "Yes, and I think your friend, Mr. Greenberg, knows something about what's going on here. He was very persistent about replacing a memory cube at Station 185 with the one he gave us."

"There definitely is something odd about that man, but I did get the sense he was holding something back from us," Rebecca said.

As they discussed what to do, some of the digital pictures they took were coming up on their display. Brett still couldn't believe it. "Any ideas on where we go from here? I'm thinking we find the fastest route to Station 185."

Troy hit the keyboard and a three-dimensional route came up. "It looks like we have two options. The first is to take the road we were on last night and head just west of the site and head northwest. Looks like a twenty-hour journey. If we bypass that road, it looks like we'll have to go around this canyon, then take this road down." He pointed to the second route. "And that could take an additional Sol. Neither sounds good to me."

"I agree. It would be safer to take the canyon route, but Ivory must be looking for us by now. He has to have both routes covered."

"So we head back to Roman?" Rebecca asked.

"It's a thought. If we can make it back alive. I was thinking of taking this route." Brett pointed to a small black line that swung around and seemed to head straight into the site.

"You're kidding me!"

"No, they wouldn't be expecting us to drive right down there and out the back road to Station 185. This MultiVec will blend in with all of theirs."

"What if they start pulling over vehicles searching for us? It's too risky"

"Any better ideas? I'm up for any suggestion."

Rebecca looked at the two of them. "What if we drive down there and steal a different vehicle?"

Troy looked over to Brett and smiled "I'm game if you are."

14

Terry McGregor set up work schedules and posted them to all the contractors that might be interested. Those interested were to contact Jane Bender, Jon Connor's new fictitious foreman. Everything would be funneled into a main board, and McGregor could set up new schedules depending on the work and those interested.

Within a few hours the replies were coming in to Jane Bender. Most of these men had come to Mars to make money to support their families back home on Earth. So, this extra work at higher wages was not going to be turned down by too many.

Within twelve hours of the posting, McGregor had more workers than he anticipated and had to assign additional work details. He quickly assigned additional details and laid work plans out for the next few sols. If he could keep up this pace, he would be close to completing the work needed to have Capricorn functional. He still needed to squeeze more out of the workers to make the deadline, but how? He had almost all the interested workers already committed. As time went, on he would lose men, not gain them, something he couldn't afford.

Terry McGregor knew if he was correct he could get Capricorn completed on time. He wanted to prove to himself that he was capable. Most importantly, he didn't want to let down those like Brett Roberts who had confidence in him. He sat back in his chair after reviewing the schedule, thinking that maybe Mars wasn't that bad a place after all.

He knew the work was just beginning, but maybe he ought to go into the Jane Bender messages and see if there were any updates. He punched in the password, and a dozen messages came on the screen. One stood out, "No materials at work site"!

* * *

Rebecca sat at the table in the galley reading as Troy walked by to get a cup of java. "As soon as it's dark we can make our way down there," he said looking over at Rebecca. "What are you reading there?"

Rebecca turned off the pocket PC and tucked it away. "Nothing. Nothing, anyway that would interest you."

"That sounded a bit sarcastic," he snickered.

"I'm sorry. You're right. I was reading the bible."

Troy took a sip of the java without responding.

"See, I am right. It doesn't interest you."

"Well, I do find it interesting that after what we have just seen that you're reading the bible. You can't believe that Jesus Christ is actually the Son of God? We know now that we are not alone."

"Actually, I believe more than ever. There are so many mysteries in this universe that we don't understand. Man cannot comprehend it all. It comes down to faith. I take it you don't believe in God?"

"Oh, I do. You're right. There is so much we can't comprehend. There has to be an almighty force out there. For every action there is a reaction. For every positive there is a negative."

"You call that religion? I call that an easy way out."

"I never said I believe in religion. Religion has always been a great tool to control the masses. Look at all the killing and wars in the name of God. Not exactly a benevolent fellow is He?" Troy took another sip of java as Rebecca rose up from her chair.

"If you read the bible and its writings about love, compassion and forgiveness, you'll understand it's the men that kill, not God."

"Didn't God make us in his image? Pretty violent species, don't you think? Look, most of us know the difference between good and bad. Everything has a consequence."

"I'm sorry, but not believing is the easy way out."

"You mean ignoring all the science we have? Not believing in hard evidence and believing in a fairy tale that says when we die we go somewhere special. I wonder which one is the easy way out?"

"I'm not saying that everything is true. Having faith takes strength. Having an excuse to do whatever you please is easy."

"Easy? I remember my grandparents dragging me to church every Sunday. The church was filled with hypocrites. They would all go up for communion without ever having gone to confession. I mean, they had to have some sin, however small. They would pick and choose what was convenient for them. They would almost run each other down in the parking lot. Those were the same people who struck their spouses, lied, stole and cheated their fellow neighbors. But all was forgiven on Sunday. That sounds like an easy way out to me!"

"You're talking about a minority of people. Religion refreshes the soul and makes you feel better about what is going on around you. It helps you take comfort and understand that although man looks for answers, we can never understand everything."

"Well, I wish I could find religion, but I haven't yet. I don't understand. You're a scientist, a geologist. Don't you believe in Darwin's theory of evolution?"

"Of course, I do."

"But doesn't that go against the church? Doesn't it contradict the Adam and Eve story?"

"Look, I'm not saying that everything in the bible is true. It may be a story to simplify and understand something. I believe in evolution, but I also think that God had a hand in how everything played out. The universe just didn't happen."

Brett had walked into the back of the galley to grab some freeze dried fruit. Troy turned to him. "What do you think about all this? Do you believe in religion, believe in God?"

Brett turned to the two of them. "After what happened to Alex, you tell me."

Troy glared at Rebecca with a puzzled look. "What happened, Brett?"

* * *

The sun was setting over Seneca Lake as a hot summer day was making way for a humid evening. Brett sat out on his deck, watching the sun sinking behind the rolling mountains. A smile came to him as he thought about the next two weeks with Alex.

After Kathleen and Brett were divorced, the time with Alex was limited. Kathleen had moved to San Diego, and with Brett working for Calprex on assignments on the Moon and space stations, it would be hard to get any lawyer to have Alex split time between them. Kathleen was an incredible mother and would provide a much more stable environment for Alex.

So Brett would get Alex a few weeks in early and late summer as well as during any other breaks he had from school when Brett was home. Brett would also find reasons to visit Calprex's office in Arizona on a Friday and take a shuttle over to the west coast to spend an afternoon with him, maybe catch a ball game.

Brett sat back thinking about how Alex had grown to be a young man. He had incredible grades, and he was the quarterback on his high school football team. He was just a plain good kid. He was accepted into the

University of Southern California and was going to major in Marine biology.

Before Alex and his buddies took off to college, they decided to take an excursion down the Colorado River. From there Alex would come to visit Brett for two weeks. Brett was making mental notes to himself. Did he have enough of the soda that Alex liked? Did he have all the food he liked?

He thought about the early mornings when the two would get up at the crack of dawn and get out on the lake and spend the entire morning reeling in the perch. They would talk about football, discuss the teams and the players, and who was going to be the surprise team. They would talk about the future. They would stay up late at night watching old reruns. Three more days till Alex came.

Brett went into the cabin to grab a beer when the phone rang.

"Hello." Nothing, but he could hear someone on the other end.

"Hello," he said again.

"Brett." He recognized Kathleen's voice.

"Brett, it's Alex." He could detect the trembling in her voice.

"There's been an accident." Barely getting the words out. "Alex's raft turned over and..."

There was silence. "What? What happened?"

He could hear the tears, "Alex is dead. He is gone."

Brett dropped the phone as the life was sucked out of him. He walked over to the window and looked out across the lake. The tears filling his eyes, he couldn't make out any shapes or forms.

"God, let this be a dream. Let me wake up!"

As he knew he was fully awake, he slipped to the ground and cried in disbelief. "Why not me? Take me!" he screamed.

Later that night Brett was on a jet to the west coast to bury his son.

"So you ask me if I believe in God. No, I do not. They say God gave up his Son for us, but I was not willing to give up mine. I see no reason to take a boy like that out of this world. If there is an almighty God, full of benevolence, have him show me the reason for taking my boy from me. There was a negative, where is the positive gained from it? No, no God, no religion, no sense."

Troy took a step over to Brett. "I'm sorry. I didn't know." Brett looked into Troy's eyes and could see how shaken he was.

"I know you didn't." Brett wiped a tear from his cheek and went up to the cockpit.

* * *

Gary Ivory looked at the coordinates. Still another day from P – Base. No one has seen Roberts or the MultiVec. He knew his men were busy but he needed to find Roberts. Setting up checkpoints and telling people to keep an eye open is not the same thing as a full out search.

He knew he would have to send an update to Afidan by the end of the week. The last thing he wanted to tell him is that Roberts' whereabouts were unknown. The more progress they were making at the site, the harder it would be to keep secret. When the news does finally come out, whoever has rights to this land would be very wealthy.

Religious groups from the Arab Republic felt they could prove that the ancient history of man was related to the history of Mars. The pharaohs and Kings were descendants of Martians. They also thought that this information would wipe out most of the other religions in the world. God did not send his son to Earth, the Martians sent theirs.

For all the religious implications, Ivory could not care less. If all went as planned, he would leave Mars a very rich man and never have to lift a finger the remainder of his life. He walked up into the cockpit where the two drivers were busy reviewing coordinates.

"We're making good time, Mr. Ivory. The weather looks favorable for the remainder of the trip."

Ivory looked out at the red boulders as the vehicle bounced along.

"Just get us there quickly and let me know if anyone finds Roberts." He turned back into the main cabin. When he did find Roberts, he knew what he would do, the same thing that he did to Mendez, kill him.

* * *

Ed stepped out of the taxi and looked up at the large skyscraper before him, the International Space Consortium, ISC. Many dreams were made and squandered in the building. Calprex had won its share of battles with ISC but had lost just as many.

ISC had been established almost twenty years ago to regulate National and Corporate interests in space. It had started as a branch of the United Nations, but as man had pressed out to the stars it had became a large and powerful group. Since corporations were investing more money than governments were, it broke away from the UN to distance itself from countries.

The International Space Consortium was made up of three branches. Twelve countries consisted of one branch, "The Locale," with the twelve seats becoming known as the Nationalist. The second branch, "Industry," was made up of twelve seats represented by twelve corporations, and nicknamed the Firm. Four seats were held by large corporations, four by midsize, and four by smaller corporations. Both the Locale and Industry seats were voted on every three years.

The next branch was made up of five chairs, and were called, "The Observers," becoming known as the Golden Five. These five held their post for twelve years. They were voted in by both the Locale and Industry. The Observers were a mix of the group and had years of experience in space. The idea was that the Observers would base their views on what was good for space exploration. These five held veto votes and two vetoes could end a proposed bill or plan of action.

All three branches had their elections staggered, and no more than one third of the seats were up for election at any one time. It seemed to work well in principle but the Observers became extremely powerful, and it wasn't long before bribes were common practice. The Nationalist and the Firm would lobby their case to the Golden Five.

Early on, the "Observers" seemed to have exploration in mind. They seemed to want to share the wealth, but as the years went on, the faces began to change, as did the outcomes. Money, bribes and threats went a long way.

Ed's hope was that the issue with the Arab Republic, and their demand of compensation for the delayed work on Capricorn, would seem so trivial that the ISC, would grant an extension along with a financial reimbursement. Ed felt that their request for land right north of Roman was ridiculous.

Ed entered the lobby and headed for the chambers.

"Ed, long time no see. I saw the claim on the docket. I wouldn't think they have anything to stand on."

"Hey, Craig!" Ed held his hand out as he continued to walk down the corridor. "I would think not, but I've seen stranger things happen. I hope they're reaching high and hoping to get something in the middle. I'm not giving anything away. This is bullshit."

"Well, we go back, Ed. You know our vote is with Calprex. Most of the chairs in the Firm agree. Some of these countries are trying to pull a fast one. Even in the Locale the United States and China agree with you. I wouldn't worry."

Ed opened the doors to the back of the chambers and took a seat. In the front of the room at the podium a dark-haired man was presenting his case in regards to a space station. Ed flipped through the sheets. "Three more cases, then I'm up," he thought.

* * *

Terry McGregor went to the work site, and sure enough there were no materials, only a bunch of angry workers.

"Hey, McGregor, what are you doing here? Trying to spy on us? We can moonlight on our time. Relin doesn't own us," yelled one of the workers.

McGregor surveyed the area for possible materials that had been overlooked. "Hmmm, yeah, I know. You guys can do whatever you want. I don't blame you. I would be doing the same thing if I could." He picked up his communicator and scrambled to find the materials as the angry group continued to ask McGregor questions.

"Who is this Jane Bender? I hope she knows she owes me credits from the time I arrived, and not the time the work gets here!" one man bellowed from the back, others cheering his comments.

McGregor felt the sweat dripping down his forehead. Did someone know what he was doing? Would he get caught? The workers were getting restless.

"Well, I've met Jane Bender only once but heard a lot about her. Bottom line is she is tough, but fair. She'll pay you what you're owed. I also hear she is generous with bonus credits if the work is good and ahead of schedule." He continued to run down possible places for the materials.

"Now how can you get a bonus if you don't have the materials?" yelled another.

McGregor could feel the unrest in the crowd. There it is. He found the materials, at least some of them. But how to let them know? McGregor yelled to the group of men, "What are you guys looking for what type of work are you contracted for?"

"It's looks like a general placement configuration for Capricorn. The standard G series material," replied a man from the front of the group.

Terry looked up at them, "Well, according to what I see here, someone moved the G series material to hanger 29, which is actually not too far from here."

"That's a couple kilometers away!" countered someone from the back.

"I'll send Bender a note about the situation. I'm sure you'll be compensated."

"We'd better McGregor, or else Relin will pay me the credits."

McGregor was nervous as they slowly left towards hanger 29. What was going on here? Someone had moved the materials and there was still a good amount missing. He took a look at what materials Relin had in Aquarius. Much of the things they would need. I guess it's time to make a few transfers, he thought. It looks like Bender is going to do some wheeling and dealing.

* * *

Ed ran his hand through his hair. It couldn't be! Something was not right. The Observers came back in favor of the Arab Republic and gave Calprex seventy-two hours to complete work on Capricorn in Roman. If the work was not completed, Calprex was to hand over land rights north of Roman to the Republic.

"I have had the utmost respect for the work of the ICS and particular the fair judgments of the Observers, but this makes absolutely no sense," Ed proclaimed as he stood and faced the Observers.

"This is not consistent with any other claims in regard to contacts on completed work. I would expect fines and extensions with penalties, but this makes no sense."

"Mr. Brocton, for years the Consortium has done exactly what you have stated, but as we expand we need to mandate higher penalties to minimize these problems."

Ed looked over as they coldly continued with their response.

"Mr. Brocton, you should be content with this outcome. If we chose to fine Calprex, it may have very well put you out of business. Be happy you have a company to go back to."

Ed looked at the five of them. He had heard their arguments for other conflicts over the years, but something had changed. These were not the same men he had admired for their honest work. Someone had gotten to them. Someone had bought them off. But why? For some land? It didn't make sense?

"Well, I am grateful to be going back to a job. A job that helps me and many others like me to fulfill our dream. A dream to explore the planets, moons and beyond. Calprex has been around as long as the ISC, and I have always thought we shared the same dream. After today I have to wonder if there are alternative motives I'm not aware of?" Ed replied, trying not to show his emotions.

"Mr. Brocton, I hope you are not implying any wrong doings?" replied former Ambassador of China, Yu Hwong.

Ed glared at them. His eyes met former Senator, Nate Stills. Ed could sense his uneasiness as Senator Stills addressed him.

"Look, Ed, we go way back. I can understand you don't understand this ruling, and that you're upset with what is playing out here. Things have changed and we need to have a firm hand so that we don't tie up this organization with insignificant disagreements. As we move forward, monumental decisions will be made and the ISC will no longer have time to listen to contract disputes."

Yu Hwong and one of the other Observers looked at the former Senator and then turned to Ed. "Mr. Brocton, your relationship and friendship with Senator Stills shows that we do not show favoritism. We must all work to move forward."

Ed turned back to Senator Stills as the Senator continued. "Ed, I'm sorry. Things happen, things change. Mars, the moon, you, and me."

"I haven't changed, but I can see you have."

"Enough. We have to move on. Good day, Mr. Brocton," broke in Yu Hwong.

15

The three had quietly got everything together for the climb down the cliff to the Pyramids. They had checked and rechecked each other's equipment. Brett placed the disk that Greenberg had given them at Roman in his backpack.

"Hopefully, no one will find the MultiVec between these boulders," Troy said to cut the silence.

"They would really have to be searching hard to find it. They have a lot of ground to cover and might not be concentrating so close to their site," Brett replied as he began to check Rebecca's suit.

The three made their way out of the MultiVec. Brett pointed to the quarry. "We should be safe going down here. This indentation of the wall should cover our descent. Problem is we'll be in total darkness."

"Better safe then sorry," Rebecca remarked as she handed the lines to Troy.

Troy anchored the three lines to the red rocks at the edge of the cliff. "It appears to be secure, but maybe we should also secure the lines as we go down."

Rebecca turned to him as she grabbed the first line. "My thoughts exactly. Let's make sure we are far enough from each other. We don't need to knock each other down in the dark. It will take us some extra time on the way down, but it would probably be safe to secure the line every 10 meters. So make sure you have enough anchors." She padded the ones attached to her belt.

Brett and Troy grabbed the other lines as the three started down. As they descended, they stopped intermittently to hammer in anchors on their lines. Brett secured his third anchor as he waited for Troy and Rebecca to catch up. He looked down and in the shade of the night couldn't make out the bottom. He glanced up and figured they had gone about 30 meters, but they still had hundreds to go. "Looks like we have a ways to go," he said. "Pace yourself."

Troy slid down next to Brett and hammered the anchor around his line to the red rock. "Brett, any guess on how far to the bottom?"

"Hard to say. Maybe another 700 meters."

Rebecca finished hammering the anchor in and turned to them. "Let's hope your right, Brett. These lines are only 750 meters."

"Maybe we should have doubled back the lines as we came down," Troy questioned.

"Yeah, I thought of that," Brett said. "But that would take a lot longer and be dangerous in the night."

The three continued on down the cliff in the darkness of the night. The minutes seemed like hours as they blindly headed down.

"Well, gentlemen after I get this anchor in, I need a break," Rebecca said as she pulled out her hammer.

Troy checked the time. "We've been doing this for about ninety minutes."

"What? It feels like hours!" she said hammering at the anchor. In the darkness she had not seem the imperfection in the rock and that the anchor was not lined up. Rebecca threw her arm back and the hammer forward. As the hammer hit the anchor, it jarred to the right, and she lost grip on the hammer. Rebecca caught sight of her hammer as it slowly fell into the darkness below.

"Damn, I dropped my hammer!" she exclaimed.

"Okay. Don't panic. We can't be more than a few hundred meters from the bottom," Brett yelled to her. "I think I can pass you my hammer as we descend."

"Thanks, Brett, but we're too far apart and it's almost pitch dark. I can barely make you out. I'll be fine."

Troy checked the gauge on his line. "Looks like we have about 100 meters of line left." He hoped they wouldn't need anymore than that.

They continued down into the deep darkness. Troy became obsessed with checking how many meters were left, doing so every few minutes, 90, 80, 70 and falling.

Brett kept looking down trying to make something out. He wanted to grab his light, but it was too great of a risk.

As they descended, Rebecca found her line drifting back and forth. "Guys, I'm sorry I'm holding you up. It's hard going down perfectly straight!" she laughed in frustration.

"No hurry. The sun won't be up for hours."

"Yeah, we'll run out of line before then!" Troy, half joking, chimed in.

The next twenty minutes the three continued to descend into the darkness without a word. They knew the sunrise was not the problem, the lack of line was.

Troy continued to monitor the gauge, 50 meters, 30 meters, 20 meters, then nothing as he felt the pull on the line. The three of them dangled in the darkness.

"Anyone have any suggestions?" Troy said breaking the silence.

"We'll have to get a light out." Rebecca said.

"No, that will give us away," objected Brett. "If they find us, you know they'll kill us. There's only one thing to do."

"What would that be?"

With that, Brett let go of his line and dropped into the darkness.

*　*　*

Gary Ivory was in the main office at P - Base. He had just reviewed the status of the excavation. He pushed the report to the side. That really didn't matter any longer. Once they have the rights to this land he was filthy rich. Only one thing, one person could put that in jeopardy, and that was Brett Roberts.

"So what type of searching parties do we have out there? Any sign of Roberts?"

A man, hesitantly approached the table. "We have four check points set up on these roads." He pointed to the three-dimensional imagine that appeared in front of both of them. "We have a few vehicles scanning these two areas. He was last seen here, so he would probably come through one of them."

"What if he's already passed through that area? Maybe he's closer?"

"Sir, I don't think so. Like I said we have checkpoints set up and have the vehicle identification number posted everywhere. If he is anywhere within a few kilometers, we'll spot him."

Ivory glanced at the three dimensional image. "What if he went a bit farther North and circled back east? That would mean your men are in all the wrong places! I want a dozen vehicles to scan out in this pattern over here," he said, pointing to the area northeast of them. "I want them checking in on the hour. I also want a few vehicles to scan the immediate area. Do you understand?"

"Yes, sir."

Ivory headed back to his vehicle. He didn't drive out here to sit and wait. He flagged his driver. "Come on, we're going for a ride. Lets take a look at what's going on out there."

They headed out to the Northeast to take a look for any traffic coming in or going out from P - Base. He was getting frustrated. It was like looking for a needle in a haystack. There had to be something, some sighting. He already was late reporting into Afidan and wanted to resolve this problem before he reported to him. He called to the driver. "I want you to signal Roberts. If he responds and we're close enough, we may be able to get a location on him."

The driver turned to Ivory. "Yes, sir."

Ivory could hear the message going out and knew Roberts wasn't about to answer his message, but it was worth a try. How many more sols until this was out in the open? He wanted off this rust-infested planet. He wanted to eat without the gritty dust in his food. His patience was running thin. He turned on his COM link

"This is Ivory. I want to talk to Oshair on Phobos. When you get a hold of him, have him contact me immediately."

He signed out and gazed out the window at the horizon, looking for a needle.

*   *   *

Nick was getting concerned about not hearing from Brett. He realized with the magnitude of the last message he had sent Brett that he would need some time, but too much of it was passing by. With Ed's news from the meeting he had had with ISC, it was pertinent to get an idea on where they stood with Capricorn. Was it possible to get the work completed or was it unrealistic? Did they need to accept the ruling and move on? Nothing made sense.

Tom Afidan was mysteriously quiet. Nick was worried he's going to be going in for the kill, trying to persuade the board of Directors to give him control of Calprex. Instead he was out roaming around, sending out a few e-mails here and there. That was unlike him, but nobody was about to complain. With all that was going on, Afidan should be here helping them find solutions.

Nothing was adding up, nothing made sense. Why did the ICS make such an uncharacteristic ruling on a trivial matter and almost hand over the land rights, to that land north of Roman, to the Arab Republic. What was there? Apparently, something of importance. They had surveyed the land and found nothing out of the ordinary. The geology reports seemed in order.

He needed to get a hold of Brett. He decided too send another message, something short and to the point. Nick needed to get a status on where they stood completing Capricorn. As he recorded the message, he decided to send a copy to Conners as well and get an update on Capricorn and the clean up.

If he couldn't contact Roberts, Nick wondered who could he trust in Roman? Nick sat back in his chair, trying to figure out an answer. He remembered listening to his father when he was younger. Anthony Gambino had been a lobbyist in Washington. He would always tell Nick, "Keep your friends close and your enemies closer." That's it! He sat forward to send a message to Gary Ivory, Jon Conners and half of the administrators in Roman.

"Urgent Priority... Due to rulings handed down from the ISC I need you to take all non-contracted personnel and proceed approximately to coordinates listed below. I want a full-scale search of the area including geological and biological testing. I also need an update on Capricorn and the probabilities of completion over the next few sols/days.

This is to take priority over any other responsibilities as per Ed Brocton. I want an update four times a sol.
Nick Gambino"

Nick sat back as he hit send, copying Ed and Afidan on the message. He wondered how long before a few people started to panic.

* * *

Brett recaptured his composure as he let go of the line and fell to the bottom floor of the canyon, a fall of approximately ten centimeters! He was surprised, having expected to fall for tens of meters, not centimeters!

'Troy, Rebecca, the drop is only a few centimeters. We've made it."

Troy and Rebecca jumped to the bottom and joined Brett, who turned to Rebecca. "Well I think it was your idea to steal a vehicle. Have any preferences? Any special color?"

She smiled but knew between the darkness and the shielded visor no one could see her expression. "I just want something fast!"

The three started to walk toward the Pyramids. As the sun began to rise, the outline of the pyramid came into sight. They were of incredible size, at least three times the size of the largest Pyramids on earth. They could hear and see the activity on the far side as they tried to stay in the shadows along the back side.

"Troy, you heard the lady. We need to find something fast. Let's walk around the back and see if we can get a view of what's over there."

"Yeah, one of those Buggy IV models would be ideal. Quick as they come around here!"

"Well, Troy, work your magic."

"Let's move around the back and get up on the ledge there and survey the area."

The three continued to move along the perimeter of the floor as sunlight began to fill the quarry. Brett stopped a few times to look up at the Pyramids. The size was incredible and that such a structure was on Mars was incomprehensible. How old were they? Who built them? What did it all mean? Brett turned and realized he was falling behind. The questions were unfathomable at this point. His problem was to let Earth know about this. Then they could look for the answers.

Troy looked up as they walked. "Well it's pretty obvious why they didn't want me in the North to work on station 185. Wonder who knows about this?"

"The Arab Republic knows. They're trying to get this land although I can't see how they'll get it. There has to be some people on Phobos in on this."

"Of course, Ivory, his men, and all these workers." Rebecca said.

"Yeah, a lot of people and no one's talked!" Troy remarked.

"No ones lived long enough to talk!"

As they continued to walk, Rebecca noticed that someone had seen them.

"Guys, don't look but there are a few workers by the edge, and they've been watching us the last few minutes."

Brett turned and confirmed what Rebecca said. A group of about six started heading their way.

"Troy, let's pick up the pace a bit, but nothing drastic, nothing that might draw more attention. We need to find somewhere to hide, somewhere soon."

Troy walked briskly as he looked for some type of opening. "I wish I paid more attention in class when they discussed Egyptian history. I think there were a few entrances to these things."

"Anywhere would be good, in or out of there," Rebecca reiterated as they turned into a shadow around the corner.

Brett looked back as the group of men began to pick up the pace, as if to catch up to them. "Keep moving. Don't look back. Turn around the next corner." he calmly said to Troy and Rebecca.

"Up there. It looks like an opening," Troy pointed up at the first pyramid.

"Quick. Let's get up there. Maybe we can lose them if they think we've just pulled ahead of them and are making our way around that far bend."

The three quickly climbed up the pyramid and disappeared into the dark opening.

* * *

Gary Ivory told the driver to take him back to camp. He was irritated and frustrated. He wanted this to all end. He knew that it was a matter of sols before it would be too late for anyone to do anything. Once things were stabilized he could take the next transport back to Earth, collect his fortune and close out mankind. He leaned back and thought about growing old on some small, lush green island, surrounded by deep blue water. If he never saw any red deserts or large mountains the rest of his life, he would be happy.

He was procrastinating sending a report to Afidan. To get this close and then lose track of Roberts, letting him possibly stumble upon this, would be the end of everything he worked for. Not only had Afidan wanted an update, but also at this stage Ivory was curious on the amount of time till the Arab Republic obtained rights to the land. Was it sols, weeks? Maybe it was already over? Well, he had put this off long enough.

He might as well send an update to Afidan. At this point no one really knew if Roberts was anywhere around. He decided to be as vague as possible when he mentioned him. He turned his chair to the computer, typed in his password.

"You have two messages." came the computer.

"Play."

Ivory sat there as he digested the message from Nick Gambino. He slammed his fist down on the armrest of his chair. He didn't need countless people from Roman up here to check out what might be going on! He looked at the coordinates and saw that they were a bit off, but close enough. Close enough to be seen. He felt the sweat rolling down his back. How was he going to stop this?

He walked to the cupboard and opening the doors, threw the contents down on the floor. "God damn it, I'll kill them all!" he screamed. He walked over to the computer, almost forgetting about the second message.

"Second message"

It was from Afidan.

"Ivory,
You've seen Gambino's message. We only need two and a half sols.
Gather together those people headed into the North region and head them
there yourself, slowly. If you take the high mountain stretch and take
your time, by the time they arrive it will be too late. Reply to this when
you are on your way."

"Damn it." he mumbled flipping the reply button and cursing to himself. He knew Afidan would not like his response.

"I'm not in Roman. I'm at P - Base looking for Roberts. We've lost track of Roberts, and I wanted to make sure he didn't stumble across anything. At this point we don't believe he is anywhere near the P - Base and as for any new visitors, they will not be allowed anywhere near the site. All measures will be taken to divert them.
Ivory"

16

The three rushed into the dark opening. They turned their lights on and proceeded farther inside. Troy led the way, looking for a passage that might give them a quick escape if needed. Rebecca followed closely behind him as Brett took up the rear.

Brett took one last look back to see if the men following had seen them. It looked like the pursues hadn't made it around the bend yet, so they at least had some time. As Brett turned back to the others, he was mesmerized by what he saw.

If he didn't know any better, he would have sworn he was in Egypt inside one of the Great Pyramids. The room had statues of what looked like half- man, half-animal creatures. There was a drawing of a mummy, and the wall was covered with hieroglyphics. He reached up to touch one of the symbols.

"Brett, lets get going. It won't take them long to look in here," Troy said over the COM link.

Brett stood back from the wall, wishing he had known a bit more about ancient history. He was wondering what the writings said. "Yeah, I'm on my way," he replied, then hustling after the other two.

Troy led the three down a narrow passageway. It was so small it was difficult for to light up much of the way. Rebecca stopped for a minute to scrape a sample of rock off the wall.

"Hey, I'd kill myself when we get back if I didn't take a few samples!" she said.

"Well, let's keep moving, I don't want that "when" to become an "if"," Troy replied.

The three continued through the narrow passage for another fifteen minutes, Rebecca examining the rocks as they made their way through, finally said "Troy any idea how far this goes on?"

Just as she finished her sentence, Troy found the answer. "Looks like we're at the end."

"Now what I remember from school is that there always seemed to be a hidden exit." Rebecca remarked, continuing to take samples.

"You're assuming these are similar to Pyramids on Earth!"

Rebecca turned back to Troy a little dumbfounded. "Gee, I guess I am."

As the two continued to talk, Brett headed back to see if they may have missed a turnoff. He ran his hands along the walls, not knowing what he was looking for.

Troy and Rebecca were now trying the same thing at the end of the passage.

"Maybe its no big deal, Troy" said Rebecca. "We can hang in here awhile then go back out."

"We may have no other choice."

Troy turned on his COM link. "Brett, you back there?"

"Yeah, just checking for a turnoff. Maybe we missed something."

"Where are you now?"

"I'm about five minutes back. I'm in that small room we passed through. It seems like a logical place to have another exit."

"We'll be there in a few minutes."

Rebecca took a look at her oxygen gauge. "How much oxygen, Troy, do you have left?"

Troy glanced down. "Wow, not much left in the first tank. Maybe a fifth of it's left."

"Yeah, that kills that idea."

"What idea?"

"Waiting them out, then leaving at night and heading back to the MultiVec. It would be too close on running out of oxygen. We should have brought three more additional canisters."

"Hey, we had a long climb down here. We didn't need to be carrying tons of canisters. Anyway the plan is to find another vehicle and get out of here."

The two started making out the light coming from Brett's helmet.

"Well, I'm assuming nothing?"

"No, but there has to be something here. Just a matter of finding it."

"Rebecca, help out Brett. I'll go a little farther back toward the entrance and look there."

Troy proceeded back to the original passage to the entrance. He felt the walls as he slowly made his way back through the darkness. He found himself stopping and glancing at the writing and pictures on the walls. Did it mean what he thought? Had mankind come from Mars? It couldn't be. According to samples taken from Mars, any life on the red planet had disappeared hundreds of millions of years before the most primitive man began walking the plains of Earth.

The light from Troy's helmet made a narrow band of light, as he made his way back to the main chamber. He glanced at his oxygen tank. Only a little bit left. He'd have to change to a new tank soon.

He stopped for a minute on coming to an unusual archway. He hadn't remembered passing it on the way in. Had he made a wrong turn or had his eyes been focused elsewhere when he passed this way before?

He scanned the arch with his light to look for anything out of the ordinary. As his eyes made their way down the left pillar, he thought he saw a flicker of light towards the main chamber.

Did he get turned around? Was Brett or Rebecca walking back to him?

"Brett, is that you?"

No answer.

He started to proceed slowly toward the light. As the flickering became more constant, he turned his light off and kept on going. Standing close to the wall as and peered around to where the light was coming from, and he could make out that he was approaching a bend. There in the main chamber were three men searching the room. It looked like the men that were following them earlier, but in their suits it was hard to tell.

Troy turned into the darkness and moved as quickly as he could without turning his light on. He held his hands out in front of him and to the side waving them. He recalled that the floor was pretty level, no stairs or boulders. He needed to get back to the small room he had been in minutes earlier. There he would turn on his light.

The darkness was haunting, no shadows, no way of knowing how far he had gone. After what appeared to seem like a good twenty minutes, he began to wonder if he was headed in the right direction. He turned back and still saw a flickering light now and then. He couldn't take the chance of turning his light on.

"Brett! Rebecca! Do you read me?" There was nothing but silence.

"Brett, Rebecca are you out there?"

"Brett here, Troy. Any luck over there? We've covered every centimeter and nothing. Not sure…"

"Listen, someone's in the main chamber. Looks like at least three. They didn't see me. I'm headed back, but it's slow going since I have my light off."

"Any idea where you are?"

"I thought I'd be in the second room by now. Hope I'm not lost."

"Okay, listen we'll head towards you. Use the COM links minimally. We don't want anyone intercepting our conversation."

"Right."

Brett and Rebecca began to head toward Troy with Troy slowly walking toward them in the total darkness. At least, he thought he was headed toward them. He knew in the total blackness of the corridor he may have become disorientated. He held his hands against the walls. He must have put some distance between the men and himself. He turned around to look for any flickering light.

His boot hit something solid, and he fell against the wall. He heard a small rumbling. He quickly realized his suit was fine, no puncture. He glanced around for any lights. Nothing. He turned on his light and saw a door had opened up, and went into a different corridor.

Troy felt a bit out of breath and checked his tank. Almost empty but fine. He knew it was the adrenalin getting to him. He looked up and saw lights coming towards him. He tried to get to his feet quickly but the lights seemed to be approaching fast. He looked around as he was getting to feet, and picked up a small rock. Better than nothing, he thought. He stood up and cocked the rock behind him.

"Troy, what are you doing?" said Rebecca confused.

"Sorry. Not sure who you were. I fell against the wall and this door opened!"

The three examined the opening as they went through it.

"No idea where it goes but I'd say we have no choice," said Brett, taking the lead. As the three proceeded away from the door, it rumbled and shut itself again.

"Must be activated by motion or something," Rebecca questioned.

"Yeah, it's not what one would expect, although so far nothing here is!"

The door sealed behind them.

* * *

Terry McGregor read the e-mail twice. Nick Gambino. McGregor had heard that name before and knew he was high up in Calprex. He knew he could get Capricorn completed if he had the manpower and the time. He checked his handheld PC. It seemed that if they worked around the clock, they could get it done in three more sols.

He wondered how to send his information to Nick Gambino? What was the time frame they were looking at? The message was already almost a sol old. Well, he was a Relin employee who was told not to work on Capricorn. He definitely couldn't send a message to Nick Gambino without jeopardizing his employment. He sat back for a few minutes until the answer hit him. Give Jon Conners the information to pass on.

He tapped his COM link, "Jon, it's Terry McGregor."

"Go ahead, I hear you."

"I want to send a message to Gambino, informing him on the status of completion of Capricorn. Considering the circumstances, I was wondering if you could send him the information?"

Conners chuckled. "Gambino has more important things to concern him than Capricorn. He wants all available Calprex people to head for the North region."

"What? I don't understand?" McGregor sat back in his chair in disbelief.

"Looks like there is some type of struggle for the land rights to the North, and he wants all available people to search the area."

"I don't believe it. It doesn't make sense."

"Well, I tell you it's happening. The people are gathering as we speak. He sent it to all of Roman's administration. Look, I have no idea where Ivory is, so I have to find someone to take them out. Don't worry about Capricorn."

There followed utter silence, McGregor feeling emptiness overtaking him. He was finally making a difference. Brett Roberts had faith in him, and he didn't want to let him down. He rose up from his chair and slowly made his way out of the office. He saw people running busily to the transport station.

A young man walked up to McGregor. "Do you know how do drive one of the transports? We're in the need of drivers."

"No. No, I don't," McGregor replied hesitantly still a bit dazed from the news. "But I might be able to find some."

"Well, here." The man beamed the orders from his handheld PC to McGregor's. "We're ordered to get as many people as possible to these coordinates. Get some drivers."

"Yeah sure. No problem." He turned to return to his office with a small spring in his step.

He glanced at the message that was beamed from the young man. It was the message from Gambino. He had to read it a few times unable to understand why Conners said to forget about Capricorn. He wanted the work continued, not stopped.

He tapped his COM link once again, "Conners, it's Terry McGregor. Look I was just reviewing Gambino's message. It looks like he still wants…"

"God bless it McGregor. Don't you get it? I'm busy. If you want to work on Capricorn, go ahead. You'll never get it done in time."

"Can you send him a message letting him know…"?

"Hey, you do it. You or your make-believe supervisor!" Conners clicked off his COM link.

McGregor sat back, re-examining the plans of Capricorn. How do I get that message to Gambino? There is no file for a Jane Bender. If he sent it on his own COM link, it would go first to Relic, then on to Gambino, that's if they forwarded it on. McGregor sat down at the terminal to put more assignments out from Bender. He clicked the message board. To his disbelief, he could send outgoing messages back to Earth. He was going to be able to let Nick Gambino know exactly where they were in regards to Capricorn.

* * *

Tom Afidan just got off the line with Senator Nate Still's office, having left an urgent message. Afidan leaned back in his chair with a smile, thinking about his dealing with Senator Stills. Most said he was untouchable, but Afidan had gone around the back way. Afidan had orchestrated Senator Still some day coming to him for help. In the end he would owe Afidan.

Almost two years ago, Afidan had hired a few men of questionable reputation to do a job for him. These men were to kidnap Senator Still's grandson. They were to take him somewhere safe and not harm him. Then they were to contact Stills asking for one billion credits. If authorities were contacted, the child would be mutilated.

Stills had been extremely successful in business as well as politics. He loved only one thing more than the two, and that was his grandson. Afidan had done his homework. The boy had two bodyguards at all times. The key was to find a moment when they weren't expecting an attempted abduction or no one was watching him. Afidan obtained information that revealed when Stills spent time with his Grandson he would take him somewhere and have the bodyguards back off and secure the grounds. For the most part, the locations of these places were not well known, not known to many with the exception of a few, Afidan among them.

Afidan's men would be waiting. It was a sunny Saturday morning when Senator Stills was walking in the park with his grandson. They stopped and sat down on a bench for a few minutes. The young boy pulled out a ball and made motions to his grandfather to play catch. Stills stood up and took a few paces back, his grandson did likewise. They threw the ball back and fourth a few times until the boy missed a throw and ball rolled near the far bushes. The boy quickly ran to retrieve the ball when two of Afidan's men appeared and grabbed the boy. Senator Stills stood in bewilderment, yelling for help. By the time the Senators bodyguards arrived, it was too late. His grandson was gone.

For the next few days a manhunt was taking place across the globe. There were no clues, and what bothered Stills was that there was no contact. Finally after a week, a message was delivered asking for 100 billion credits or the boy would be killed. With all the power, wealth and friends Stills possessed, he could never come up with 100 billion credits. He turned to friends and even his enemies for help. He offered 500 million credits, his entire fortune to whomever could return his grandson safely.

Afidan waited a few days for the news to travel and watched and observed as some of the most powerful men in the world tried to find out where the boy was. Another week went by and the search was going nowhere. Afidan had it leak out that if Stills wanted the boy, Afidan had contacts.

Within a few days Senator Stills did a background check on Afidan and called him asking for his help.

After the brief phone call with the Senator, Afidan picked up the phone.

"Ivan, I need a package picked up on Friday. Make sure the handlers are handsomely paid."

By the end of the week "Ivan" made his way into an abandoned building on the outskirts of Prague.

A large, stout man was standing guard at the door. "Ivan, do you have the money? Did they pay the ransom?"

Ivan proceeded through the door carrying a suitcase. "We didn't get exactly what we wanted, but I think it will work."

The man followed him inside as two other men met them in the parlor. "Is the boy fine? Any problems?"

"No, none," said one of them. "Do you have the money?"

"Where is he? They insisted on his safety." Ivan chuckled.

"Frigen A. Show Ivan. He's a bit hungry, but not harmed," said the tall thin man as he pointed to the door.

Ivan opened the door a crack and saw the young boy watching television.

He closed the door and walked back to the three men. He picked up the suitcase and placed in on the table.

"Well, it's not exactly 100 Billion but..." he pulled out two small automatic pistols and shot the three men dead. He turned to the door and approached the boy.

"Don't be scared. I'm here to take you to your Grandfather."

Tom Afidan had called Senator Stills and told him he had found his grandson and that the senator should meet him in Prague. By the end of the day, Still's limousine was pulling up to one of the finer hotels in the city. He raced up the red-carpeted stairs.

"Senator Stills, Mr. Afidan has been expecting you. Follow me."

The two of them, along with Senator Still's bodyguards, proceeded to the elevator.

"Is he injured? How does he look?"

"I believe he is in perfect health and unharmed."

The elevator chimed as it came to a quick stop and the doors opened to reveal a large room with plush lavender carpeting. A small fountain was in the middle of the room. Stills scanned the room quickly and found his grandson.

"Grandpa!" the boy screamed as he ran over to hug him.

Nate Stills held the boy and wept. After a few minutes, he stood up and went to Tom Afidan.

"I can't tell you how appreciative I am." He fidgeted nervously. "About the reward, I will need time to liquidate my assets. It may take a month for the full amount. Do I send the money to you or Calprex? Who?

"Senator Stills, although I do work for Calprex, I have friends and business acquaintances in many places. The people who tracked down your son and killed the kidnappers do not want the reward."

Puzzled Nate Stills starred at Afidan. "I don't have anything else of value."

"Let's just say you owe us a favor or two."

"Now look! I would do anything to get my Grandson back, but this sounds like blackmail."

"Call it what you will. The favors will have nothing to do with breaking any law or have any effect on anyone's health. Let's just say there may be a few small votes or rulings we would like to see."

"If you're talking about the ISC, I can't compromise my position. Surely Calprex understands this!"

"Senator, of course, this is all confidential, but I couldn't give a rats' ass about the future of Calprex. The people I work with have more important things to think about."

"You must know there are five Observers. My vote may mean nothing!"

"Then you have nothing to worry about, Senator Stills. If our favor is so outlandish, your colleagues will surely vote against you. So please relax."

The Senator took the young boy by the hand and quickly exited the room. Over the course of a year, Afidan had never made contact with the Senator. The last few months, however, Afidan had communicated with him quite often.

Afidan sat back in his chair as his secretary buzzed, "Sir, Senator Stills is on the line."

Afidan leaned forward. "Senator, thank you for calling back so quickly. I need a small favor."

There was a long silence. "Tom, your last favor had me voting for something I didn't believe in. Turning my back on my friends, who just happen to be your employer, doesn't make sense."

"Senator, how is your grandson. What grade is he in now?"

"Look, I appreciate you getting my grandson back, but you told me you would never ask me to do anything illegal or unethical."

"I don't believe I ever said that. I'm just asking a few small favors, which I don't think is illegal. I need you to call an urgent meeting with the ISC."

"What for?"

"I want you to ask Calprex if they will have the work completed on time, and if they can't, to hand over the territory immediately."

"What? The deadline is less than seventy-two hours away. By the time I get the ISC together for a meeting we're talking 48 hours."

"Senator, every hour is important to the Arab Republic."

"This is very irregular. What will they say?"

"Frankly, I don't care. All things considered, it's the least you owe me. Please let me know what time the council will be meeting tomorrow."

Afidan disconnected.

17

The three walked for what seemed like hours in the dark corridors of the pyramid, Rebecca taking as many digitals as she could.

"This is just amazing. I wish we could stop to examine some of this," she said.

"I understand," Troy said, quickly running the light in front of him. "But we have to keep moving. If Earth becomes aware of this, there'll be time for all of us to examine the artifacts. Hell, Brett may be in charge and we'll get first dibs.

"I'm not sure I'll be in charge," said Brett. "But if we can find a way to get to Station 185, you're right, Troy, we'll be able to examine everything."

They worked their way for a few more meters and noticed a light approaching. As they drew closer, they came to an opening overlooking a large chamber. The chamber was hundreds of meters high and enormously wide as well. The three looked down on the activity below.

"Do you see that?" Troy said, bewildered. "They aren't wearing any suits, no gear!"

"Yeah, the door back there must be some type of seal."

Hundreds of meters below them were hundreds of men and women busy at work. Small vehicles scooted from one side to the other.

Rebecca picked up her binoculars and glanced across the room. "Over five hundred meters across!"

Brett reached for his faceplate and lifted it up. He took a long deep breath as the other two looked at him.

"Brett, you should have taken a reading before taking your helmet off," responded Rebecca.

"Maybe, but if they're not wearing helmets down there, then I'm not either."

Nodding, Troy and Rebecca removed their helmets.

Troy scanned the floor of the pyramid. "Looks like a few small vehicles over to the right. If we can make our way down there, maybe we can drive one right out of the door and all the way to Station 185."

"If it was only so easy. What do you think Brett?"

"I think we should make our way down to the rovers. What we need to keep an eye on is where they are headed. Are there any checkpoints or possible roadblocks? If we do take off in one of those and were caught before we leave, it's all for nothing."

"What if you're right and we get out of this big chamber and when we're about to leave the pyramid, they stop us and ask about the cargo or papers. I'm not even sure what's going on here," said Troy, the three beginning to slowly make their way down.

"What if we stowed away until we got out, then take it over?" Rebecca suggested.

Brett smirked. "Well, I like the stowing away part, but trying to take over a vehicle by force, that could be difficult. Troy, what are your thoughts?"

"I agree. Sounds good getting in one of those, but how do we know which one will be leaving?"

"Any other ideas. Can you two think of anything?" Brett asked. "I hate to say this, but let's play it by ear, get out of here and see what happens. If we can get aboard one of those, we will. If not, there has to be some other way out of here."

"I agree, Brett, there isn't much of a choice. Look at your oxygen levels. Once we were to go outside, at best we have an hour left. We need to find some type of vehicle."

"Yeah, we really only have one choice."

The three proceeded down a winding path, keeping an eye on the activity below.

"You think anyone has seen us?" Rebecca said, worried.

"No, I've been looking around. They're all pretty busy. You see anything, Troy?"

"The vehicles seem to be exiting around that far corner by that large statue, accelerating them up that road. And what happens after that, is anyone's guess. I've also noticed that no one seems to checking any vehicles. So we might be able to just take one."

A few workers passed them with small bags filled with artifacts.

"Looks like everyone is concerned about themselves and their work. Lets keep moving."

Brett looked up at the top of the pyramid. It appeared even more massive from the bottom. He couldn't help but wonder who had constructed this and what relationship it might have with Earth.

An older man walked up to the three. "Hey, you guys. You busy? I need some help here. I need to get these crates to the transport outside. Can you help me load them?"

"Sure. We were almost done in here anyway. Can you give us a ride out when you're done?" Troy asked.

"Sure thing."

Troy picked up a small crate and carried it to the back of the hatch "We're kind of new here. Never expected this when we came to Mars!"

"How long have you been here?" the man asked.

"A few months." Rebecca looked at Troy cautiously.

"You move around good. Looks like you've mastered the Mars gravity."

Rebecca didn't want to get into anything lengthy. "We've all trained on Earth in simulators."

"That makes sense. I'm actually surprised they haven't sent more people here. What are they saying on Earth?

Brett placed another crate inside the back. "What does Earth say about Mars?"

"Mars, yeah. But what are they saying about the Pyramid?"

Troy looked at the man confused. "Honestly they don't…"

Brett stepped in front of Troy. "They don't know why we aren't sending more people!" He glanced at Troy giving him a quick wink. The two lifted a large crate into the cargo area of the vehicle.

"It must be madness back home. I always thought there was life here. I mean, life here at one time. Sure makes you want to rethink a lot of things."

"It sure does." Troy glanced at Rebecca.

Rebecca handed an electronic checklist. "Looks like it's all loaded. We really appreciate the lift."

"No problem. You missed your transport?"

"Yeah, how did you know? I hope we won't get into any trouble."

"Don't worry about it. It's not like anyone's going to pull us over."

The three looked at each other and smiled. The doors closed then and the transport rolled up the road and into a dark roadway.

"Ever get lost in here?" Rebecca asked.

"Actually, I did once, but I remembered what a few guys told me when I first started. Always head west and upward, and you'll end up finding a way out."

"Really? What's the reason for that?"

"No idea, but a few people were lost and found months later. This is one monster of a pyramid."

The transport finally made it's way out of the pyramid.

"It's always beautiful at this time, " said the driver, the sky a brilliant pink. "The sky's so bright this time of day. Well I have to take these to cargo bay fifteen. Where can I drop you guys off?"

Brett turned to Troy. "To be honest," Troy said, "we're a bit worried about being seen. We're kind of late and like to pop in unnoticed."

"Hey, I understand. I'll take you to the rear entrance of the infirmary. Then make your way from there." He turned to the three. "How does that sound?"

"Perfect!" Brett exclaimed. The three looked at the small city that had formed on the north side of the excavation.

The old man slowed down. "Never can get used to this sight. You have those two Pyramids, a ridge of Mountains to the Northwest, and the canyon that runs northeast."

Rebecca smiled at the old man. "Yes, it's quite majestic."

"Yeah, something else, isn't it? Look, I'll circle to the back. No one should notice you."

"Perfect!"

* * *

Ivory had been very busy gathering men, transports and a few laser cannons to meet any company that would be coming from Roman. He kept checking the messages. He had received a message from a scout that said three unidentified people were walking around the east side of the pyramid. The message was hours old and god knows what that was about. It could have been as harmless as being only a few workers taking a look around or possibly a few more men stealing some artifacts for themselves. If it was the latter, that could be dealt with later. But where was Roberts? Surely not inside the Pyramid. Well, sooner or later he would show up.

He had sent a message earlier to Jon Conners wanting to make sure they took the identical route that Brett Roberts had taken to the North Region. He wanted them to go through Baron's Pass.

What else bothered him was that there was no return message from Afidan, who sure couldn't be happy about not being in Roman himself to lead this caravan toward the North region. Ivory could see that the last of the transports he had requested had just met up with him. He tapped his COM link.

"We've worked very hard the last few months. We have one final job to do to insure that all your dedication and hard work is handsomely compensated. I've downloaded a file to all your vehicles. It gives you specifics coordinates and responsibilities. I don't want any man or vehicles, to get past you. Use every tool available to stop them. Is that understood?"

A chorus of acknowledgments came back in return. "Yes, Sir."

"If things move quickly back on Earth, we may not have to do a thing. It may be too late for anyone to stop us." Too late for Roberts anyway, Ivory thought. "We'll be headed for Baron's Pass and should be there by early tomorrow. Review the information and make no mistakes!"

Ivory had sent them detailed information on where the people from Roman were located, and had picked Baron's Pass to cut them off. It was a small canyon, and he could pin them down there indefinitely. On each side of the canyon he was placing three transports with laser cannons.

The convoy of Transports, MultiVecs, and Mars rovers raced south to Baron's Pass. The red dust filled the pink sky as Ivory looked out the windshield. He was getting tired of Mars and all of its problems. He was tired of all of the dust everywhere he went. The dust in his cut chaffed his legs. His eyes were always irritated, and he could feel the fine grains of sand in everything he ate. Once this land was secure, and in the hands of the Arab Republic, he hoped his sols on Mars would be numbered.

The COM link came on, "Sir, we've had a report of three unknown people wandering on the far side of the large Pyramid."

"Find out who it is immediately. I want to know who it is."

"Yes, sir. We've had people searching the far side as well and the interior of the pyramid. It may just be a few workers trying to loot a few artifacts."

"Whoever it is I want them found!"

Ivory leaned back and smashed the dash as he turned to the driver.

"We're turning around. Tell the rest to continue to their designated sites. They have their orders and should contact me when a sighting is made."

"Yes, sir."

Ivory looked out at the swirling dust as the vehicle turned to return to P - Base.

"Damn Roberts. I've had enough of him."

18

The three went through the airlock of the back entrance of the infirmary. They took off their helmets, but remained in their suits. They received a few stares from the people passing through, but for the most part it seemed everyone was preoccupied with what they were doing.

"Brett, I think we need to find something to eat. We haven't eaten all day." Troy said to the two others.

"Probably a good idea if we come across anything, but top priority is finding a vehicle to take us out of here."

"I know. Can't go without food and water though."

"Brett, he's right," said Rebecca, being just as hungry. "We might be out there for days. We probably should have packed more food, water, and supplies."

"Easier said then done. That was some cliff we came down. I can't imagine us carrying much more," Brett pointed out.

"Yeah, you're probably right," Troy said, scanning the hallway.

Rebecca slid into a supply closet and came out with a few bags of water. "Well, this is a start!" she said transparently with a grin.

"Don't go waving those around," Troy cautioned.

Brett came up on the far end of the hallway. "Garage." The sign read.

"Here we go." The three put their helmets back on and walked into the garage.

Troy quickly glanced around to see if anyone was paying attention to the three of them. "So far so good,"

Brett gestured to an EX – Rover. "Those are fast, or so I hear?"

"Yes, they are. Don't have a lot of room, but probably the fastest thing in here," Rebecca replied also scanning the room.

Brett opened the hatch, and the three entered the vehicle. They pressurized the EX - Rover and took off their helmets.

"Nice little sporty thing isn't it?" Brett said as he examined the control panels.

"That was too easy," Troy declared. "They're not going to let us just drive this out of this garage."

"Well, let's see," said Brett with a grin, turning to Rebecca.

"Troy's right. We've come too far to get caught here," exclaimed Rebecca.

"So far there hasn't been any check point or people questioning anything. I think these people here all have too much to do or frankly don't give a crap!" Brett interjected.

"But if you're wrong? They're not going to let people just drive anything out of here?" Troy questioned

"Okay. You two get out of the vehicle!"

"What!" Rebecca exclaimed in astonishment.

"You two go back to the infirmary entrance that we entered by. I'll pick you up in about ten minutes."

"And if they stop you?" she asked.

"Then you two continue without me. You have the disks right?"

"Yeah, right here in my pocket." Troy patted his chest.

"All right, now get out and meet you in ten."

The three put on their helmets as Brett released the hatch, and Troy and Rebecca jumped out. Troy gave him the thumbs-up as Brett slowly accelerated the EX - Rover. Troy and Rebecca returned to the entrance, looking back for a moment to see if Brett had run into any problems. Everything looked fine as they saw the garage door open and the rover rolled out.

"Is he always right?" Troy quipped.

"Yes. Don't you hate that?"

Troy and Rebecca returned inside and quietly made their way back to the entrance in which they came a few minutes earlier. They both placed their helmets on, snapped the gloves and went out. There waiting for them was the Rover.

"What took you two so long?" Brett chuckled.

The hatch closed behind them and they headed along the rim of the excavation. Troy plugged in a few things into his PC. "It looks like there is a direct route. Let's see turn right at the next turn, an entrance down to Aries canyon should be there."

Brett made the turn, and sure enough they saw an opening in the mountains. Waiting at the entrance was a line of numerous vehicles.

"Looks like they're on to us." Rebecca sighed.

"I don't know. What do you think, Brett? I think they're looking for us but don't know we're here," said Troy.

Brett slowed down and zoomed in with one of the sensors. "They're searching in both directions. They don't know where we are. Troy, is there another route?"

Troy plugged in a few coordinates, "Damn. There's another route, but it will take us out almost a day."

"Looks like there isn't any other choice. Plug in the route, and lets take a look."

Within minutes Brett was circling around the west to another entrance out of the small city. "Guys, I hate to tell you this, " he finally said. "But I think we're back where we started."

"What are you talking about?"

"The MultiVec is somewhere over this ridge."

"Damn, you're right. We are close. A kilometer or so from here."

"No, can't be." Troy plugged in a few numbers.

Brett continued to drive toward the other exit. "It doesn't matter. We needed this rover."

"Yeah, your right."

The rover clipped along for another ten minutes before coming to another roadblock.

Troy zoomed in a sensor to get a better look. "Okay any ideas now? We've run out of exits. Anyone have a plan?"

Brett sat back and put the engine into neutral. "How far are we from that MultiVec?"

"A few kilometers. Why?"

"Brett, what are you thinking? Just go back to Roman?" Rebecca asked.

"No, I have another idea. Do you think the MultiVec could make it over the ridge?"

"Well, it's pretty steep going up, but if you can shift the power to the front wheels, it's probably possible. What's your plan?"

"If we can get the MultiVec over the ridge, you two take the rover and wait by the first entrance. I'll distract them with the MultiVec. They're looking for us in the MultiVec!"

"No, Brett, you can't do that," Rebecca objected. "It's too dangerous. When they catch you, they'll..."

"Look, if they all start after me, you can slip out down the passage. I can buy you enough time and then I'll stop and let them catch me."

"Troy, tell him he can't."

Troy looked at Brett, then back to Rebecca. "Actually, it sounds like a good plan. If they don't see us they'll be chasing him."

"What if they hurt him?"

Brett reached out and held her hand. "They're not going to do anything to me."

"What about us. They'll want to know where we are?"

"I'll tell them you're back with Ali." He smiled as she gave him a hug.

"You'd better be careful, you fool," she replied.

"Troy, make your way as close to the MultiVec as possible. Does this thing have a winch to help us get the MultiVec over the ridge?"

"If it doesn't the MultiVec has a portable one that we can attach to the rover." Troy glanced at the map on the monitor. "We should be there in less than an hour."

"That will be fine. Should give us some daylight to get everything set up and we can pull it over the ridge during the night."

"Boys, boys, I hope you know what your doing," Rebecca remarked, shaking her head.

An hour later the rover was on the top of the ridge above the MultiVec. It was what Brett had been hoping for as the sun began to set. Brett and Troy were getting into their suits as Rebecca scanned the area to make sure they were alone.

Troy checked the seals on Brett's suit. "We should be fine even though this rover doesn't have a winch. When we get down to the MultiVec, we can detach the winch and bring it up here. A little more work, but shouldn't be a problem."

"Thank God for the low gravitation. Otherwise we'd need a winch to bring up the winch!" Brett replied.

Troy laughed. "It's actually not that big. It's just an extra hike back up the ridge." Within minutes the two were making their way down the ridge.

"I don't care how strong the winch is, Troy. This is going to be tough bringing the MultiVec up here. Not only is it steep here, it's extremely rocky."

"Yeah, I see that. Maybe you should head to the right and I'll go left. Let's see if it looks better somewhere else."

"Sounds like a good idea. Go out for about ten minutes and then meet back here. The suns going down, and we won't have much time."

Troy went left and surveyed the landscape. It didn't look much better. Small scattered boulders would make it almost impossible to get up the ridge. He continued looking for a gap where they could bring up the MultiVec. After ten minutes, he turned back, hoping that Brett would have had better luck than he had.

Brett had headed to the right and had found similar landscape Troy had. The boulders were scattered, almost in uniform perfection, as if they had been placed there. He glanced at the time. A few minutes and he would have to head back.

The shadows were getting larger as the sun sank seemingly rapidly to the horizon, the rocks and boulders cast long shadows along the red clay. At first Brett thought he was seeing things. He looked down at his feet, took a few more steps, and looked up again. The shadows thrown by the rocks laid out a path up to the top of the ridge.

He glanced at the time on the monitor on his wrist. By the time he got back to Troy and got everything set up it would be totally dark. He needed to copy or mark the path. He thought of what he had in his backpack, but not enough of anything. He took off his backpack, hoping there was something in there, but when he opened it, there was nothing.

He looked down at the items in the pack and pulled out a metal bar. He raced to the first boulder and scraped the metal rod against the boulder. The boulder was soft, and he was able to carve an arrow on it. From there he raced to the next boulder and carved another arrow. One by one he scurried from boulder to boulder before the sun set.

Troy was starting to worry. He knew using the COM link at this range could be picked up. One thing he had learned about Brett was that Brett was reliable. Troy watched the sun set as the sky took on a dark blue. It was becoming very dark and without lights it was going to be difficult to get the MultiVec up over the ridge let alone look for someone!

He glanced at the time. Brett should have been back 15 minutes ago. He turned on the headlight on his helmet and headed toward the area Brett went into. He angled the light sharply toward the ground so, as not be seen by anyone passing by.

It was getting darker every minute, and he was getting concerned that Brett might be injured and he wouldn't find him. He turned on the COM link at a low frequency. "Brett. Brett you there?" There was nothing but static. He continued to walk on.

"Brett can you hear me?"

"Troy. Its Rebecca, is there a problem?" came a voice.

"Brett and I got separated. We had the COM links on low frequency and apparently he can't hear me. He can't hear us!"

"Will you two be quiet!" snapped Brett. "Troy, I see your light, I'll be there in a minute. Low frequency only!"

Troy looked at the horizon as he saw Brett approaching him.

"I found a road up the cliff," said Brett.

"A road?"

"Well, more like a path. The shadows from the setting sun laid out a route up the cliff. We'll still need the winch, but it will work. We'll have to rearrange the winch a few times as we move through the boulders."

"I'm not sure if I know what you're talking about, but just tell me what you need me to do."

"First thing is to get the MultiVec to about 100 meters to right."

Within a few minutes the MultiVec was in place.

"Troy, I'll take the portable winch up about 20 meters past the first boulder and bring you up. Once we get to that point, we'll make sure the MultiVec is secure, then I'll move the winch to the next boulder. We'll have to do it about five times, but it looks like the only way."

"Okay, I'll take your word on it. When you're in place, let me know, I'll give it full throttle."

Brett worked his way up the first boulder on which he had carved an arrow in earlier. He proceeded another few meters and set up the portable winch. He secured the winch then the line.

"Nice and steady, Troy. Straight ahead."

Troy accelerated slowly and headed straight for Brett. The MultiVec climbed up the incline.

"Another few meters, Troy, then slow it down. Place the brake on. Once it's secure, I'll move to the next boulder."

Troy maneuvered the MultiVec and parked it as Brett made his way up. For the next few hours the two maneuvered the MultiVec up the path that Brett had found earlier. At the conclusion of each section Brett noticed that the motor on the winch was getting warm, beginning finally to smoke. What the two didn't realize is that the line from the winch was taking its toll as it made its way across the rocks along the ridge. Brett went up over the crest of the ridge. He saw the rover sitting a few meters to his left. He started to set up the winch.

"Okay, Troy. Give me a few minutes. Then you're finally at the top."

Troy secured the winch, checked the line. "Looks good, let's go."

Troy accelerated as the winch helped pull the MultiVec up. Twenty meters out from the MultiVec the line rubbed against a jagged rock. It was becoming more frayed with every meter. Brett knew the winch unit was getting warm, and although he had some concern earlier about it burning out, in fifty meters it wouldn't matter any more.

"How far Brett? Hard to tell in the dark?"

"Maybe forty-five meters. Keep it coming nice and slow."

The frayed line came up against a sharp rock, and as the winch pulled the line snapped.

Troy was sitting at the controls as he felt the line let go. The wheels began to slip. He tried controlling it by hitting the accelerator harder. "What the..." The MultiVec began to slide back. The incline was too much.

Brett knew instantly that the line had snapped as the line dropped to the ground and began to reel in at a high speed. Brett turned back to the winch, the end of the line that was dancing wildly out of control heading directly at Brett. He jumped to the side and rolled quickly toward a boulder. The line just missed him and coiled up on the winch.

Meanwhile, the MultiVec slid down the cliff and crashed into a series of boulders that stopped it from falling any farther.

Rebecca was monitoring the last few moves in the rover. "Troy! Brett! Are you okay?" There was nothing but static. "Either of you. Do you hear me?"

Brett rolled over and looked for the MultiVec, which had slid back a good hundred meters. "I'm fine, Rebecca. Troy, are you okay?"

"Shit man, yeah. That was some ride."

"Is the MultiVec damaged?"

Troy looked at the gauges and could still hear the engines running.

"I think it's fine, but we've just wasted a good hour."

Brett got to his feet and examined the path of the MultiVec. "Maybe not. It looks like a direct shot back up. I'll just need to get a line back down to you."

Brett turned to look back at the winch, which was still rotating. He quickly went up and turned it off. He examined the remaining line.

"Do we have a backup line, Troy, that's long enough to get you up here?"

"Yeah, we should. I'll take a look."

Brett cautiously made his way down to the MultiVec. As he got closer, he could see the dents along one side.

"Boy, it's amazing you're not more banged up than you are. That is one ugly vehicle you're in."

"Well, it gets uglier. There's no back up line."

"Damn it. Any ideas?"

"No. So all this for nothing."

"Guys, the MultiVecs usually have a tow line attached to the back."

Brett raced to the back and tried to find the tow. It was pretty smashed and nothing looked useable in the back. "What am I looking for here? It's pretty banged up."

"They are usually under the rear headlight. The cover will have a small marking that looks like a coil of rope." Brett brushed away the red dust to look for it. "Yeah, I found it."

"Open it up and hit "Full Release." You should be able to walk the line up to the winch and pull it up in reverse." Brett pulled on the cover until it came off. He released the line and began to walk it up the cliff.

"Let's hope this works." Brett's feet slipped as he made his way up. "Damn, this may take some time to get up to the top."

"Take your time, buddy. I want to make sure this thing is ready to go. I'm reading a small leak. Hopefully, I'll find it by the time we're ready to go." Troy replied.

Within the hour the leak was fixed, and Brett had attached the line to the winch.

"You ready? Here we go." Brett turned on the winch as Troy put the MultiVec in reverse. The vehicle abruptly swung around and was headed up the cliff in reverse.

"Hard to tell if I'm going straight, Brett. Let me know if I sway to one side."

"You're looking good. Keep it coming."

Brett heard a pop and looked at the winch that was smoking.

"Keep it coming, Troy. The winch is overheating. If it burns out, hit reverse full speed."

"I understand. How far am I? What's it look like?"

"Another forty meters. Keep it straight."

The winch was smoking hard as it pulled the vehicle up the cliff.

"Troy, accelerate it slowly, but keep accelerating until you feel you're losing control."

Troy accelerated as he attempted to keep it moving straight up the cliff.

"More to the left. Keep it coming another twenty meters." Brett turned to the wench but couldn't even make it out through the smoke. He looked back at the vehicle and then heard the winch die.

"Hit it hard!"

Troy opened up the MultiVec full as it jumped over the crest of the cliff and spun to a stop.

"Nice job, Troy."

Rebecca joined them in the MultiVec as they performed a few more diagnostics on it. Troy went over to the table where Brett was double-checking a few numbers.

"Everything is checking out. Looks banged up on the outside, but she appears to be fine."

"So boys, where do we go from here?"

Troy looked at Brett "What do you think. We'll need about thirty minutes."

Brett opened up one of the cots, "First thing is, let's get a few hours of sleep. Then in the morning, you two get near the entrance to Aris Canyon, and I'll drive right up in the belly. I can keep them busy." He laid down on the cot and closed his eyes.

Rebecca looked at him, then at Troy, "I hope you two know what you're doing!"

19

Brett sat in the MultiVec waiting for Troy and Rebecca to signal that they were in place. Brett would need to get the attention of everyone and clear the path so Troy and Rebecca could go unnoticed as in making their breakout down into Aris Canyon.

His communicator blinked as he responded. "Roberts here."

"Brett, we're in place." Rebecca replied, Brett sensing her concern. "They seem to be gathering here, almost like they're waiting for you."

"I hope they are! Remember to wait till it's all-clear. You don't want anyone following you."

"If you give us a thirty-minute head start, Brett, I don't think they'll be able to catch us," Troy interjected.

"Brett be careful," Rebecca said. "Don't do anything foolish. Like Troy said, we only need you to keep them busy for thirty minutes, then you can let them catch you."

"Don't worry," responded Brett, then pulled the MultiVec out into the clearing and headed one kilometer south of Aris Canyon. He drove quickly across the clearing, stirring up the red sand. Brett viewed the scanners as he proceeded, but so far nobody had noticed. He needed to get their attention, but how? He drove the MultiVec in a large circle trying to disturb more sand and get their attention. He still didn't see anything on the sensors.

Brett stopped the MultiVec, thinking if he only knew where Ivory was he'd send him a message. That was it, the messages. He could retrieve the messages from earlier, and they would pick up his location. Brett flipped on the communicator.

"You have two messages." the communicator announced.

"Let me hear both messages"

"Brett, it's Nick. I'm not sure how to tell you this." Brett could sense the concern in his voice. *"I was just notified that there was an accident. I'm afraid it's Kathleen. It looks like she accidentally took an overdose of medication. I'm afraid by the time they reached her it was too late. I'm sorry Brett. Kathleen died."*

Brett stared out the window at the pink sunrise, his eyes filling up with tears. Somehow he always felt this day would come, but would never be ready for it.

"She seemed to be writing a letter to you, but never completed it. She said she missed Alex and was looking forward to being with him. She also wrote that it was always difficult for her to tell you that, she did love you. Brett, I'm sorry. I'll arrange everything back here on Earth. Get back to me when you can. We'll proceed with whatever will work for you."

Brett sat in the cockpit with tears slowly running down his face. Now he was alone. His heart was pounding, yet he felt dead. Why now, when he was away. Again, he was away and unable to be there. He trembled in his seat as he absorbed the news. Memory's raced through his head. He had loved her. Did she ever realize how much?

Back in Roman Jack Lucinie picked up the signal from Roberts and quickly got a fix on it. He yelled over to one of the technicians, "Get me Ivory," and shortly he was talking to Ivory.

"Sir, we've picked up a signal. It's Roberts. He's checking his messages. We have him pinned down. Sir, he's less than a kilometer from you! I'm downloading his coordinates to you."

* * *

Ivory uploaded the coordinates as he sat in his cockpit. He could quickly see there were many other vehicles closer to Roberts. Ivory sent out the coordinates to all his people and got a message over the COM link.

"This is Ivory. I've just sent you Roberts coordinates. He's less than a half a kilometer from you. I want him stopped at all costs!"

Troy heard and received the coordinates in their vehicle. "They've found him. We just need thirty minutes. Once they've cleared the opening to the canyon, we'll need thirty minutes."

"Thirty minutes is a lot of time," Rebecca said setting her coordinates on Brett's exact location.

"He's just sitting there waiting for them! What is he doing? They're going start firing lasers within minutes." Just as if they heard her, the large tractors fired up their lasers and locked in on Brett's hull.

"Troy, he isn't moving! They'll breach the integrity within seconds!"

Brett sat in his seat, empty and lifeless. He could hear the tractors and other vehicles heading towards him. He even felt as if he was being fired upon, then thought he heard the voice of Alex.

"Remember what you told me? You have to continue to carry on and keep alive those you love in your heart."

He felt a laser then hitting the hull. He hit the accelerator and headed away from the canyon. He wiped his face as he zigzagged across the Martian dessert. The red dust flew across the dessert, deflecting the strength of the laser cannons. He also knew that the lasers needed to be locked in on one spot for at least a half a minute to breach the hull.

He sped wildly across the sand, feeling dead inside. Rebecca and Troy watched as over a dozen vehicles abandoned the canyon's entrance to pursue Roberts. Troy signaled Brett. "We're off, thirty minutes, buddy. That's all."

Troy accelerated down into Aris canyon as Rebecca focused on the sensors watching the chase behind them.

"He seems to just be dodging the lasers," she said. "They seem to be gaining on him. If they ram into him, they'll immobilize him."

"Don't worry. I'm sure he knows what he's doing." Troy looked at the coordinates to Station 185. It was still almost three hours away. They needed that thirty-minute head start.

* * *

Ivory was headed toward the chase. Roberts had been nothing but a problem for him since his arrival. He wanted to put an end to Roberts and his friends. It would be too late for anyone to help or do anything about it. Soon Calprex would sign over the land to the Arab Republic, and the masquerade could end. He could then go back home with enough money for 100 lifetimes.

Ivory monitored the progress as he drew closer to Roberts. "That fool, he's driving across the desert like a desperate animal." He scanned the monitor and turned to the satellite's view. He saw Robert's vehicle with a dozen others pursuing him. He also noticed two other vehicles to the southwest, three still farther back, then him and one vehicle near the entrance to the canyon.

His vehicle was much more agile and weighed considerably less than the Transports and Robert's MultiVec. He would be in the chase within another ten minutes. In the meantime he didn't care if someone took care of Roberts, but there was a part of him that wanted to do it personally.

Ivory picked up the COM link. "This is Ivory. Continue to pursue Roberts. The two vehicles that are coming in from the southwest are to head to coordinates 235 by 110. If Roberts makes a break, you'll be there to cut him off. I also see three other vehicles behind me. Hold your positions and cut off an escape route to the east. I also want the vehicle near the entrance to the Aries canyon to stay put and block off that escape route. Those in pursuit, try to disable him. If possible, I want him alive." At least for a few extra minutes, he thought.

Brett was still in a daze. He knew his life was in danger. He knew he had vehicles in hot pursuit and that Troy and Rebecca needed another twenty minutes to get a safe head start. With all this in mind he felt numb and alone. There were so many things he wished he had told Kathleen. There were so many things that he had told Kathleen that he knew she didn't understand.

She had been his true love, the wind in his sails. Even in the bad times, she had been the one he had wanted to talk to, the one he had wanted to celebrate with. Over the last few years they had both been shells of the people they had once been. How did their dream of their life together, their dream of a family together, go so far astray? How did it get to this point?

Brett's stomach felt as if he had been hit over and over. His head was lost in thought as the tears flowed. "Why? God, why her and not me?" Brett slammed his fist down on the steering wheel.

As he continued to maneuver across the desert, he made apparent turns to interrupt any lasers hitting his hull directly. The sand was still being churned up, billowing up thick red dust behind him. He saw he was running out of room. He was headed straight for the cliff of Aries Canyon, which had a drop of nearly two kilometers down.

His eyes were burning from the salt in his tears. Troy and Rebecca still needed time, but he seemed to be running out of it. He accelerated the MultiVec and headed straight for the cliff. The wheels spun and through the red, Martian sand flew high into the sky. The vehicles in pursuit were having a difficult time getting a fix on him.

Ivory continued to gain on the group. He was coming in at an angle and could see Roberts headed for the cliff. The cloud of sand blinded those in pursuit.

"The bastard's going to go right off that cliff and take everyone with him!" he thought.

Roberts saw the edge of the cliff and turned the wheel sharply to the right. The wheels locked, and the vehicle still continued to move forward. He held the wheel tightly as he could feel the wheels spinning out of control. The pink sky filled the windshield as he came near on the edge. The wheels still continued to slide on the fine sand.

Was this the way it was going to end, he thought? Did it matter anymore? He could feel the front left wheel fall a meter but then seemed to hit a rock again as it fought to get traction. He continued to fight the wheel, even though he didn't have a fight left in him. He thought back to a time when he, Alex, and Kathleen were together in their small home. He had no fear of death, just regret for all of his failures.

He heard Alex's voice once again, "Remember to continue", as all the wheels found traction. He turned to the right as the vehicle came to a stop.

The ones in pursuit were not as fortunate. They never saw the cliff with the dust of sand blinding them. The first few vehicles went over before they had any idea the cliff was there. The next three attempted to stop but were too late as they skidded off the cliff and fell to the canyon floor. Two others collided with each other, one pushing the other over the side.

Brett's MultiVec continued to turn as he regained control. He saw through the windshield his pursuers plummet to their deaths. There were still a few that had averted the cliff and were almost upon him. One shot its laser, and Brett could tell it was on his hull. He attempted to turn away from the oncoming vehicles, but they were too close. He looked at the clock. Twenty-three minutes and counting. He had given Troy and Rebecca all the time they needed. He turned back to his pursuers and turned down his engines. He knew what he needed to do.

Ivory was less than a kilometer away and moving fast towards Roberts.

"Fire your gun, I want you to burn a hole in his hull!"

The oncoming vehicles, which had lasers, fired on the MultiVec. Ivory sped towards them as the MultiVec didn't attempt to maneuver away from the oncoming laser beams. In less than a minute the hull would be penetrated, and Roberts would no longer be a problem for him. Ivory scanned the monitor barking orders to the vehicles to the southwest and east of him. He glanced again. Where was it? Where was the vehicle that was near the entrance to Aries canyon?

A large pop was heard as the hulls integrity was breached. Ivory knew that whoever ever was in there would be dead within a minute of the hull being breached. Ivory pulled up to the group that surrounded the MultiVec. "Send in a party and verify they're all dead." Ivory commanded. Ivory was wondering where the other vehicle disappeared to. His sensors couldn't pick anything up. Wherever it was, it was now out of range.

Within minutes, three armed men left one of the transports and walked over to the MultiVec. One by one they entered the vehicle cautiously, and without any difficulty. Ivory looked on, monitoring the conversations, while waiting for the confirmation. There was a part of him that thought maybe one of them might have gotten a suit on. The three men entered the galley and saw nothing. The first man pointed his weapon toward the cockpit, the other two men heading toward the front.

"Cover me," said the one, then he charged into the front of the MultiVec. "What the...?"

Ivory stood up. "What's going on? Are they all dead?"

"Sir, there is no one here. It looks like some type of remote mechanical device is attached to the steering column. I'm really not sure what it is."

Ivory could hear another voice. "What is that? Never seen anything like that. It might be rigged with an explosive."

"Listen, you fools, check the entire vehicle and for the three of them, or better yet, their remains."

"Yes, sir. We'll continue to search the MultiVec. Once it's secured, should we get someone here to check for explosives?"

"You're giving them way too much credit. Remove the device and take it back to base. We'll go over it there." He added briskly. "Do you think you can handle that?"

Ivory thought back to twenty minutes ago when he was in pursuit of the MultiVec. What happened to the vehicle near the canyon? It did not join in on the pursuit, why? Where was it now?

The intercom signal came on. "Sir, no one dead or alive is in this vehicle. We'll take it back to base."

Ivory glanced at the holographic map in front of him. He noted his position, the bases, and the entrance of the canyon, then saw Station 185!

"Damn him! Roberts is in the canyon! I want half of you to go along the cliff of the canyon heading north. I want the two Laser Tractors to follow me in the canyon." He changed the frequency to the party in the MultiVec. "Are you sure there is no one in the vehicle?"

The third man in the party had taken a quick look in the other cabins of the MultiVec. "Yes sir. No one is in here."

"All right. One of you take the vehicle back to base. The other two return to your vehicles. Now let's get a move on."

* * *

Troy kept looking at the scanners to see if anyone were following them, "I don't see anyone. So far, so good. We still have a long way to go. I'll feel a lot better when we get closer."

"How far are we?" asked Rebecca.

"The computer reads 203 kilometers. Estimated arrival is just over two hours."

"God, a lot can happen in two hours. Is this the only route to Station 185?"

"It's the route that is logged in by the computer. There may be another route that isn't on any of the maps." He flicked on a screen depicting the course. "You can see we're going to be headed through the canyon and then up the slope here to the station. The only other way would be along the perimeter of the canyon, but that route is quite a bit longer."

"Let's hope no one's already there!" she said, pointing to the route along the perimeter.

"I think Brett's keeping them busy."

"Troy, you don't think they'll hurt him?"

"Even if they do stop him, there would be no reason to do him harm. By the end of the day everyone on Mars and Earth will know what's going on down here."

"I hope you're right. I don't trust Gary Ivory. He is a vindictive man!"

"But he's not stupid. With everything going on, he won't do anything. Look, they'll chase Brett down, corner him and then take him to Ivory. By then the whole thing will be in the open. Don't worry."

"You're probably right, but I have a bad feeling."

Troy also had an uneasiness but didn't want to worry Rebecca any more than she was.

They made their way through Aries Canyon. The walls of the canyon climbed seemingly high into the sky. The morning sun cast a shadow over the near side.

Troy thought he should probably change the subject. "So it must have been some river to make this?"

Rebecca turned to him. "Yes, the reading we got from almost every canyon on Mars shows that Mars did indeed have large rivers running throughout."

"I've been to the Grand Canyon as a kid, and I know how big it is, but I bet you could fit that inside here."

"Oh easily. You could have a few inside here and wouldn't even notice them."

She continued to discuss the geology of Mars for another half hour. Troy nodded and smiled but was wondering what was going on back at the Pyramids.

20

The three men searched the MultiVec one more time, one of them saying, "Do you know anything about wiring? Explosives?"

Responded another, "Look, I'm a friggin driver. This is getting to be much more than I bargained for."

The third man chimed in, "Why don't we decide who will take this thing back. No sense in three of us going up if this thing is rigged."

"So then how do we decide who takes this thing off?" He pointed to the steering column. "And takes this piece of junk back?"

"I have three children back home," argued one of the other two.

"Don't give me that shit. I don't have any but my life is as important as yours!"

The one reached over and picked up three plastic pointers. He cracked a piece off one and then held the three in his hand. "Short stick stays." The first man slowly picked a stick from his comrade's glove. It was full length. The second man reached out and pulled out a stick, the short one.

Two of the three men left the MultiVec had headed back to their transports. The lone man in the group stared at the wire and the contraption that was on the steering column. He followed one of the wires to see if it led to an explosive or a transmitter. If it truly was remote it must have some type of transmitter. After following a few wires, it seemed they we're all loose wires going nowhere in particular. Was this series of wires just produced to stall for time, he wondered. He grabbed the unit and tossed it in behind him. Maybe it was a remote receiver of some type, but he'd let the people at base figure it out.

He sat in the cockpit chair and reached with his gloves for the steering column. He felt uncomfortable. It was a long ride back, and he would prefer to take his suit off. He sat there for a minute and decided it would only take a few minutes to fix the hole. He continued back into the main cabin where the hole was located. He examined the hole, which was about three centimeters in diameter. He searched the cabinets for patches and tools.

He placed a patch and smeared some silicone sealant across the entire area. He waited a few minutes, made a few checks and found he was only losing minimal pressure. It was good enough for him to be without his suit so that he could drive this thing back to the base in a bit more comfort. He sat in the cockpit and started up the engines to head back to base.

* * *

Corey Davis was the driver of one of the MultiVecs headed up to the Northern Territory. He was happy to get out of Roman after being cooped up there for so long. Give him the opportunity to drive a MultiVec and he was like a kid on Christmas morning. So when the order came for all non-essential personnel not being used in the construction of Roman, specifically Capricorn, were to ride out into the Northern area, he quickly volunteered to be one of the drivers.

There were eight others in the vehicle including two geologists, a technician, a cook, a nurse and two mechanics. Dale Oshioki, one of the geologists, grabbed the seat next to Corey. "Well I think we both have a few friends out there ahead of us. Any idea what's going on?"

Corey turned and seemed a bit confused. "What? I'm not sure what you mean?"

"Troy Smitts. He works with you?"

"Oh, yeah."

"He left with my colleague and Roberts a few days back. I just wonder what's going on? I wonder if what we're doing has anything to do with them. I wonder if they're lost or injured."

"I'm not sure, I only know that they need many people searching the area. Maybe they are lost. Aren't you guys supposed to do some testing?"

"Yes, but it really wasn't clear. Only at the specified coordinates that they gave us are we to take a series of tests and look for abnormalities."

"They'll probably tell us more as we get farther out. We have at least another sol or two to reach the area."

"Do you even know why they went out in the first place?" Oshioki asked as he looked over some geologic readings.

Corey turned with a smirk, happy to finally have an answer. "Yeah, you mean Troy? They went to fix weather station one eighty-five. A bunch of the weather stations went down after the storm. I actually went out to repair a few myself. Troy wanted to handle this one personally. He thinks we weren't getting accurate readings in the first place."

"So now they're either lost and we have to find them. Or maybe they found platinum, gold or something of value and want our help. All I know is I'm glad they're my friends or I'd be pissed. I have a lot of work to do back at Roman."

Corey pulled up a map on the monitor. "Mr. Conners gave us this route to take. He didn't mention anything about looking for them, just your tests."

"Well then, maybe it's something they found. Something we can mine for."

"Yeah, all I got was an order that we head north and let you guys run a full series of testing. At this point I'm just following the other transports."

"It must be a good fifty transports. They must have found the mother load." He grinned at the possibilities. He then glanced back at the route Corey had put up. "Interesting. We're headed to areas we were restricted from testing in the past. Maybe I won't be pissed after all."

* * *

Robert's MultiVec was headed back to the P - base. The driver kept an eye on the pressure gauge. He felt patch should hold till he got back to base. He was about 93% pressure and estimated he was losing about 1% every twenty minutes. He knew that as long as it was 90% or above no suit was needed. He also knew the base garage was only another thirty minutes away.

He switched the COM link to scan as he listened to the communication from the base. Nothing really interesting, but it beat listening to the noise of the engine. The additional noise also didn't help him hear the floorboard in the main cabin move. A hand in a glove of a space suit was holding the side of the floorboard as it pushed the floor up and to the side.

Quietly, Brett Roberts, in a full space suit, pulled himself out of the small storage area under the floor. He could see that the driver had not heard him, being focused on where he was driving. Brett took a double look to make sure he was the only one left behind. He noticed the driver had patched the hole and depressurized the MultiVec.

Brett walked to the side hatch and opened the door. He knew before he could turn to the cockpit that the driver was dead. His blood would have boiled out of his body. Brett had seen men die like this before and it wasn't a pleasant sight. The MultiVec came to a halt, and Brett dragged the body out of the cockpit and tossed the body outside. He grabbed a blanket from one of the bunks to wipe down the mess.

He closed the hatch and started to depressurize the MultiVec. He grabbed a tarp and tossed it over the main seat in the cockpit. Even with the body gone and things had been somewhat cleaned up, Brett knew that the smell of the driver's fluids and blood would be tough to take. He found a small sheet and folded it over and made a scarf that he would use over his face when the MultiVec was depressurized.

His next job was to find out where Troy and Rebecca were and how far Ivory and his men were from them. He turned the MultiVec towards the south ridge of Aries Canyon. He would never be able to catch-up with them by going through the passage Troy and Rebecca took. As he raced along the ridge he scanned the sensors to see if he could get a fix on anything. He was too far away to pick up anything.

He needed to find a quick way to get to Station 185, but the computer had already given them the shortest route, the one Troy and Rebecca were presently taking. He needed someone's help, but whose? He turned on the MultiVec's COM link.

"I need some help and am looking for someone who has yet to let me down!" He wondered if his friend was listening.

"Hello, is my friend out there?" he said, not really expecting an answer.

A few minutes went by and nothing. Nothing gained, nothing lost, he thought. He continued to head along the rim of the canyon, keeping an eye on the sensors and scanning all the frequencies to get an idea of what was going on. He briefly picked up some communication, which sounded to be drivers in pursuit, but he was only guessing and it was gone as quickly as it came.

His thoughts returned to Kathleen as he continued to press on along the rim of the canyon. He drove for over an hour, hoping to find a way down to the canyon floor. He was scanning the frequencies, attempting to pick up any communication, trying to find out where Rebecca and Troy were.

He found it difficult to stay focused as he thoughts drifted toward Kathleen. Had she realized that he had truly loved her? Could he have done more? His thoughts regressed to what his, what their lives, would have been had they stayed together. His dream of what his life should be, slowly fell apart, and now twenty-five years later he was once again all alone.

The transmitter crackled on and off as it scanned, attempting to get a strong signal. The sun began to set and the pink sky took on a blue hue. His eyes watered as he continued on, not focused on anything, an empty feeling consuming him.

The transmitter came to life, "Brett. Brett, you out there?"

Brett could sense the anxiety in Rebecca's voice.

"Yes, I'm here," said Brett.

"Are you safe?"

"Yes. I'm driving along the rim of the canyon." Brett paused trying to gain his composure. "Where are you?"

"Troy's been making good time. He says were about an hour away. We'll load the disk and be on our way."

"I'm not sure what that disk will do but they're probably about forty-five minutes behind you. I'll try to get a look in a few minutes and see if I can find you or Ivory and his men. From this vantage point I should be able to see for kilometers. That's as long as the Sun stays up."

"Well, we should be okay. Why don't you get back to Roman? We'll catch up with you."

There was a pause, and Brett didn't reply.

"Brett, is everything okay? Are you injured?"

"I'm not hurt. It's, … it's nothing. Keep moving. Get to Station 185."

"How did you get away from them?" Troy asked.

"I'll tell you later. Just get that disk in and get the hell out."

"Why don't you get back to Roman? We'll be at Station 185 all set in less than an hour."

"Thanks, I'll stay up here. Make sure the two of you get back safe."

"We'll be fine. Go back home."

Home, where was home, Brett wondered? "I'll be fine. Get a move on and work quickly. Keep me posted."

Rebecca got back on. "Brett, everything will be fine. I'll see you back at Roman."

21

Brett had no intention of returning back to Roman without Troy and Rebecca, and continued to drive along the canyon. He felt tired and worn out. He wanted to wake up from this bad dream. He approached a small peninsula-type ridge that overlooked the entire canyon. He focused the sensors on the canyon. He was hoping that Troy and Rebecca were at the weather station. If there was any type of movement, he should be able to pick it up. He scanned back and forth, but nothing was showing up. Were they that far ahead of him or was he looking in the wrong spot? He continued to scan, but nothing.

Maybe the windshield was blocking the scan. He decided to get into a suit and take a look outside. As he reached around to slip his arm into the suit, he felt old. All the aches and pains seemed to catch up to him. It seemed to take him an hour to get dressed in the suit. Without double-checking any of the seals, he went out of the hatch with a portable scanner, which he pointed down into the canyon due east. Still nothing. He turned back to look at the other end of the canyon. Where could they be? He pointed the scanner to the other end, just to check if it worked. Maybe it would pick up something.

The lights flashed as something came into view. He narrowed the field down and he could see about a dozen vehicles racing east. Maybe Troy and Rebecca had more time than he thought. He quickly scanned east of the vehicles. Nothing, just the red desert. Then he saw it. Not more than a few kilometers ahead was a rover stopping near a weather station. How could this be, Brett thought. He had passed everyone. They were minutes behind them. He had to warn them. He tried the COM link in his suit even though he knew he was out of range. He had to get back to the MultiVec and warn them. His feet felt heavy as he ran to the MultiVec.

* * *

Troy could see the two tall antennas in the setting sun. Station 185 was similar to most of the weather stations surrounding Roman. It had three large dishes and multiple antennas, electronic wind tunnels, and a series of other instruments that were used to measure winds, temperature and the relay of the information to satellites circling Mars and then to Phobos.

It had a large base that actually could be use as a shelter for short-term use. The main entrance was double sealed and pressurized. It had a central control room, which could be employed to adjust directions of the dish and to check the signals. A small room contained a variety of supplies for the possible repairing of the equipment. There was also a ladder that led up to a small loft that could accommodate two people if someone needed to spend the night.

"We should be there in a few minutes. Get the suits ready. Let's move fast." They said as he went over the last ridge in front of the station.

"Yeah, Brett had said they're only about forty-five minutes behind us."

Rebecca pulled out two suits and tanks as she placed the disk on the console. She could feel Troy slowing down the rover as she quickly got into a suit, helping Troy then with his. They fastened their helmets, depressurized and open the hatch. The hatch closed behind them as the two walked over to Station 185.

"Do you know where this disk is supposed to go, Troy?"

"I think I have a pretty good idea. There are a few different layouts for the weather stations. It should be inside on the front top panel." The two had their COM links set to short-range messages as they walked towards the station.

It was too late for them to hear the message from inside the rover.

"Are you there? Are you there? They are only minutes behind you! Hurry! Get out of there. Get out!"

Troy opened the door, the two then entering the dark room. The lights slowly flickered on as the door closed behind them. He hit a series of controls and the room pressurized. The second door opened and the two entered the station. They both walked forward, Troy taking off his gloves and helmet. He could smell the stale, musty air. Rebecca had her gloves and helmet off on making her way to the control panels.

"Is that it?" she asked.

"I'm not sure. If not, it looks something like that." Troy walked over and pulled out the disk. "No, not this one," He glanced at the control panels. "Here it is." He pulled out the disk and placed the new one in.

"Is that all?" Rebecca asked.

"Just one more thing. Let's hit reformat." Troy hit the button and watched the bars move across the screen as Station 185 reformatted. Station 185 would become fully functional.

"What's that?" Troy said as hearing noise coming from the outside. Rebecca quickly looked at the panels and, finding the monitors, and turned them on. "Looks like we have company."

* * *

It was a quiet day in the newsroom. Mary Ann Franklin was double-checking her next piece on Mars. It was old news, nothing really exciting happening. Her last few stories were far from stellar and this wasn't going to help. It was her third network in four years and probably her last chance in the National media.

She walked into the projection booth. "Hey guys, what's going on today?" she said, strolling into the room and setting them up for a favor. "You guys don't seem too busy." She perched herself on a tall stool along the wall and crossed her long legs.

"Always delighted when you honor us with your presence, Mary Ann" said the older technician obviously sizing her up.

"Harry, you're just a dirty old man. You're old enough to be my father, well almost!" she replied grinning at him. The two other technicians, to the right of Harry, ogled over her as well.

Louis, who was finishing up some splicing, was not as excited about Mary Ann. "Ms. Franklin, I know you're not here for some chit chat. I'm sure you need a favor. So what is it this time?" said Louis, not even lifting his head as he continued his work.

Harry turned to Louis. "Take it easy, man. It's our job to help the reporters out. Do what you're doing. We'll take care of it."

"Thank you, Harry." Said Mary Ann. "All I really want is the latest feed from Mars. I need some scans of the surface showing the canyons and mountains."

"See, Louis, that's not too bad. Sit right over here, Mary Ann, and let's see what we can find for you." As he patted the chair next to him, Mary Ann slid off the stool and made her way to the monitor.

"Let's see, this should give us live shots of the surface. About two kilometers out ought to give you a nice view."

"Yes, that looks good. Can you move around and just record it all. Then we can edit it after." Said Mary Ann.

"Hmm, sounds like work Harry," Louis grunted.

"Mary Ann, don't listen to him. It's no big deal. Look at the mountains."

All the eyes were glued on the monitor.

"What was that?" she said, sitting up in the chair.

"Where?"

"Move it back a bit. There, right there. Can you get in any closer?"

"Sure."

The picture became closer.

"Holy shit!" they cried in unison and bewilderment.

"Are you recording this?" she said, with excitement in her voice.

"Every second. Louis, look at this. It's a frigin pyramid!"

*   *   *

Troy and Rebecca had quickly sealed the door, then barricaded the entrance with anything they could find. Troy pushed over a large cabinet on top of a metal desk.

"How long do you think we can keep them out, Troy?"

"I'm not sure. Probably not long. It all depends on what they have with them."

Rebecca looked at the monitors. "Well, they've tried the keypad and that's failed. It looks like they're waiting."

"Let them wait all they want. Time is on our side."

The second monitor showed two more vehicles heading from the horizon. The red dust swirled into the pink sky. "Looks like they're waiting for whoever that is," Troy said as his eyes darted from one monitor to the other.

"Do you think it's Ivory?"

"I don't know, but I really don't want to wait to find out."

"I don't think we have a choice."

"Maybe we do," He looked down at the floor.

"What, is there a way out of here?"

"I'm not sure. I don't think so, but this station's pipes and equipment are under this floor. If we can get in we might be able to hide there till they leave."

Rebecca's eyes went back to the monitor. "We'd better hurry. Whoever is in the transport is almost here."

Troy swept the floor back and forth with his feet. He went down on his knees near the far wall. "This may be it." Troy reached for a flat metal bar. "Here we go!" He pried the floor panel up and pushed it to the side.

Just then they heard a blast at the door. Troy looked at the monitor. On top of the transport was a laser.

"Looks like sooner then later!" Rebecca exclaimed as she ran grabbing their helmets and gloves to the opening in the floor. "Jump in!"

Rebecca went down with Troy quickly following. The laser blasted a hole in the door as Troy slid the floor panel across to close the opening. The debris from the blast tossed their barricade across the room. A group of men in suits rushed into the weather station.

Below, Troy and Rebecca crawled through the winding pipes and cables making their way to the other side of the station. Above them they could hear the footsteps as the men stormed the weather station.

Five armed men entered the station looking for the occupants of the rover outside. They searched the station and went through the debris from the blast.

Gary Ivory walked into the station.

"Where are they? Where is Roberts?"

"No one is here, sir. They must have left before we got here."

"I want every inch of this place searched. I want every scrap turned over, every nook and cranny checked and double-checked." He looked behind him.

"Where the hell is the technician? I need this station fixed!"

Two men came into the weather station with two small boxes. "We'll be able to see if they were able to disable the feed." They hooked a few wires up to the monitors and did a few tests.

"Looks like they were able to block our feed, but we can get it up within a few minutes."

"Damn it, I want Roberts found." Ivory turned back to the two men working on the monitors. "How long was the block down for?"

"Looks like..., here it is..., sixteen minutes, twelve seconds. The block is back up. Sir, the Pyramids may have gone unnoticed."

"I doubt it. They'll be sending flyers over the coordinates within the hour. We need to get back to the site and prepare."

"Should we leave anyone here at the station?"

"No, it's too late. I need every available man and woman to prepare for the onslaught of unwanted quests."

"Should we call in the group waiting at Baron's Pass?"

"No, not until they've dismantled the convoy. Let's get a move on."

* * *

The Secretary of Defense sat back in his chair engaged in a conversation with the President of the United States. "Yes, sir. Most of the media has been tracking it for over ten minutes. The Chinese and Europeans saw it immediately." He wiped his brow as he kept his eye on the monitor. "I agree, sir. Yes, we need to send every available person to Mars. I can have a few hundred troops ready for a transport before the day is over.

Mr. President this is uncharted waters. I suggest we get as many people and supplies headed to Mars. It will take them months to get there. What actions they'll take, we can decide over the next few months. My advice is get up there fast. You know everyone else will."

He took a sip of water. "Mr. President, consider it done. I will keep you apprised of the men and material that we send out." He turned the communicator off and switched to the monitor, mesmerized by the view of the pyramid.

As his eyes were fixed on the screen, the view changed from the pyramids to a mountain range. He tapped the communicator. "Did someone change the view? Get that back on."

"Sir, no one changed anything. It's the same coordinates, but now the pyramids are gone!" came a reply from the communicator.

"Get me General Strawkowski. I want to know what the hell is going on!"

"Yes sir."

Gerald Patterson had been an advisor for two Presidents and now was in his second year as Secretary of Defense for a third President. Over the last few years he had deployed troops to control a few small skirmishes in South America, but for the most part everything had gone smoothly, that is, until today!

"Sir, General Strawkowski is on the line."

"General, what the hell is going on? One minute the entire friggin World is looking at two Pyramids on Mars and the next minute they're gone! I want answers, now!"

"We're looking into that right now. We've run a preliminary test of the feed, and it's no a hoax. Those are actual pictures from Mars. We've contacted Phobos to get some still shots, but it will take thirty minutes to get a reply. We're also sending multiple flyers over the coordinates."

"If those are actual shots of Mars, General, who is blocking them? Who has land rights to that area?"

"I'm not sure who is blocking the view, but we'll get an answer on that soon. We do know the land is deeded to Calprex, Inc. They're the company building Roman just south of that area."

"I want to find out who is blocking the feed and why? I want to know everything about Calprex, including who works for them, what contracts they have, and when everyone there takes a shit! Do you understand?"

"We're already looking into it. I'll have the answers for you shortly."

"General, I need them fast! This could get very ugly."

"I understand."

Patterson killed the line, stood up and looked out into the dark sky. He glanced up at the sky, suspecting he would know where to look for Mars. After a scan, his eyes focused on the Moon.

He wondered what it all meant.

*   *   *

Troy turned on the small light on his gauges to check how much air they had left.

Rebecca looked at him, then checked her gauge. "Is that right? How long have we been down here?" Rebecca tapped her COM link.

"I know. I'm low to. I have about twenty minutes left in mine. We've been under this floor for at least an hour. I think they've been gone for some time but it's hard to tell with these helmets on."

"Yeah, I could feel the vibration as they drove away. The question is, is anyone still here?"

"Considering our situation," he said as he glanced at the air gauge, "does it matter?"

"Good point. Let's get out of here."

The two crawled their way back to the floor panel, opening through which they had entered. Troy slowly lifted the panel, and the two cautiously lifted themselves up into the station.

"Stay here and let me take a look around." Troy headed in the spot where the front door had been an hour before.

A large hole had been blasted through, allowing men to enter and open it up further from the inside. The red, Martian dust blew through the opening. Troy checked the loft and the control room. It looked deserted. He tapped the COM link "Looks like we're alone." He made his way to the control panel.

"Rebecca, can you hear me? Looks like we're alone," he said. There was no answer. Troy turned around and saw Rebecca bending over on her knees. "Rebecca are you all right?"

"Yeah, just a little nauseous. I'll be okay once I can get out of this suit. Let's get in the rover and get back to Roman."

Troy helped Rebecca to her feet, and the two headed out the door.

Troy scanned the area looking for the rover. "It's gone. The bastard took the rover."

Rebecca glanced at her oxygen gauge. "It doesn't look good, Troy. I have about fifteen minutes left."

Troy glanced at his as well. "Yeah, same here." He hit the distress beacon on his COM link.

"If someone is around, maybe they'll hear it."

"I hope you're right. We should change the mix rate of oxygen and try to move and say as little as possible. We might be able to stretch it another ten minutes."

"That's optimism if ever I heard it! But I'll take ten minutes."

They both adjusted their gauges and sat against the wall. Rebecca sat back thinking that there was no one left behind to carry on her memory. She and Brett had become very close since he had come to Roman, but they could have shared much more. She grabbed her stomach as she became queasy.

Troy rehashed in his mind his entire adult life and how he had made one mistake after the other. He would die here on Mars and no one would give a damn.

"What a wasted life!" he said out loud.

"Troy, save your voice. You're going to waste oxygen."

'It doesn't matter if I die in ten minutes or twenty. I'm still going to die today."

"Someone might hear the distress signal, Troy."

"Who will hear it? Ivory isn't going to come back for us. Brett's headed back to Roman. We're going to die out here."

"Don't get worked up. Relax and pray."

"I told you I don't believe in God."

"I do. So pray for me, pray with me, pray for a miracle."

Troy sat back and tried to remember the Sunday morning that he had stayed with his grandmother and went to church with her. "Our father…"

Rebecca grabbed Troy's hand as they waited for their tanks to empty. She barely had enough breath left to speak.

"Troy, I don't think it was a wasted life. You seem like a good guy to me."

"Thanks. But I did waste it. If I could do it all over, it would be different." He closed his eyes.

Rebecca thought she felt a vibration but figured then that she was becoming delusional from lack of oxygen. Her body felt heavy as she tried to twist her head back to look at the monitor. She thought she saw something on the monitor, but everything was getting blurry. She thought she saw someone in front of her. "Brett?"

"Save your strength. You're fine now," Brett said as he tapped both Rebecca's and Troy's air line into a free tank of oxygen. "Both of you take nice slow breaths, nice and easy."

Within thirty minutes the three were on the MultiVec.

"Buddy, I thought you were headed back to Roman. Thank God you followed us instead," Troy said, grinning happily.

"Troy, did you say 'thank God'?" Rebecca chuckled.

"I felt I needed to."

Brett went into the cockpit. Rebecca followed him in as Troy was completing a diagnostic on the transmitter in the back of the vehicle.

"I think, Brett, there is something you should know..." She looked into Brett's eyes and could see they were swollen with tears.

"Brett, what's wrong? Are you okay? Are you hurt?"

"No, I'm fine. I'm not injured it's just..." He took a deep breath. "It's Kathleen. She's dead." The words were so hard to say. His eyes were filling up with tears.

Rebecca put her arms around him. "I'm so sorry. I know you shared so much together." She held him tightly as tears began flowing down her cheeks. She would have to wait to tell him later.

Troy walked up to the front and saw the two embarrassed and crying. "What's going on?"

Brett looked up but could not get the words out.

"Troy, Brett's ex-wife is dead."

"Oh God, I'm sorry." He placed a comforting hand on Brett's shoulder. The three sat for a few minutes.

Brett turned to the dashboard and plugged in a few coordinates. "Lets get back to home. The place is going to be hopping soon."

Troy thought about the choice of words, home. The word felt right, maybe Mars was home.

They fired up the engines and headed back to Roman.

22

Nick Gambino needed answers, and fast. Brett still had not gotten back to him in response to the previous messages he had sent out. Everyone else would give him the runaround. He walked over and sent Brett another message. He had nothing to lose.

Buddy,

Look, I know the news must have been difficult to take but I need your help. I need it now! I need you to tell me what the hell is happening over there? A few hours ago live satellite pictures of Mars showed two large Pyramids. These Pyramids are in the area you're in. What's going on?

The view of the Pyramids disappeared after about 15 minutes. Earth is buzzing. Every media picked up the feed and ran it. Most of the governments are deciding what to do. Ed is meeting with ISC, which is holding a special session. Ed will have the main floor in the first hour claiming members of the ISC were aware of this and that was their reason for their ruling on the dispute with the completion with Capricorn.

At this point Ed needs answers. We need to know exactly what it was that Earth saw a few hours ago. Were those two Pyramids, and if so, who built them? Ed also wants any information on the timetable of Capricorn. We need you.

Nick

Nick hit 'send' and glanced at some of the incoming messages from Roman. They were all hours old. He reviewed the message from Jane Bender and saw that Capricorn should be completed within two days. Bender had sent numerous graphs, charts and work orders showing the status. In every message he could tell Bender was worried about the budget used. At this point it was irrelevant.

Nick made an electronic file of all the completed work on Capricorn and sent it to Ed in case he needed it when he talked to the ISC. He had wanted to go to Washington to support Ed, but Ed needed him here, needed him to find the answers. He hoped to get as much information to Ed in time for his meeting.

He glanced at his watch. Another ten minutes before Brett would even receive the message. Ten minutes. Brett hadn't even replied to any messages over the last few days. Ed would have the floor of ISC within two hours and Nick needed answers. He felt helpless just sitting at his terminal waiting for replies.

Nick's COM link chimed, "Sir, there are a few men from the Defense Department here and are insisting on seeing you."

Nick sat up straight in his chair. "That's okay. Send them in."

The door opened, and two men in uniform walked in and approached Nick's desk. The first was a black man with gray sideburns. He was easily over six and half feet tall. He was in good shape and didn't appear much older than Nick, but his eyes betrayed his true age of around sixty years.

The second man was much shorter, had a clean-shaven head and looked like he worked out every free minute he had. The older of the two put out his hand.

"Mr. Gambino, I'm Major Robinson, and this is Lieutenant Cooper."

Nick shook hands with the two men.

"I can't say I know why you're here. I don't know if I have the answers you're looking for, but hope to have some soon."

"Mr. Gambino, how long have you been aware of the Pyramids?"

"Same time you guys have. Found out when it was on the satellite."

"Are you saying you did not know anything about them before today?"

"Of course not!"

"So Calprex had nothing to do with building them?"

"What? Are they man made?" Nick sat momentarily stunned in his chair. "Look, I have not known about these Pyramids, and as far as I know, no one in Calprex has either. This is just as much a shock for us as it is for you. Ed Brocton, will be presiding at the ISC later today. It appears that someone in the ISC was aware of the Pyramids since they ruled on the land rights going to the Arab Republic."

"Yes, Mr. Gambino, we are aware of the situation there, and we're following it closely. At this time I need you to come with us. We need to ask you more detailed questions."

"Are you kidding? I can't leave, not now!"

"I'm sorry. You really don't have much of a choice in this matter. You can come peacefully or in handcuffs."

"What, are you arresting me?"

"No, sir. Just bringing you in for questioning."

"On what grounds. I've done nothing wrong."

"On the grounds of National Security. We'll determine if you've done anything wrong."

"May I have a lawyer?"

"For what, Mr. Gambino? You said you did nothing wrong. This is only for questioning."

Nick went to the rack and grabbed his jacket. "Let's get this over with. I have a lot of work to do back here."

The three walked out of his office and down the hallway. Nick saw men and women in military uniforms going through filing cabinets, computers and questioning employees.

"What the hell is going on?"

"Sir, someone here has known about the situation on Mars. We need to find out who."

* * *

Terry McGregor sat at his desk in total exhaustion, bewildered at the sight of the Pyramids that were also seen by everyone on Mars. How could something like this go on without someone slipping and letting it get out? The Pyramids were larger than anything on Earth. Hadn't someone been able to see them from a ship coming in? Maybe that's why Roman was being built. This magnificent city is being built for the Pyramids.

The more he thought about it the less he believed it. Why keep it a secret and why such an urgency to complete Capricorn? Since McGregor had arrived, he had dealt with missing equipment. Rumors were always rampant that others were signing other workers in. It was all making sense to him. The manpower and equipment used to uncover the Pyramids must have been astonishing.

McGregor was working in Capricorn when the live pictures were linked in to all the monitors in Roman. Some, like McGregor, were astonished, while others just fixed their eyes on the screen. Conversations broke out on estimates of the size of both Pyramids. "Look, if that little dot to the right is one of the Worms, you do the math!" he remembered one of them saying.

So that's what McGregor would do. He used conservative numbers and began tabulating the size of the Pyramids, the amount of material moved along with what equipment would be needed to do such a massive task. McGregor sat at his desk and put down some numbers on the keypad. He had also pulled up the numbers of missing material and equipment and cross-referenced them too.

"That's it! All of this came from Roman. No wonder."

He franticly continued to compute numbers and sat in amazement, wondering how these resources could be diverted without anyone knowing. McGregor estimated the dig had been going on for at least one year. He sat and thought about all that time and manpower used and now over a year out, it's uncovered. How many people with whom he had he been working knew about this? Who could be trusted? He knew from the first day Roberts could be trusted, but besides Roberts he didn't know. He would have to proceed cautiously.

As he continued to tabulate the numbers, he decided to send them to Brett Roberts and Nick Gambino. Maybe they would need them.

* * *

Gary Ivory knew the next Sol would determine if he would end up being a very wealthy man or a man on the run. By the time he was almost back to the Pyramids he received confirmation that Earth was aware of the Pyramids. He was also notified that dozens of ships from Phobos had flown over the site.

Although he realized it was out and it didn't matter, he still wanted Roberts to pay for this. They had worked so hard for over a year, and to get this close only to have this happen. Well, maybe it was too late, maybe the Arab Republic had the rights to the site. In that case he would live his remaining days a wealthy man.

The driver glanced back at Ivory. "Sir, an urgent message coming in."

"I'll take it in the back." Ivory walked to the rear of the vehicle and sat at the monitor.

Even before the face appeared on the screen Ivory knew it would be Afidan.

Earth is aware of the Pyramids. As of this message the rights to the land have not been released to the Arab Republic. You must hold and secure the site and allow no one in. Within the next day we'll know if the land is released or if we'll need to fight to keep it. Most of the governments are sending men from Earth and also men already stationed on Mars. Secure the site and stop all those who attempt to get near the site. The next 24 hours are vital. I am leaving on a transport with 500 men and will arrive on Mars in sixteen weeks. You need to hold out till then.

"Fight to keep the Pyramids"? Ivory thought it peculiar the way he had phrased it. Yes, he would use all the means available to him to stop anyone from getting near the Pyramids. He had the resources to hold the

Pyramids for a few months, but if troops were coming from Earth before Afidan, he wouldn't have a prayer. He was hired to run the operation of uncovering the Pyramids and keeping it under wraps. He was not interested in fighting a war to hold onto them.

Something seemed different in this message, but he wasn't sure what. He decided to play it one more time before he deleted it. Ivory analyzed the actions and appearance of Afidan on the message. He didn't appear as cold or as forceful as he had in previous messages. Earth uncovering the Pyramids should have sent him overboard, yet he seemed calm.

Was Afidan worried about the message being decrypted? At this point it didn't matter. He was actually on his way to Mars! He noticed that Afidan didn't have his usual business attire on, but an Arab tunic. Was Afidan a member of the Republic and just playing the part? After a few minutes he became exhausted over trying to figure out what it all meant. He replied that he understood and deleted the original message.

"Damn Roberts!" as he pounded the side panel. "I was so close and now I have to hold off intruders. I'm not interested in some Holy War."

He tapped the COM link. "This is Ivory. Move us to red alert immediately. I want all of the laser cannons up and ready. I want them visible for anyone monitoring." He sat in his seat, exhausted.

He was hoping that this would all be over within weeks, but now he knew it would be at least four to six more months on this cold, red rock called Mars. Within thirty minutes any ships passing over the Pyramids would see eight large laser cannons ready to blast anything that got close to the site whether it was from land or above.

The co-pilot called back to Ivory. "Sir, we received word that everything is all set at Baron's Pass." Baron's Pass. Ivory had almost forgotten about it. "Proceed there immediately. I want to make sure a message is delivered." A message of both death and destruction.

* * *

The convoy was buzzing about the Pyramids. As they drove to the North region, they had picked up the link from Phobos. Uliga Sukora was in charge of the convoy. She was the department head of microbiology and had spent more time on Mars than any other person in the convoy. Her years of experience and ability to take charge and her type "A" personality would not allow anyone else to direct this group.

She had made the executive decision to drive straight through to the Pyramids with no stops. She had asked that each crew rotate the driving responsibilities so that they would make it to the Pyramids one sol earlier, allowing everyone to still be as fresh as possible. She also had set up a

Mars 185

COM Meeting within the convoy, trying to determine once they arrived what needed to be done.

Dale Oshioki was included in this meeting. "Uliga, so much depends on what's been going on there already. A lot of the information, the questions we're asking ourselves right now, may already be available. Has anyone attempted contacting them?"

"We've sent messages to Jon Conners, but he has no idea who is there and how to communicate with them. He said he has set up long range scans on communication and hopes to find some traffic and pin it down."

"That guys useless," came a voice over the link.

"I hope Conners gets a hold of them so we know who is there. What about Calprex? Has Gambino sent any directions?"

"Yes and no."

"What do you mean?" came a voice from another transport.

"His message was brief and vague."

"What did he say?" Yet another voice.

"His message reads… I realize you're aware of the Pyramids by now. Continue on route until you reach the destination. Calprex was unaware of any activities in this area. Calprex owns the rights to this land and whoever is there is trespassing and in violation of ISC Mars Treaty. Please proceed, but be cautious and do not take unnecessary chances. I will update you on any further information received. Gambino."

Sukora couldn't make out the numerous comments that were spoken all at once.

"Please one at a time."

"We should stop right now. We have no idea who is there." Came a nervous voice.

Dale Oshioki interjected. "Look, whoever is there may not be happy to see us. We're crashing their party, but keep in mind, that party is in our house. This is the biggest moment of our lives and I am not interested in sitting idly by."

"I agree," came a chorus of voices.

"I came to Mars to find something new, find excitement. Full steam ahead," said Charlie Bolton from one of the transports.

Dale replied "I agree, Charlie. Uliga, have you heard back from Gambino?"

"No, just that message. Hopefully, we'll get a reply soon."

Sukora patiently listened to everyone. "Look, we could go on and on and get nowhere. I want you all to electronically send me your proposals. I'll take those along with information from Gambino and set up a game plan. Sound good?"

"Let's make it happen!" bellowed Bolton

"Uliga, works for me," chimed in Dale.

Within a few minutes, everyone had disconnected. Dale looked at his watch. Soon it was time to relieve Corey and take over some of the driving. He went up to the cockpit and sat in the empty chair. "How you holding out, Corey?"

"Great! This is so exciting. I mean, now we know what we're looking for!"

Dale, who was now more impatient than ever, "Yeah, I don't think I'll be taking samples in search for precious metals, it'll be more like samples on as to date the construction of those Pyramids."

"So you think those were found and not built by someone, I mean, someone from Earth?" Corey asked staring out the windshield and keeping an eye on the transports in front of him.

"Well, we won't know for sure until we get there, but what would the reason be for being so secretive about building Pyramids? I mean, if you plan on building a pyramid, just do it. Also, I don't think anyone could have built anything that big in such a short time. That would take decades to complete."

"Yeah, but what if someone figured out how to? What if these Pyramids are a hoax, just a ploy to get people out here?"

"If that was the idea, it worked, but I doubt it. We don't have any equipment on Mars to chisel the boulders like that. Hell, we're still studying the rocks and for someone to find a quarry that large, I just can't comprehend it."

"Comprehending the other alternative isn't easy."

"Hell it isn't. It's something that most of us have thought for sometime. We are not alone! I can't wait to get some samples for dating. This is the greatest discovery for mankind."

"And we're here! Here on Mars."

"Yeah, so where are we? How long till we get there?"

Corey tapped the map as a 3-D projection came up. "Looks actually like we're here. If we drive all night, we should make Baron's pass by morning. Then less than a sol to the Pyramids."

The anticipation in the other transports, MultiVecs and assortment of other vehicles, was similar. Men and woman who could have only dreamed about this were on their way to see what surely was the greatest discovery of mankind.

23

Brett had circled back up to the top of the canyon and was headed back to Roman. He still wanted to think it was all a bad dream. He wished to wake up, smell fresh cut grass and be back home, back home and twenty years earlier. He wanted to change all that had happened, stop all the pain and death.

Troy sat quietly as they proceeded up the canyon wall. He could see the deep pain that Brett was in and felt that if Brett needed to talk, he was there. As they circled above the canyon wall, Troy could still see the tears in Brett's eyes.

"Hey, let me drive for awhile. You need some rest."

"No, this helps me not to think, not think as much, I think?"

"Look, you're in shock. Go lay down. If you don't fall asleep, I promise to let you have the wheel."

Rebecca had overheard them talking as she went up in the cockpit.

"He's right, Brett. Let me get you something warm to drink. At least sit down and close your eyes for a few minutes."

Brett couldn't look at either one of them as he gazed out at the path in front of them. He was too tired to argue. "Fine, it's all yours. Maybe sleep would do me some good," he replied, not believing a word he had said. He stood up and headed back to the rear of the MultiVec. Rebecca followed him and gave him a drink.

"Here, drink this. It will help you sleep."

"What is it?"

"Don't worry about what it is. Just drink it and lie down."

Brett looked up into Rebecca's eyes and took the cup from her.

"Thanks." He took a few sips as the drink started to warm him up. He placed the cup to the side then and laid back, closing his eyes. Rebecca covered him with a blanket and then headed to the cockpit.

"Is he all right?"

"I think so. I gave him something to help him sleep. He'll feel better when he gets up."

"How close was he with his ex?"

"You know, I don't think they kept much contact after his son was killed, but I knew he loved her all these years."

"What about you?"

"What do you mean, what about me?"

"You guys seem pretty close. This must be a bit awkward?"

"I guess it could be, but I know Brett. He has a practical side to him, but there is a romantic side trying to get out. I know he wanted to live in the perfect little world with a loving wife, kids, dog and a picket fence, but he knows like we all do that's not real. Brett and I were close friends when we worked on the moon together, and when he came here our friendship has evolved into something more. We'll just have to see what more ends up being."

Troy could see her eyes were moist and said, "According to this route we should be at Baron's Pass by night fall, maybe a bit longer."

"Do you think we should travel at night? Ours lights might be seen."

"Yeah, but they may not even be looking for us anymore. We'll see where we are at nightfall."

Rebecca stood up. "I'm getting a cup of java, do you want any?"

"Yeah, thanks."

Rebecca walked to the back to get a couple of cups and to check on Brett. She looked at him as he lay in the cot, appearing to be twitching sporadically. She wished she could do something for him, but knew it would just take time for him to heal.

* * *

The ISC had called a special session to discuss the Pyramids. Ed Brocton was given the floor, the Pyramids being on Calprex land or at least their land for another few hours. The "Observers" did not want to hear anything from Brocton, but they had to give into the demands of both the "Locale" and "Industry" branches of the ISC.

Ed patiently waited as the opening comments from the "Observers" went on for an unusually long time. Ed glanced at his watch, less than two hours before the land rights north of Roman were handed over to the Arab Republic. Yu Hwong was the last of the Observers to declare his opening remarks.

"In closing, I would like to change the agenda slightly. I would like to call up Muhammad Elbaneh up to discuss what he has seen and documented from the city of Roman, specifically Capricorn."

There was a rumbling in the audience.

"Quiet, or you'll be removed from these chambers," interjected Senator Stills, looking a little uneasy.

Muhammad Elbaneh walked up to the podium. He was a tall slender man with jet-black hair and dark eyes. He calmly addressed the audience. "Ladies and Gentlemen, Observers, members of the ISC, I appreciate this opportunity to share with you some things of great importance. I work with the Arab Republic and for the last six months we have been waiting for the completion of Capricorn. We had paid upfront millions of credits just to have one delay followed by another. We have sent men a few months ago to survey the work that is being done, or should I say not done in Roman."

Ed listened, wanting to interject a few questions but knew there would be time after his initial remarks were made.

"As you can see, these pictures were taken just two days ago." As a three dimensional picture came up, he continued. "Capricorn is not even half- complete. This laboratory, where we have plans to do many experiments, is not even close to completion."

One picture after another came up showing an empty shell of Capricorn with little if any work completed. Ed was steaming as he pulled out his PDA. He quickly sent a note to Nick.

Nick,

I need your men to take pictures of Capricorn and the work that is completed. Make sure you get the laboratory and send it to me immediately!"

Ed

Ed focused on Elbaneh's comments.

"I also propose this to you. I feel that Capricorn and all of Roman is behind schedule because of this!" A picture of the Pyramids was projected.

"My colleagues and myself have concluded that Calprex has known about these Pyramids for over a year and have been using resources and manpower to uncover and keep secret their findings."

Ed wanted to go up and smack him, but he would have his time soon. He glanced at his watch. Was his watch correct? In less than thirty minutes the North region would be handed over to the Arab Republic unless something was done about it.

"I also believe that that man," as he pointed to Ed, "has been making a mockery of the ISC. He has known what has been going on for sometime now. I ask you all, how could he not?"

The room erupted into a frenzy.

Senator Stills stood up. "Quiet! Quiet I said!" The room continued to be in an uproar. Nate Stills looked around the room. He turned back to Yu Hwong who just sat there with a smug look on his face. His eyes met

Yu's as Hwong gestured with his hand not to try to quiet the crowd. He wanted the confusion to continue.

Ed, sitting toward the front of the chambers, stood up. Many people screamed and yelled at him. He raised his hands in the air and walked up to the podium until the room became quiet.

Yu Hwong stood up. "Mr. Brocton, you do not have the floor yet. Not until Mr. Elbaneh has finished."

"Mr. Hwong, with due respect to protocol, I believe Mr. Elbaneh has made some wild accusations and the chambers want to hear what I have to say." Ed turned to the room and raised his arms as if asking them what they wanted.

A chorus of people screamed to let Ed have the floor. Finally, with some hesitation Yu Hwong gave Ed the floor. Ed glanced at his watch again as he knew the minutes were moving quickly.

"Ladies and Gentlemen, let me first say the accusations of Mr. Elbaneh are just that. There is no truth behind them. He is part of Arab Republic and is trying to put doubt in your mind. He wants you to stop and think, at least for twelve more minutes. At that time the Arab Republic will get control of the land. I ask you to vote now. Vote now to delay the rights of the land to change from Calprex to the Arab Republic. Aren't there a lot of questions that need to be answered before we move forward on such a monumental week in the history of mankind?"

Yu Hwong's voice cut through the others. "If there was any wrong doing by the Arab Republic, we can change the ruling and give it back to Calprex."

"You say that, Mr. Hwong, but the rules of the ISC have different laws on land rights of corporations verses Nations. If the Arab Republic is awarded this land, the ISC or any other group cannot take any actions for at least six months. By that time they'll have thousands of people there. The Pyramids will be in total control of the Arab Republic."

Senator Stills looked at Ed. "Ed, what about the images showing that Capricorn is nowhere near completion?"

"First, those pictures could be months old, Nate. I ask that we send a neutral party to observe the conditions of Capricorn. I have sent a message to my people asking them to send images of the completed work. I may have them as soon as within the hour."

"Is this true about the ruling?" yelled a voice in the chambers. Again the chamber became loud.

Senator Stills looked over at Hwong and then addressed the answer. "Yes, Mr. Brocton is correct on that ruling. But if there are wrong doings, we can take back the ruling."

"It will be too late, Senator Stills, and you know it. Ladies and Gentlemen, members of the Locale, members of Industry, I fear something that what I had hoped would not happen, has! I believe someone has gotten to the Observers."

The room exploded with comments.

Yu Hwong, stood up. "Mr. Brocton, those are the last words you will have on the ISC floor, ever!"

"Mr. Hwong tell us why you made such a bizarre ruling on the land rights in the first place. Why have you stalled this morning? Aren't you trying to stop what I've ask for?"

Ed turned to the floor of the chambers. "We have two minutes to overrule their findings at least until a neutral party has a look. All in favor?"

A chorus of agreement echoed throughout the chambers.

"This is not protocol on a vote. This will carry no weight. This can not be enforced!" With that statement, one by one the members of the Locale and Industry stood to vote yes on waiting to give the rights to the Arab Republic.

Ed was somewhat relieved and checked to see if Nick had sent him the information. Nothing. He needed that information! What was Nick doing? It was unlike him not to even acknowledge receiving the message.

* * *

Uliga Sukora was in the first transport of the caravan heading for the pyramids. The sun was rising over the mountains to the North. Sukora's goal was to reach Baron Pass by morning, and it appeared she was on schedule. The problem was that many of the other transports had fallen behind overnight.

Sukora tapped her COM Link to the other transports. "Looks like we've made it to Baron's Pass, that is, at least about half of us. We have another twenty vehicles scattered as far back as an hour time-wise. We'll continue to proceed into Baron Pass for another few kilometers and then we'll hold up until the others catch up."

Consequently, as the first morning's light hit the west face of Baron's Pass, twenty vehicles were slowly entering into the narrow canyon. Baron's Pass was discovered over twenty years ago by Sir Richard Baron, one of the first explorers in this part of Mars. This passage had eluded many of the satellites in mapping due to its high cliffs. From above it appeared to be a broken riverbed. Sir Richard Baron had established a series of supply caravans to outlying colonies. Before the pass had been discovered it took almost a week to cross the mountains. Baron's Pass cut it down to twelve hours.

The bottom of the canyon was dark, the sunlight hitting only the wall. Uliga Sukora's transport stopped in the middle of the canyon as she focused the monitors on the canyon's rim. The walls were almost three kilometers straight up.

"How many are in the canyon?" Sukora asked the driver.

"It looks like we have twenty-three here. Oshioki and Bolton should be here within ten minutes. Another sixteen behind them. Farthest one is about forty minutes."

"In that case, I'm going for a walk. I want to see this sight with my own eyes, not by camera. Let me know if you get any new orders from Roman."

"Not a problem. Enjoy."

"Sure no one wants to join me?" she asked.

"No, thanks. I'm too tired to get a suit on. I can see it just fine through the windshield."

"Suit yourself."

Uliga Sukora quickly got out of her overalls and into a suit. She had one of the technicians check her seals and then was on her way out.

At about the same time as Sukora was getting dressed, Corey Davis was turning into Baron's Pass. "I didn't know this was a race. Driving this thing in the dark isn't that easy."

Dale took a gulp of some hot java, "Relax, kid. We're all going to get there at the same time. These MultiVec are a lot heavier than those transports. We were climbing up some steep mountains last night."

Corey, still keeping his eyes on the pass, "Yeah but the last message from Sukora seemed like we were holding her up."

"Uliga is a good woman. A bit competitive, but all of us are, or we wouldn't be here. Look, we're in the middle of the pack. There they are." Dale pointed out the windshield.

High above the convoy on the cliffs of Baron's Pass sat waiting Ivory and his men. Waiting for this moment. Gary Ivory had arrived at nightfall and wanted to be present as the convoy would be crushed. Ivory looked down into Baron's Pass as the convoy slowly entered.

"Sir, it looks like they're stopping?"

"Stopping for us. How wonderful. Maybe they'll place a bull's eye on their hulls?" he snickered.

"Sir, sensors are picking up numerous vehicles following, some as far back as thirty kilometers. Do we wait?"

"Looks like at least twenty five vehicles there. We'll wait a few minutes." He tapped his COM Link. "Everyone hold your fire until I give the word. I want you to concentrate on the three transports in front. Remember to keep the beam straight. Now, on my word." His mouth twitched as he thought about Roberts. Was Roberts down there? Probably not, but it would solve most of his problems if he could get rid of Roberts along with everyone else.

Ivory checked the monitors. All laser guns were in place. He placed four on the near side and another three on the far side. The transports looked like little toys from up on the cliffs.

"Let them have it. Now!"

Uliga Sukora was walking off to the sides of the transports. She looked up to the top of the cliffs. She had to stare almost straight up, almost losing her footing as she glanced from one side to the other. She thought she saw a bright light flash to the side. Must be the sun on some metallic rock, she thought.

She felt so alive on this Mars. She loved the bigness of everything. She smiled as she thought about reaching the Pyramids tomorrow. She turned to her transport as she saw a laser hitting the hull. She ran to the transport, tracking with her eyes, the laser up to the top of the cliffs.

She tapped her COM link. "Turn on the engines and move! Move, damn it!"

There was a brief reply. "We're losing hulk integrity and..." Then static. She knew the laser blew a hole in the transport and that everyone inside was dead. She looked at the two transports next to hers, lasers also blasting them.

"It's Sukora. Everyone get your ass in gear! We are being fired on from lasers from above. Move, move!"

The laser moved systematically to the next few transports, blasting laser at the hulls.

Corey Davis saw the transports in front get knocked off one by one.

"B-18 this is MV –47. Do you read me? Do you read me? T-88, B-9, anyone?" he cried panic in his voice.

Dale heard him. "What's going on?"

"Lasers from above. They're shooting at all of us."

"Move this thing kid, move it!"

Corey accelerated the MultiVec.

"Keep moving back and forth. The key is not to let the laser hit any one spot for more than a few seconds."

The MultiVec turned back and forth and it spun back toward the front of Baron's Pass. Uliga Sukora started back to her transport, making it only in a few meters before she saw the remains of a few of the crew members. Her stomach wanted to heave, but she knew she certainly couldn't afford to get sick in the suit. She turned and ran back outside.

"It's Sukora. Everyone get your suits on and get your ass out of this canyon." She looked around and could tell it was too late, seven vehicles lying motionless. The other twenty had turned and were making swerving maneuvers as they headed back to the front of the pass.

The red dust swirled in the sky as she turned back up and looked at the top of the cliffs. She could see the lasers from both sides coming down on the convoy. She could hear the panic on the COM Link.

She recognized Charlie Bolton's voice. "Pete you have a laser chasing you up your ass! Swing right. Shit, swing harder!"

As she stood by the seven transports that were first hit, the dust began to settle with the other vehicles heading back out. She saw the laser hitting them one by one, although she realized that even if their hulls were breached, everyone should have their suits on by now.

Her eyes followed the lasers and she was mortified as she followed two lasers blasting into the cliffs above the convoy. Within minutes, hundreds of thousand of kilograms of rocks would crush the retreating convoy.

"Turn around, damn it. Listen, it's Sukora. There are blasts into the cliff wall above you. Turn back towards me. It's your only chance." With those words she heard the eruption as areas of the cliffs began to fall down on the convoy.

Corey Davis was scared as he kept his eyes in front of him and listened to his friends die. He was too scared to hand over the driving to anyone else so he could get a suit on. Through all the communication he was able to pick up Sukora's message and slammed on the brakes to turn back toward the middle of Baron's Pass.

"Kid, what the hell are you doing?"

"Saving our lives." Or so he hoped.

He went full speed straight back to the seven lifeless vehicles. Charlie Bolton's vehicle and a few others had also heard the message and had turned back up the pass. The massive boulders fell upon the remaining convoy. Corey could hear the boulders hit behind him. The dust and rocks made visibility zero as he continued to accelerate full speed straight ahead.

Dale heard a large jolt hit the MultiVec but they continued to move, in their attempt to outrun the avalanche of rock. He glanced out the windshield, wondering if it were too late? Was anyone going to get out of this convoy alive?

24

Nick Gambino sat in a small conference room for over twenty-four hours. The two goons who had brought him were doing the typical good cop, bad cop routine, and trying to get him to confess to something he knew nothing about.

"Look, I have no idea what the hell you're talking about."

"I think you're in a shit load of trouble, Nick. If you just tell us who else is involved, you might get a break," the lieutenant advised him.

"Listen, you can ask me all you want. I'm as startled as you are about this. If you get me out of here, I might be able to find out what's going on."

"You mean let you out so you can warn your colleagues?"

"This is so typical, as you two dick heads work on me, the person you should be looking for is getting away! You just don't get it. You have the wrong guy." The two stared at each other as Nick's frustration was now just erupting into anger.

The lieutenant hit the table. "You're lucky I can't hit you!"

"Like I've said hundred a times, I want my lawyer here. If you have something, charge me or release me."

"We're not the police!"

Major Robinson came between the two of them. "Nick, we've secured multiple coded messages that are linked to you and sent to Roman."

Nick looked up. "And? That's my job. I contact people on Roman daily."

"Why scramble them?" the major asked.

"We use secure channels. We don't scramble or code any messages."

"Well, take a look at this log," the major said, throwing a folder on the table. "It's a series of messages that were sent from Calprex to someone on Mars. We still haven't figured out the code, but we will."

The lieutenant grabbed the folder. "See this on all the messages? Does the word Beatle mean anything? All the messages stamped with Beatle are linked back to you, so we know you sent them. To who, Mr. Gambino, who?"

This went on for hours, back and forth and getting nowhere. They had left Nick in the room alone for over an hour. Nick was getting tired, hungry and just plain pissed. Nick looked up at the clock in disgust. It may be the most important day in history and instead of helping find answers as to what was on Mars, he was in here.

The door swung open. Only major Robinson came in. He had a tray of food and coffee and placed it in front of Nick.

"Mr. Gambino, tell me about Tom Afidan."

"What besides that he's a ...... Jesus Christ! It's him?" He took a swig of the coffee.

"It looks like that. He encrypted all the messages and actually tagged them to you just in case something like this happened."

Nick took a bite of the sandwich. "friggin bastard. Can I go?"

"In a minute. Please a few more questions."

"Are you kidding me? I have a shit of work to do. I have to find out what the hell is going on."

"I'll make a deal with you. You tell me about Tom Afidan, I'll tell you what we know."

"Alright. That's fair. Calprex hired Afidan a few years ago. He worked for a competitor and the stockholders wanted him. I never trusted the guy, most of us didn't, but the bastard knew how to make money." Nick took another bite of the sandwich. "He brought a lot of his own people in."

"Was Gary Ivory one of these people?" the major asked.

"Yep, he brought him in and put him in charge of security in Roman."

"Well, they must have thought we would never break the code. It was in ancient Arabic, probably decoded on the other side from Ivory. We're still going through the messages now."

"Your turn. What about the Pyramids?"

"They're real. We've had numerous confirmation on fly-bys, photos from satellites, when we could see the Pyramids. The ISC retracted the ruling on the land rights to the north. Almost every country with capability has sent ships to Mars in the last twenty-four hours. Some information we are getting is suggesting that they have a defense system around the Pyramids, which includes multiple laser cannons and an elaborate defense shield against proton bombs. It's not going to be pretty. We need someone down there to knockout the block they are using. We need to find out what's down there. Is there anyone down there who can help us?"

Nick took the last slug of coffee and stood up. "I might just have the man for you. Send the information to my office. I need to take a shower"

"One man! I hope he can do it."

"Me, too." Nick wondered what was happening down there? He hadn't heard from Roberts in days.

"I'll have the information sent to your office. We need that block down, and down for good."

"Well I'm sure you'll excuse me, but I have a lot to do." Nick wondered, was Brett still alive?

* * *

Gary Ivory felt a feeling of exuberance as he looked down into Baron's Pass. The red dust prevented him from getting confirmation of what he knew had to have happened and that was that the convoy had perished. He knew they had knocked out at least eight transports before they knew what was happening. The remaining convoy that had turned and run had been buried under the avalanche of rocks and boulders.

He was growing impatient, the dust seeming to hover over the canyon.

"Sir, it could take hours before we can see down there. Should we wait?"

"As much as I'd like to see the scene, we need to get back to the base and set up a perimeter there. I almost hope someone down there is alive. What better way to spread the news to stay away than a sole survivor making it back to Roman." Ivory snickered.

"Yes, sir. I'll contact the others to return back to base."

"Do that." But he wanted to see his work. No other convoys were headed for the P-Base yet?

"Now that I think about it, we'll wait here while the others go back. I've got to see what it looks like down there. Send everyone back and we'll stay behind."

As Ivory's vehicle stood on top of the cliff, the other vehicles with the laser cannons started their engines and began on their way back to P - Base. He knew he should probably head back with them but for all the shit he took, this was a small treat for him. He double-checked the reports on P-Base, sent a few messages to confirm the work was getting completed, and then just waited for the dust to settle.

"Magnify the view. We must be able to make something out by now."

The technician made a few adjustments. "That's the best we can do. There isn't a lot of light down there, so that doesn't help."

The driver chimed in, "We have a vehicle coming from the other end of Baron's Pass."

A smile came over Ivory face. "As soon as it's in range, I want to find out who it is."

David Czaplicki

* * *

Troy had made it to the North side of Baron's Pass by nightfall. Brett was still sleeping, so they decided to stop and catch a few winks. The following morning Rebecca woke up early and grabbed a mug of java and went on the gravity bike. She would be happy to get back to Roman.

Brett awoke and went into the galley and got some water.

"Did I wake you, Brett?" she asked with a warm smile.

"No. I can't believe I slept that long. Where are we?"

"I fell asleep before we stopped but Troy said he wanted to make it to Baron's Pass before he got some sleep."

Brett looked out the windshield. "Yeah, I think that's where we are."

"You feeling any better?" she said, getting off the bike.

"Thanks, I think so. It was such a shock. It still is. I'm sorry."

"You don't have to be sorry for anything."

The two stood there for a minute in silence holding each other's hands. The MultiVec began to shake. Troy fell out of his cot. "What the hell is going on?" he screamed.

Brett held on to the chairs and counters as he tried to make his way to the cockpit.

"Rebecca, it can't be an earthquake?"

"No, no chance at all." She was hanging onto a railing.

Brett made it to the front and took a look outside. "It's coming from Baron's Pass. Looks like some type of explosion. Smoke and dust all over."

The rumbling and shaking came to a stop as all three looked out into Baron's Pass.

"Let's get out there and see what the hell is going on," said Troy, turning on the engines and starting into Baron's Pass.

They proceeded into the narrow canyon, seeing the dark clouds of dust just a few kilometers into the canyon.

"What the hell is that?" Troy said.

"Whatever it is, it must be what shook us a few minutes ago," Brett said as he tried to get some readings with his sensor. "The dust is making it impossible to read anything. Keep driving. Maybe we'll pick something up as we get a closer look."

Rebecca watched the clouds of dust pouring out towards them. "You don't think we have to worry about that reaching us, do you?"

Troy looked like a little kid watching a thunderstorm rolling in. "One way or the other, we'll reach it. Either us to it or it will come here. The walls of Baron's Pass are too high for anything to escape. Whatever force took place, the energy and power needs to funnel out."

189

"Are you sure it's safe? What's the speed on that thing?" she asked.

Brett was trying to read the instruments. "Probably Troy should be reading this, but if I'm reading this correctly, it's moving at about 175 kilometers an hour."

"Wow!" Troy yelled. He stopped the MultiVec.

"Brett you drive. I want to set all the instruments and get as many readings as I can. This is awesome." Brett took the driver seat and continued to drive into the rolling clouds of red dust.

Troy was reading an assortment of instruments. "Okay, there will be a strong gust hitting us just before the clouds hit us. We'll get tossed a bit but just stay straight and keep going forward. It should dissipate in a few minutes. Hang on. It should be here any second."

Rebecca strapped herself into the seat in the back. Brett double-checked the harness.

"Here it comes!"

The MultiVec shook as an air mass of sand hit the vehicle. Within seconds the rolling clouds engulfed the MultiVec. Brett thought that they had gone airborne for a second but knew it was too difficult to tell. The MultiVec shook back and forth as Brett tried to keep the vehicle straight as they continued on. Although Troy was being bounced around, his face was down reading all the data.

"This is incredible! Wow. Brett, just take it in nice and straight. We should be able to get some better visibility soon."

As Troy had said, within minutes the winds died down and they were able to make out objects within the pass. "Yeah, it's getting better, but still hard to see."

"Looks like visibility is about .5 kilometers. Just keep it slow."

Rebecca had unbuckled herself and was making her way to the cockpit. "What happened? This is not the same Baron's Pass we came through a few sols ago."

Brett turned to both of them. "Well I have a geologist and meteorologist here. What are your best guesses?"

Rebecca eyes were still focused on what lay ahead of them. "I'd say an avalanche of some type." She turned to Troy "What do you think?"

"That sounds just about right. The high walls here, the force of clouds, yeah, I'd agree."

The dust was starting to settle. Rebecca kept her eyes focused on the rocks in front of them.

"What's that over there?" She pointed to their right.

"What? I don't see anything," Brett questioned.

"Move to the right, over there."

"It's a transport," Troy said with shock.

"Over there. There's another one. Oh my God, what happened?" she said in disbelief.

* * *

Gary Ivory watched as the MultiVec made it's way into Baron's Pass. He could see the bellowing thick clouds of dust rolling quickly towards it. He realized that in a minute he wouldn't be able to make any identification.

"Can you make it out? Any ID numbers?"

He knew that it wasn't one of his men down there. It was either someone lost, a scout from the convoy that had slipped by them, or maybe even Roberts?

"Run the ID numbers in the computer. I want to know who that is."

As he watched, the cloud of dust overtook the vehicle in the canyon.

"Sir, it was too far away to get anything. We'll have to wait for everything to clear."

Ivory pounded the counter. "I want to know who it is!"

The MultiVec pulled up against the lifeless transport. Troy hit the COM link.

"Anyone read me? Anyone there?" All they heard was static.

Rebecca turned to Brett. "Depending on what's in this dust, there might be some interference on the communications. There has to be a high concentration of iron. Mix that with a few other metals and the COM links will only work short range."

Brett nodded, listening to her explanation of the composition of minerals as he went in the back to pull their suits out.

"All right, now let's go and take a look."

The three quickly got their suits on and headed out.

"It's pretty thick out there. Let's stay together," Brett told the other two as they opened the hatch. Rebecca nodded in agreement.

They approached the first transport Troy pointing out the burn marks in the hatch. "Those aren't caused by any avalanche."

Brett tapped his COM link. "Anyone home? Anyone there?" He went to the hatch and banged on it a few times. But, there was no answer.

He opened the hatch and stepped inside. The door closed as he opened the decompression door. On the door opening, he saw the crew, or what was left of them, sprawled across the Transport. He tapped the COM. "They're all dead in here."

"Same thing in this one," responded Troy.

Rebecca continued to walk deeper into the settling dust. "Something's moving over here. Guys over here!"

She thought she saw a flicker of light or movement. Maybe the dust was playing games on her eyes? She continued to proceed farther out.

"Rebecca, wait up. Don't get too far ahead of us."

"I'm right over here. Keep coming."

Brett and Troy caught up to her as the three scanned the area. The wind was starting to pick up and drove the dust away.

"Over there!" Troy gestured.

There were a few Transports near a pile of boulders, a group of people huddled outside. It appeared that they were pulling others out of the Transports. The three ran over to the group.

"Hello. Do you need some help?"

A few of the heads looked up. "Yes. Is that you Brett?"

"Yeah, and..."

"It's Dale Oshioki."

Troy walked up to them. "What the hell happened?"

Still a bit dazed, replied Uliga Sukora, "We were ambushed. Ambushed from above. The bastards took out the first few from above with laser cannons."

Charlie Bolton placed his hand on Sukora's shoulder. "Sukora was able to warn us that they were blasting the transports. Most of us turned to get out of range, then they turned the lasers on the cliff and the mother fell on us."

Brett looked up but couldn't see more than a few meters as the dust was still settling. "How many of you were there?"

"We started with almost fifty vehicles, over five hundred men and woman," Oshioki explained.

"We have no idea how many of us are left," Bulton interrupted. "Maybe some survivors on the other side as well."

"Has anyone been able to make contact with anybody?" Rebecca asked

"We're having trouble with communications, even with each other. Must be some type of electric charge when the cliff came down."

Brett looked around watching the injured being pulled out. He turned to Troy and Rebecca. "Help them with the injured. See if you can patch up some of the Transports back there. Bury the dead and get everyone back to Roman."

"Okay not a problem, buddy," said Troy. "What are you going to do?"

"First thing is to get out of Baron's Pass and get some help here. Then, ...well, don't worry about it."

"What are you going to do, Brett?" Rebecca said with concern.

"Don't worry." Brett turned to make his way back to the MultiVec.

* * *

Brett Roberts made his way out of Baron's Pass. As he turned the final bend, he was wondering if anyone would be able to receive his message. Station 185 was back to jamming satellite feeds as well as communications. Brett wondered how far out the signal went. He tried to remember if they had any communications near Baron's Pass on the first trip to the Northern region. He couldn't remember.

Brett turned on the communication full power. "This is Brett Roberts. Does anyone read me?"

Nothing. He tried again.

"Hello, anyone out there?"

"Go ahead. This is Phobos," crackled a voice.

"We need a rescue team sent to Baron's Pass. An avalanche has killed and injured hundreds of people."

"Where are you located at this point?"

"I'm at the north end of the Pass."

There was a long silence. "Stay there until we reach you."

Above the canyon Gary Ivory was listening to the conversation Brett Roberts was having. He smirked as he wrote a note and handed it to the driver in the vehicle. The driver read it and spoke into the COM link.

"I repeat. Stay there until we reach you. Do you understand?" Ivory's man calmly said into the COM link.

"Affirmative." Came Brett's voice.

The driver turned the COM link off as Ivory chuckled. "How perfect. He plans on waiting for us. It looks like you were correct. That was Roberts who left Baron's Pass. Circle around and get over there so I can finish this once and for all."

25

Brett sat waiting wondering what time they would arrive. He probably should check with them soon. Hopefully get an answer. He attempted to contact Troy and Rebecca but with no luck. The COM link blinked as it picked up an incoming message. Brett smiled to himself. They must be reading my mind, he thought as he tapped open.

A bright red light appeared.

"High Security. Please fill in identification number."

Brett punched in his ID number.

"Password?"

Again he punched his password in.

"Brett,

I'm not sure if you have any idea how they are blocking the view of the pyramid, but we need to interrupt it somehow. We need to find out what's going on over there. Find out if anyone knows what happened the first time it went down. Somehow, some way we need to see what's going on at the Pyramids. Multiple sources say there might be laser cannons.

It appears there might be some type of showdown. Just about every country that is capable of sending troops and men to Mars has done so! It looks like it's going to get pretty ugly over there. See what you can do to help us. Then make sure all our people are out of harms' way. I haven't heard anything from you in days. Please reply.
Nick"

Brett sat back and listened to the message. Station 185 had been unguarded when they had left the other day. He looked above the dashboard to see if the spare disk was still there. Sure enough it was. He could probably make it to Station 185 before Ivory thought of guarding it. He sat and thought as the message played again. The message ended and the computer voice came on.

"You have one saved message."

The saved message started playing as Brett was thinking about Station 185.

"Brett, its Nick. I'm not sure how to tell you this."

Brett heard the message play and his hands began to shake. He turned on the engine and headed for Station 185.

* * *

Gary Ivory and his men arrived at the North end of Baron's Pass. "Where the hell is he?" Ivory screamed.

"We can't find him on any sensors. He must have headed back into the canyon." Replied one of Ivory's men.

"Call him on the COM link and see if you get an answer.

"Brett Roberts, this is rescue one. Do you read? We are near the North end of Baron's Pass. I repeat. Do you read me?"

There was just static. "Damn it. We can't go in there."

"Yes, I read you," said Roberts over the COM link.

Ivory frantically wrote down what he wanted the driver to ask.

"We are having problems finding you. Did you go back into Baron's Pass?"

"Negative. I have something I need to do."

Ivory looked a bit confused, then wrote down another response.

"Can we assist you in anything?"

"No, just help the people in Baron's Pass."

Ivory once again jotted down a few notes.

"We have a large team here. We have personnel to help you if need it?"

There was just silence followed by, "Negative. I'm fine."

"Damn him. Head back to P – Base, but I want every frequency monitored."

"Yes, sir."

Troy and Rebecca had helped the others get all the injured out. They had buried the dead from the first transports that had been hit. A few of the crew were patching the hulls.

Troy walked over to Sukora. "You okay? How are the Transports looking?

Sukora was still a bit flustered. "I'm fine, but we need to get these injured back to Roman. Looks like about four Transports should be good to go soon. I only wish we had enough people to fill them up."

"Brett went out to try to get some help. Hopefully we won't have to wait to get to Roman, and some one will come to us."

"I hope you're right."

Charlie Bolton walked over to them. "Looks like we're ready to leave. We have most of the serious injuries in the two big transports. They should be more comfortable there."

"Rebecca and I will need a lift," Troy interjected.

"Not a problem. My transport is just about empty."

"Great. Let's go."

The transports crawled out of Baron's Pass, having to take a much longer route over the mountains to get back to Roman. Rebecca walked up to Charlie, who was in the cockpit driving. She took a seat next to him. "Hope you don't mind. I want to try to raise Brett on the COM links."

"Be my guest, young lady."

"Brett, are you out there? It's Rebecca. Can you hear me?" She tried for almost a half hour until finally hearing a faint reply.

"I'm fine, Rebecca. I have some unsettled business to attend to."

The reception was bad but she was able to understand him.

"What are you talking about, Brett?"

"Don't worry about it. Did the rescue team get everyone out? I'm having trouble hearing you."

"What rescue team? No one came?"

Troy had overheard the conversation and joined Rebecca and Charlie in the cockpit.

"I had made contact with someone who was sending a rescue team," said Brett.

"Brett, it's Troy. No one came. Do you know who you talked to?"

"No, there was a lot of static."

"Yeah, we're getting a lot of static now, too. We're on our way back to Roman. Are you headed there?"

"No, I'm headed back to Station 185."

"What for?"

"Look, I'm having trouble with my communications. Send Nick Gambino a scrambled message. Update him on what happened in Baron's Pass and tell him that I received all of his messages and that I will take care of it."

"Take care of what?" Rebecca interrupted.

There was no reply just static. Rebecca turned to Troy. "Troy, we have to go help him. He's going to do something stupid."

Troy glanced at Charlie. "She's right."

Before he could reply, Charlie swung the transport around. "Hell, lets' go do it!"

"Sukora, it's Bolton. We have to make a stop. We'll meet you back at Roman."

Troy sat down and began his message to Nick Gambino.

Ivory smiled as he overheard the conversation on his COM link. "That's it. Come back to me." He turned to the driver. Let's get to Station 185 on the double." He sat back and thought about how he would kill Roberts.

* * *

Brett knew that he still had a backup disk from Greenberg and could reprogram Station 185. He wondered though if that failed, could he just shut down the station? His mind drifted then from Station 185, to Kathleen, and Alex and Rebecca.

His life was filled with so many emotional highs and lows. How he would have settled for a life in the middle, a boring life. If he had to do it all again, he would change things.

Tears rolled down his cheeks as he realized he wouldn't have changed anything. He loved Kathleen and would till he died. Together they had brought the most special boy into this world. A day never went by when Brett didn't think of Alex.

Brett also had a love for adventure, a love for space. He wouldn't have been happy with a life behind a desk, a life boring and dull. If he had a choice to do it all over, he would go for it all, just as he had.

The red link on the MultiVec communicator lit up. He hit the message.

"My friend,
I'm sorry for not replying earlier. I was not available. Place the disk once again into Station 185. Once it's reprogrammed, destroy whatever you can.
A friend"

Brett deleted the message. Was Greenberg his mysterious friend, he wondered. Brett felt hollow and tired as he raced back across Mars to take care of Station 185 once and for all. The pink, midday sky had given way to a dark, red glow. The shadows from the mountains painted numerous shades across the landscape.

Brett clicked the map. Just a few more kilometers to go. He wanted to take care of the station, then start heading back to Roman before nightfall. He noticed a few dust devils off to the east as his mind drifted to thoughts of Kathleen.

Brett felt an eruptive jolt as the MultiVec was blindsided from the rear. His helmet on the other seat crashed against the windshield. He held on as the MultiVec spun around.

"Going somewhere?" came the voice of Ivory on the COM link.

Brett regained control of the vehicle and swung around and headed for Station 185. Ivory's vehicle came up to the side of Brett's MultiVec and bumped it as the two raced across the Martian terrain.

"Ivory, it's all over. Everyone knows about the Pyramids."

"Oh, it's over, over for you," Ivory responded as his vehicle rammed the side of Brett's.

Brett swung the MultiVec into Ivory's. "It's over for you and Afidan. Within months thousands of troops will be here."

"I'm not worried. I'll destroy the Pyramids rather then have them fall into someone else's hand."

The two continued to bump each other as metal and debris were coming off both vehicles. A light flashed on the dashboard, followed by a computerized voice.

"Integrity breached. Leak on right side panel."

Brett reached for his helmet rolling on the floor of the cockpit. The MultiVec swayed as Ivory's vehicle clipped the back end.

"Pressurization 92%"

Brett grabbed the helmet with one hand, snapping it on. Ivory's voice continued on the COM link. "You should have stayed back on Earth. You may have lived longer."

Ivory's transport jarred up against the side, the two vehicles becoming locked together as the twisted metal wrapped and intertwined with each other.

"Pressurization 90%"

Brett secured his gloves and placed his harness on as the two vehicles rolled along together as one. Ivory screamed at the driver. "You idiot, break free of him."

"Sir, we're trying." A light flashed in the cockpit. "We have a leak somewhere."

Ivory held onto a beam as the vehicles bounced. "What the hell are you doing?"

"Sir, he's fighting us for control. The MultiVec has more weight. If we can't break free, he'll end up with control."

"You're worthless!" Ivory screamed.

Brett could feel the power of the MultiVec, but it was still a battle as they continued on. He looked out the window and saw a tall, slender boulder off to the left. He turned the MultiVec in that direction hoping to take Ivory with him as both vehicles fought for control in continuing together across Mars at high speed.

Ivory's driver saw the boulder at the last minute but it was too late to do anything as the two vehicles slammed into the boulder. The vehicles separated, Ivory's beginning to tumble numerous times. The MultiVec flipped over once and came to a stop with the engines dying out.

"Pressurization 73%" came the voice from the computer.

Brett was happy to have his suit on, happy to be alive. He released the harness and stood up. He scanned the area in search of Station 185 and Ivory. He could make out the antennas over the ridge to the north. Ivory's vehicle was upside down about hundred meters away.

He checked the gauge on his air tank. Less than half. Definitely enough to get him to the station, but he would need more oxygen until someone found him. He grabbed the disk from the dashboard and looked for another canister of oxygen. He searched the entire cabin but found nothing. He turned on the COM link.

"Anyone out there? This is Roberts. I'm at Station 185. My vehicle's hull is breached. I have enough oxygen for two hours. Anyone out there?"

There was nothing but static as Brett wondered if the communicator had been damaged. He took one more look for another tank as he hit the distress signal, then left the MultiVec and headed for Station 185 on foot. Hopefully, the station had a working communicator and he could get some help.

Brett slowly made his way across the pink dunes. It was farther than he had thought but finally made it. The beat-up station was still abandoned, just the way they had left it the other day.

He passed through the blown open doors and proceeded to the main control panel. He dislodged the disk in the main frame and replaced it with the one in his suit. He watched the monitor as a program booted up and installed. He flicked on the stations communicator.

"This is Station 185. I'm in need of assistance. Please respond." Brett continued to send out the message but didn't hear anything but static.

Well, no time to waste, Brett thought. He needed to demolish as much of the station as possible. He took a piece of metal from the floor and smashed the control panels. He went on his knees and opened up the panels below the controls. There were hundreds of wires, computers chips and circuits. Brett recklessly pulled and tore out everything he could.

He stood up and looked for the maintenance room. He thought that maybe he could do some damage there and then head back to the

MultiVec and hope someone picked up his signal. He activated a shutdown as the few lights that were on flickered off. Brett was drawn to the monitor, it reporting that there was an error in the deactivation. It didn't matter, he thought. He did enough damage.

He walked back to the MultiVec to check the messages but found nothing. He tried sending a few more times but again only static. He was hoping that with Station 185 out of commission he would be able to contact someone. He feared it was broken and that he was probably wasting his time. He glanced at his tank. Just over an hour.

He looked out of the windshield and saw Ivory's vehicle tipped over. Maybe their hull wasn't breached or possibly their communicator was working. He grabbed a small metal pipe and decided he had nothing to lose.

As he approached the turned-over transport, he noticed a side panel had been split off. Brett knew with the integrity breached the best he could hope for was that their communicator working. He pulled opened the door and hoisted himself up to the turned-over vehicle.

As he entered, he saw the remains of someone in the main cabin, the blood having been boiled out as the Martian air ripped through them. So this is how Ivory met his fate. The exhausted vent had been punctured as gray smoke drifted throughout the transport. He made his way through the twisted metal, up to the cockpit. There he saw two men. The driver, who was still harnessed in the seat, had met the same fate as the man Brett had seen as he entered. The other man was in a suit but was lying motionless.

Brett noticed the light on the communicator flickering as he reached for them.

"Not so fast!" The person in the suit swung around and knocked Brett back into the main cabin.

Brett recognized the voice from earlier. It was Ivory. Brett looked up as he saw Ivory pull out a Martian pistol and fired. Brett threw himself behind debris as he tried to make his way to the back. Ivory chased behind, him tripping over the driver. Another shot was fired that ricocheted above Brett's head.

Brett grabbed a bar and dove out the hatch. He rolled back under the opening of the hatch, under the flipped over transport, and waited for Ivory to exit.

"Roberts there's nowhere to hide out there!" Ivory chuckled.

Roberts could hear Ivory make his way across the Transport. He looked at the bar that he had picked up as he had rolled out of the transport. Not much of a weapon he thought. He turned to both sides, looking for something else since he knew that Ivory would be stepping down in front of him within seconds.

As Ivory left the transport, Roberts picked up a small twisted piece of metal and reached out to grab Ivory's leg. With a violent slash, he had cut through Ivory's suit. He quickly jumped on Ivory, fearing that Ivory would have enough time to turn and get one last shot off. Roberts was right. Ivory was able to get one more shot off.

26

Troy turned to Rebecca. "Yeah, this distress signal is from Brett's vehicle."

"Do you have a readout on where it is?"

Bolton turned to Rebecca. "Station 185. We should be there in about an hour."

Rebecca felt a bit nauseous and pressed her hand against her stomach. She would tell Brett when she saw him.

Charlie Bolton continued, "Looks like the others have made contact with Phobos and are sending down multiple teams to help the injured and look for more survivors."

"Do you think anyone from Phobos can get to Station 185 within the hour?" Rebecca asked.

Troy turned to her as he could see the concern in her eyes. "We'll get there before anyone from Phobos could. Don't worry. He'll be okay."

She forced a smile. "I hope so. Then we're all going back to Roman."

"Yeah, I'm starting to miss that place."

Charlie Bolton continued driving as he checked the map. "Fifty minutes till we're there."

Rebecca looked out at the red mountains on the horizon.

* * *

Brett heard Ivory's last shot. He figured he would have the split second to get it off. He saw Ivory's lifeless body fall to the ground. Brett was almost afraid to look at the gauge on his wrist. After a few seconds, he figured maybe the bullet didn't penetrate his suit. He lifted his arm and saw the status was normal.

He glanced at the air tank. Twenty minutes, he figured. He made his way back inside the flipped-over transport and made his way to the communicator.

"This is Roberts. Anyone out there?" He flipped to a few other stations and repeated the message.

"Brett, it's Rebecca. Are you okay?"

"I'm glad to hear you. I'm fine but I'm running a little low on air. I'm at Station 185."

"Buddy, we're headed your way. Should be there in forty minutes, tops!" Troy interrupted.

"That's going to be cutting it close, maybe too close. I don't think I have enough air left to last that long."

Rebecca turned to Troy. "Listen, Brett, don't talk. Save your breath. Reset the settings on your tank. Cut the oxygen by ten percent. That should give you a few more minutes. Sit down and relax."

Charlie Bolton accelerated to full speed. "Hang in there. It's opened the engines up the whole way."

Brett changed the setting on his tank and sitting back, looked out at the majestic red mountains. "Okay, you guys, do your best to get out here. I'll be waiting. I'm in Ivory's transport. It's the one flipped-over."

"Is Ivory there?" Troy asked.

"Yes, but he's dead."

"Well, tell us about it later. Save your breath. We'll check in every few minutes." Troy said.

"Okay."

Brett looked out as the red sky was slowly changing over to the blue hue of evening. He sat looking out, thinking about Kathleen. He wished he would have never come to Mars. He should have been there for her. Maybe he would change things if he could. Maybe he would change things so he could be with Kathleen and Alex.

What a great family had they started out as. He and Kathleen were so in love so many years back. Alex had been such a special boy. Yet it had all fallen apart. So here he was all alone on Mars.

"Brett, how are you doing?" Rebecca asked.

"Okay." He looked at his tank. It showed almost empty. "How far away are you?"

Troy interrupted. "Fifteen minutes, buddy. Just hang on."

"I'll try," Brett said, wondering how much time he had left. The gauge read empty but hopefully there was enough to get him by.

"We'll check back in a few minutes. Just relax," Rebecca said, hoping she could do that. She held her stomach, which carried Brett's child.

Brett tried to slow down his breathing as much as possible. He reflected back on his times in Ithaca. The best days of his life.

"Don't worry. We're almost there." came a voice that Brett knew. It wasn't Rebecca's or Troy's. "We've been waiting for you." It was Alex.

"Brett, just breathe slowly and close your eyes. We're coming to get you." It was the voice of Kathleen.

"Dad, we'll all be together. Just the three of us."

Brett could see both their faces even though he knew his eyes were closed. They held out their hands to him as he reached out to grab them. He held Kathleen with one and Alex the other as they picked him up and they all embraced. Brett felt a heavy weight lifted off his heart as they held hands and walked off.

* * *

"Brett! Brett, can you hear me?" She turned to Charlie. "How far? Why isn't he answering?" Rebecca screamed.

"Seven, maybe eight minutes."

"Okay, I'm going to get the suits ready. Troy find a few spare tanks for me."

He turned to her. "Not a problem. They're all ready by the suits."

Rebecca turned to the back as Troy looked at Charlie. "Let's hope he's just lost consciousness. This last incline is pretty steep. It's probably closer to ten minutes before we get there."

"Just do what you can," Troy replied.

Just as Charlie Bolton had mentioned, it took them ten minutes to get to Station 185. Rebecca and Troy were all suited up and ready when they got to the transport. They raced inside and found Brett. Rebecca quickly replaced his tank.

"Breathe, damn it. Breathe!" she screamed.

Troy lifted him up. "Let's get him back in our MultiVec. We can give him CPR."

The two quickly got him inside and removed his helmet. Troy tilted his head back and blew short puffs into his mouth. For ten minutes he tried CPR but it was no use. Brett Roberts was dead.

"Why, god, why?" Rebecca cried as she held Brett in her arms.

Troy was on his knees with his hand on her shoulder as a tear fell from his eye. "I'm sorry."

David Czaplicki

EPILOGUE

Nick Gambino received the news by the end of the day. Another colleague, another friend, dead on Mars. He also knew there would be many more. Brett was able to knock out Station 185, and live feeds on the Pyramids were being examined around the clock.

There was an elaborate defense system in surrounding the Pyramids. Countries and major corporations would fight for the mysteries of the Pyramids but Nick's only concern was about the people he sent up to Roman.

He had reviewed the numerous reports funneling in over the last few days. He decided to place Uliga Sukora in charge and surround her with a council of five others to help manage the situation. One of the five was Jon Conners. He still was a little unsure about him, but Jon had been an assistant to both Mendez and Roberts and would be needed.

He also asked that Troy Smitts and Rebecca Marceau be added to the council. He figured anyone that Brett had trusted and was close to the situation was someone he wanted on his side. He knew that they all had an incredible amount of work ahead of them. It was not going to get any easier.

He looked up at the picture of Mars that hung on the far wall of his office. I guess Mars is the God of war, Nick thought.

With hundreds of ships, thousands of personnel headed to Mars, a new war would be taking place. A war to uncover the secrets of the red planet.

2240009

Made in the USA